THE DEATH OF BUNNY MUNRO

Also by Nick Cave

And the Ass Saw the Angel

THE DEATH OF BUNNY MUNRO

Nick Cave

HarperCollins*Publishers*Ltd

Published by HarperCollins Publishers Ltd, by arrangement
with Canongate Books Ltd., Edinburgh.

First Canadian edition

HarperCollins books may be purchased for educational, business, or sales promotional
use through our Special Markets Department.

HarperCollins Publishers Ltd
2 Bloor Street East, 20th Floor
Toronto, Ontario, Canada
M4W 1A8

www.harpercollins.ca

Library and Archives Canada Cataloguing in Publication
Cave, Nick, 1957–
The death of Bunny Munro / Nick Cave.
ISBN 978-1-55468-540-0
I. Title.
PR9619.3.C4D43 2009A   823'.914   C2009-903147-7

Printed and bound in the United States
RRD 9 8 7 6 5 4 3

For Susie

PART ONE

COCKSMAN

1

'I am damned,' thinks Bunny Munro in a sudden moment of self-awareness reserved for those who are soon to die. He feels that somewhere down the line he has made a grave mistake, but this realisation passes in a dreadful heartbeat, and is gone – leaving him in a room at the Grenville Hotel, in his underwear, with nothing but himself and his appetites. He closes his eyes and pictures a random vagina, then sits on the edge of the hotel bed and, in slow motion, leans back against the quilted headboard. He clamps the mobile phone under his chin and with his teeth breaks the seal on a miniature bottle of brandy. He empties the bottle down his throat, lobs it across the room, then shudders and gags and says into the phone, 'Don't worry, love, everything's going to be all right.'

'I'm scared, Bunny,' says his wife, Libby.

'What are you scared of? You got nothing to be scared of.'

'Everything, I'm scared of *everything*,' she says.

But Bunny realises that something has changed in his wife's voice, the soft cellos have gone and a high rasping violin has been added, played by an escaped ape or something. He registers it but has yet to understand exactly what this means.

'Don't talk like that. You know that gets you nowhere,' says Bunny, and like an act of love he sucks deep on a Lambert &

Butler. It is in that instance that it hits him – the baboon on the violin, the inconsolable downward spiral of her drift – and he says, 'Fuck!' and blows two furious tusks of smoke from his nostrils.

'Are you off your Tegretol? Libby, tell me you've been taking your Tegretol!'

There is silence on the other end of the line then a broken, faraway sob.

'Your father called again. I don't know what to say to him. I don't know what he wants. He shouts at me. He raves,' she says.

'For Christ's sake, Libby, you know what the doctor said. If you don't take your Tegretol, you get depressed. As you well know, it's dangerous for you to get depressed. How many fucking times do we have to go through this?'

The sob doubles on itself, then doubles again, till it becomes gentle, wretched crying and it reminds Bunny of their first night together – Libby lying in his arms, in the throes of some inexplicable crying jag, in a down-at-heel hotel room in Eastbourne. He remembers her looking up at him and saying, 'I'm sorry, I get a little emotional sometimes' or something like that, and Bunny pushes the heel of his hand into his crotch and squeezes, releasing a pulse of pleasure into his lower spine.

'Just take the fucking Tegretol,' he says, softening.

'I'm scared, Bun. There's this guy running around attacking women.'

'What guy?'

'He paints his face red and wears plastic devil's horns.'

'What?'

'Up north. It's on the telly.'

4

Bunny picks up the remote off the bedside table and with a series of parries and ripostes turns on the television set that sits on top of the mini-bar. With the mute button on, he moves through the channels till he finds some black-and-white CCTV footage taken at a shopping mall in Newcastle. A man, bare-chested and wearing tracksuit bottoms, weaves through a crowd of terrified shoppers. His mouth is open in a soundless scream. He appears to be wearing devil's horns and waves what looks like a big, black stick.

Bunny curses under his breath and in that moment all energy, sexual or otherwise, deserts him. He thrusts the remote at the TV and in a fizz of static it goes out and Bunny lets his head loll back. He focuses on a water stain on the ceiling shaped like a small bell or a woman's breast.

Somewhere in the outer reaches of his consciousness he becomes aware of a manic twittering sound, a tinnitus of enraged protest, electronic-sounding and horrible, but Bunny does not recognise this, rather he hears his wife say, 'Bunny? Are you there?'

'Libby. Where are you?'

'In bed.'

Bunny looks at his watch, trombones his hand, but cannot focus.

'For Christ's sake. Where is Bunny Junior?'

'In his room, I guess.'

'Look, Libby, if my dad calls again . . .'

'He carries a trident,' says his wife.

'What?'

'A garden fork.'

'What? Who?'

'The guy, up north.'

Bunny realises then that the screaming, cheeping sound is coming from outside. He hears it now above the bombination of the air conditioner and it is sufficiently apocalyptic to almost arouse his curiosity. But not quite.

The watermark on the ceiling is growing, changing shape – a bigger breast, a buttock, a sexy female knee – and a droplet forms, elongates and trembles, detaches itself from the ceiling, freefalls and explodes on Bunny's chest. Bunny pats at it as if he were in a dream and says, 'Libby, baby, where do we live?'

'Brighton.'

'And where is Brighton?' he says, running a finger along the row of miniature bottles of liquor arranged on the bedside table and choosing a Smirnoff.

'Down south.'

'Which is about as far away from "up north" as you can get without falling into the bloody sea. Now, sweetie, turn off the TV, take your Tegretol, take a sleeping tablet – shit, take two sleeping tablets – and I'll be back tomorrow. Early.'

'The pier is burning down,' says Libby.

'What?'

'The West Pier, it's burning down. I can smell the smoke from here.'

'The West Pier?'

Bunny empties the tiny bottle of vodka down his throat, lights another cigarette, and rises from the bed. The room heaves as Bunny is hit by the realisation that he is very drunk. With arms held out to the side and on tiptoe, Bunny moonwalks across the room to the window. He lurches, stumbles and Tarzans the faded chintz curtains until he finds his balance and steadies himself. He draws them open extravagantly and vulcanised daylight and the screaming of birds deranges the

6

room. Bunny's pupils contract painfully as he grimaces through the window, into the light. He sees a dark cloud of starlings, twittering madly over the flaming, smoking hulk of the West Pier that stands, helpless, in the sea across from the hotel. He wonders why he hadn't seen this before and then wonders how long he has been in this room, then remembers his wife and hears her say, 'Bunny, are you there?'

'Yeah,' says Bunny, transfixed by the sight of the burning pier and the thousand screaming birds.

'The starlings have gone mad. It's such a horrible thing. Their little babies burning in their nests. I can't bear it, Bun,' says Libby, the high violin rising.

Bunny moves back to the bed and can hear his wife crying on the end of the phone. Ten years, he thinks, ten years and those tears still get him – those turquoise eyes, that joyful pussy, ah man, and that unfathomable sob stuff – and he lays back against the headboard and bats, ape-like, at his genitals and says, 'I'll be back tomorrow, babe, early.'

'Do you love me, Bun?' says Libby.

'You know I do.'

'Do you swear on your life?'

'Upon Christ and all his saints. Right down to your little shoes, baby.'

'Can't you get home tonight?'

'I would if I could,' says Bunny, groping around on the bed for his cigarettes, 'but I'm miles away.'

'Oh, Bunny . . . you fucking liar . . .'

The line goes dead and Bunny says, 'Libby? Lib?'

He looks inexplicably at the phone as if he has just discovered he is holding it, then clamshells it shut as another droplet of water explodes on his chest. Bunny forms a little

'O' with his mouth and he shoves a cigarette in it. He torches it with his Zippo and pulls deeply, then emits a considered stream of grey smoke.

'You got your hands full there, darling.'

With great effort Bunny turns his head and looks at the prostitute standing in the doorway of the bathroom. Her fluorescent pink knickers pulse against her chocolate-coloured skin. She scratches at her cornrows and a slice of orange flesh peeps behind her drug-slack lower lip. Bunny thinks that her nipples look like the triggers on those mines they floated in the sea to blow up ships in the war or something, and almost tells her this, but forgets and draws on his cigarette again and says, 'That was my wife. She suffers from depression.'

'She's not alone there, sweetheart,' she says, as she jitters across the faded Axminster carpet, the shocking tip of her tongue protruding pinkly from between her lips. She drops to her knees and takes Bunny's cock in her mouth.

'No, it's a medical condition. She's on medication.'

'Her and me both, darling,' says the girl, across Bunny's stomach.

Bunny seems to give this reply due consideration as he manoeuvres his hips. A limp, black hand rests on his belly and looking down Bunny sees that each fingernail has the detailed representation of a tropical sunset painted on it.

'Sometimes it gets really bad,' he says.

'That's why they call it the blues, baby,' she says, but Bunny barely hears this as her voice comes out in a low, incomprehensible croak. The hand twitches and then jumps on his stomach.

'Hey? What?' he says, sucking air through his teeth, and he gasps suddenly and there it was, blowing up from his heart,

8

that end-of-things thought again — 'I am damned' — and he folds an arm across his eyes and arches slightly.

'Are you OK, darling?' says the prostitute.

'I think a bath is overflowing upstairs,' says Bunny.

'Hush now, baby.'

The girl lifts her head and looks fleetingly at Bunny and he tries to find the centre of her black eyes, the tell-tale pinprick of her pupils, but his gaze loses its intent and blurs. He places a hand on her head, feels the damp sheen on the back of her neck.

'Hush now, baby,' she says again.

'Call me Bunny,' he says and sees another droplet of water tremble on the ceiling.

'I'll call you any damn thing you want, sweetie.'

Bunny closes his eyes and presses on the coarse ropes of her hair. He feels the soft explosion of water on his chest, like a sob.

'No, call me Bunny,' he whispers.

2

Bunny stumbles in the dark, groping along the bathroom wall for the light switch. It is somewhere in those dead hours, the threes and fours, and the prostitute has been paid and packed off. Bunny is alone and awake and a mammoth hangover finds him on a terrifying mission for the sleeping pills. He thinks he may have left them in the bathroom and hopes the hooker didn't find them. He locates the switch and fluorescent tubes buzz and hum awake. Bunny moves towards the mirror and its merciless light and despite the hot, toxic throb of his hangover – the dry, foul mouth, the boiled skin, blood-blown eyes and his demolished quiff – he is not displeased with what greets him.

He is afforded no insights, no illuminations, no great wisdoms but he can see immediately why the ladies dig him. He is not a toned, square-jawed lover boy or cummerbunded ladies' man but there's a pull, even in his booze-blasted face, a magnetic drag that has something to do with the pockets of compassion that form at the corners of his eyes when he smiles, a mischievous arch to his eyebrows and the little hymen-popping dimples in his cheeks when he laughs. Look! There they are now!

He throws down a sleeping tablet and for some spooky

reason the fluorescent light short-circuits, and flashes on and off. Bunny sees, for a split second, his face X-rayed and the green bones of his skull leap to the surface of his skin. Bunny says to the grinning death's head, 'Oh, man!' and throws down a second tablet and makes his way back to bed.

Showered, quiffed and deodorised, Bunny hunches over a tabloid in the breakfast room of the Grenville Hotel. He wears a fresh shirt patterned with oxblood lozenges and feels like shit, but he is relatively optimistic. You've got to be, in this game. He sees the time is 10.30 a.m. and curses to himself as he remembers a promise he had made to his wife that he would be back early. The sleeping pills still course around his system and he is finding that it is taking a certain amount of effort to turn the pages of the newspaper.

Bunny feels a ticklish interest around the back of the neck, a feathering of the hackles, and realises he has earned the attentions of the couple breakfasting on the other side of the dining room. He clocked them when he came in, sitting in the striped light of the louvred window. He turns his head slowly and deliberately and their eyes meet in the manner of animals.

A man with reptilian teeth, the bright spot of his scalp blinking through his thinning hair, strokes the jewelled hand of a woman in her mid-forties. He meets Bunny's gaze with a leer of recognition – they're both on the same game. The woman looks at Bunny and Bunny checks out her expression-free eyes, cold beneath her Botox-heavy brow. He takes in her bronzed skin, peroxided hair and gelatinous lips, the freckled cleavage of her vast modified bosom, and experiences a familiar tightening in his crotch. Bunny zones out for a while and then in a flash remembers the woman, a year ago, maybe two, in a hotel on Lancing seafront, pre-surgery. He recalls waking in a horror of confusion, his body smeared alarmingly in her orange fake tan. 'What?' he cried, slapping at his discoloured skin. 'What?' he cried, in panic.

'Do I know you?' says the man across the breakfast room, glassy-eyed and adenoidal.

'What?' says Bunny.

The muscles around the corners of the woman's mouth retract causing her lips to stretch laterally, and it takes Bunny a moment to realise that she is smiling at him. He smiles back, his dimples doing their thing, and Bunny feels a full-boned, bubonic erection leap in his tiger-skin briefs. The woman throws back her head and a clogged laugh escapes her throat. The couple rise from the table and the man moves closer to Bunny, like a skeletal animal on its hind legs, patting the breadcrumbs off the front of his trousers.

'Oh, man, you're a trip,' he says, in the manner of a wolf. 'You really fucking are.'

'I know,' says Bunny.

'You're out of this fucking world,' says the man.

Bunny winks at the woman and says, 'You look good,' and means it.

The couple exit the dining room leaving a sickly ghostage of Chanel No. 5 that compounds Bunny's hangover and makes him wince and bare his teeth and return to the newspaper.

He licks an index finger, flips a page and sees a full-page CCTV grab of the guy with the body paint, the plastic devil's horns and the trident.

'HORNY AND ON THE LOOSE', says the headline. Bunny

tries to read the article but the words just don't want to do what they were invented to do and keep breaking formation, reordering themselves, scrambling, decodifying, whatever, generally fucking around, and Bunny gives up and feels a mushroom cloud of acid explode in his stomach and blow up his throat. He shudders and wretches.

Bunny looks up and becomes aware of a waitress standing over him holding in front of her a full English breakfast. Cheeks, chin, breasts, stomach and buttocks – she looks like she has been designed solely with a compass – a series of soft, fleshy circles, in the middle of which hover two large, round, colourless eyes. She wears a purple gingham uniform, a size too small, with white collar and cuffs, her hair raked back in a ponytail and a nametag that says 'River'. As Bunny disimagines her clothes he thinks for a fraction of a second of a pile of custard-injected profiteroles, then a wet bag of overripe peaches, but settles on the mental image of her vagina, with its hair and its hole. He says, closing the newspaper with a careful, disbelieving shaking of the head, 'This world, I tell you, it gets weirder every day.'

Bunny taps at the tabloid with a manicured nail and looks up at the waitress and says, 'I mean, have you read this? Jesus.'

The waitress looks at Bunny blankly.

'Well, don't. Just don't.'

She gives her head a little jaded jerk. Bunny folds the paper in half and moves it out of the way, so that she can put the breakfast down.

'It's not something you want to read over breakfast, particularly when you've got a bloody cement mixer in your skull. Christ, I feel like someone actually *dropped* the mini-bar on my head.'

Bunny notices obliquely that a shaft of yellow sunlight has crawled across the dining room and moved up the inside of the waitress's leg, but because the waitress has started to jiggle impatiently, it gives the surreal impression that a light is short-circuiting up inside her dress or that there is a sort of seepage of luminance over the pale dough of her inner thighs. Bunny can't decide which.

He stares down at his breakfast, adrift in its sullage of grease, picks up his fork and with a sad poke at a sausage says, 'Jesus, who cooked these eggs? The bloody council?'

The waitress smiles and covers her mouth with her hand. Around her neck, hanging on a delicate chain, is a dragon's talon made of pewter holding a small glass eyeball. Bunny catches her smile, unguarded in her enormous, toneless eyes.

'Ah, there we go. A little drop of sunshine,' says Bunny, squeezing his thighs together and feeling a pulse of pleasure register around the perineum or wherever.

The waitress fingers her necklace and says, 'You want tea?'

Bunny nods, and as the waitress moves away, he clocks the sudden and self-conscious seesawing of her retreating haunches and Bunny knows, more than he knows anything in the whole world, that he could fuck this waitress in the blink of an eye, no problems, so that when she returns with his cup of tea, Bunny points at her nametag and says, 'What's that? Is that your name? River? Where did you get that?'

The waitress places her hand over the nametag. Bunny notices the frosted, achromatic nail polish she is wearing corresponds in a suppositional way with the non-colour of her eyes. They both have something to do with the moon or the planets or something.

'My mother called me that,' said the waitress.

'Oh, yeah? It's pretty,' says Bunny, bisecting a sausage and forking it into his mouth.

'Because I was born near a river,' she says.

Bunny chews and swallows and leans forward and says, 'Good job you weren't born near a toilet.'

A crease of ancient pain ruckles around the waitress's eyes, diminishing them, then they clean-slate, blank-out, and she turns her back and begins to walk away. Bunny laughs, apologetically.

'I'm sorry. Come back. I was joking.'

The breakfast room is empty and Bunny clasps his hands together in panto-supplication and says, 'Oh, please,' and the waitress slows.

Bunny zones on the afterpart of her lilac gingham uniform and a glitch in the pixels of the crosshatched pattern causes time to deregulate. He begins to see, in a concussed way, that this moment is a defining one for this particular young lady and a choice is presenting itself to her. It is a choice that could mark this waitress's life for ever; she could continue to walk away and the day would roll on in all its dismal eventuality or she could turn around and her sweet, young life would open up like, um, a vagina or something. Bunny thinks this, but he also knows, more than he knows anything in the world, that she will, indeed, turn around and willingly and with no coercion step into the slipstream of his considerable sexual magnetism.

'Please,' he says.

He contemplates getting down on one knee but realises that it is unnecessary and that he probably wouldn't be able to get up again.

River, the waitress, stops, she turns and in slow motion lies back in the water's drift and floats towards him.

'Actually, River is a beautiful name. It suits you. You've got very beautiful eyes, River.'

Bunny recalls hearing on *Woman's Hour*, on Radio 4 (his favourite show), that more women prefer their men to wear the colour maroon than any other colour – something to do with power or vulnerability or blood or something – and is glad he has worn his shirt with the oxblood lozenges. It just makes things that bit easier.

'They go deep,' he says, spiralling an index finger hypnotically. 'Way down.'

He feels a simple shift inside him, and the miserable machinery that has been grinding mercilessly in his brain all morning suddenly and effortlessly self-lubricates and moves into something sleek and choreographed and he almost yawns at the inexorable nature of what he is about to do.

He throws out his hands and says, 'Guess what my name is!'

'I don't know,' says the waitress.

'Go on. Guess.'

'No, I don't know. I've got work to do.'

'Well, do I look like a John?'

The waitress looks at him and says, 'No.'

'A Frank?'

'No.'

Bunny limps his wrist, goes ham-homo, and says, 'A Sebastian?'

The waitress cocks her head and says, 'Well . . . maybe.'

'Cheeky,' he says. 'All right, I'll tell you.'

'Go on, then.'

'It's Bunny.'

'Barney?' says the waitress.

'No, Bunny.'

Bunny holds up his hands at the back of his head and waggles them like rabbits' ears. Then he crinkles his nose and makes a snuffly sound.

'Oh, *Bunny*! Suddenly River don't seem so bad!' says the waitress.

'Oh, she's got a mouth on her.'

Bunny leans down and picks up a small suitcase by his chair. He puts it on the table then shoots his cuffs and snaps the locks. Inside the case are various beauty product samples – miniature bottles of body lotion, tiny sachets of face cleanser and little tubes of hand cream.

'Here, take this,' says Bunny, giving River a sample of hand cream.

'What's this, then?' says River.

'It's Elastin Rich, Extra Relief Hand Lotion.'

'You sell this stuff?'

'Yeah, door to door. It's bloody miraculous, if you must know. You can have it. It's free.'

'Thanks,' says River, in a small voice.

Bunny glances up at the clock on the wall and everything slows down and he feels the thunderous journey of his blood and his teeth throb at their roots and he says, quietly, 'I can give you a demonstration, if you like.'

River looks at the tiny tube of lotion cradled in the palm of her hand.

'It's got Aloe Vera in it,' he says.

3

Bunny turns the key in the ignition and his yellow Fiat Punto splutters sickly to life. A low-level guilt, if you could call it that, a nagging consternation that it was now 12.15 and he was still not home, rankles at the borders of his consciousness. He has a vague, unsettling memory of Libby being particularly upset the night before but he can't bring the reasons to mind and, anyway, it is a beautiful day and Bunny loves his wife.

It is testament to Bunny's irrepressible optimism that the glory days of their courtship refuse to relinquish their hold on the present so that it does not really matter how much shit intersects with the marital fan, when Bunny brings his wife to mind, her arse is always firmer, her breasts are shaped like torpedoes and she still possesses that girlish giggle and those happy lavender eyes. A bubble of joy explodes in his belly as he emerges from the car park into the glorious seaside sunshine. It is a beautiful day and, yes, he loves his wife.

Bunny manoeuvres the Punto through the weekend traffic and emerges onto the seafront, and with a near swoon Bunny sees it – the delirious burlesque of summertime unfolding before him.

Groups of scissor-legged school-things with their pierced

midriffs, logoed jogging girls, happy, rumpy dog-walkers, couples actually copulating on the summer lawns, beached pussy prostrate beneath the erotically shaped cumulus, loads of fucking girls who were up for it – big ones, little ones, black ones, white ones, young ones, old ones, give-me-a-minute-and-I'll-find-your-beauty-spot ones, yummy single mothers, the bright joyful breasts of waxed bikini babes, the pebble-stippled backsides of women fresh from the beach – the whole thing fucking immense, man, thinks Bunny – blondes, brunettes and green-eyed redheads that you just got to love, and Bunny slows the Punto to a crawl and rolls down the window.

Bunny waves at an iPodded fitness freak in Lycra shock-absorbers who maybe waves back; a black chick bouncing across the lawns on a yellow moon-hopper (respect); a semi-naked schoolgirl with a biscuit-sized fucksore on the base of her spine, that turns out, wonderfully, to be a tattoo of a ribbon or a bow – 'Gift wrapped,' yells Bunny. 'Can you believe it?' – then he wolf-whistles at a completely naked chick with a full Brazilian wax job, who Bunny realises, on closer inspection, is actually wearing a skin-coloured thong as anatomically integrated as sausage skin; he waves at a threesome of thunder-thighed Amazonian goddesses in Ugg boots volleying an outsized blow-up ball (they wave back in slow motion). Bunny hits the horn at a couple of surprisingly hot dykettes, who flip him the finger, and Bunny laughs and imagines them dildoed-up and going for it; then sees a knock-kneed girl in pigtails licking a red-and-blue striped stick of Brighton Rock; a girl wearing something unidentifiable that makes her appear as though she has stepped into the skin of a rainbow trout; then a nanny or something bending over a pram and the bright white spot of her panties and he blows air through his teeth and hammers the horn. Then he clocks a forlorn-looking, big-boned office girl that has been separated from her hen party, zigzagging drunkenly across the lawns, alone and disorientated, in a T-shirt that says 'SQUEAL LIKE A PIGGY' and carrying a large, inflatable penis. Bunny checks his watch, considers it, but cruises on. He sees a weird, veiled chick in a bikini with a Victorian bustle and then waves at a cute little junkie who looks a lot like Avril Lavigne (same black eyeliner), sitting on a pile of *Big Issue*s in the doorway of the crumbling Embassy apartments. She stands and shuffles towards him, skeletal, with giant teeth and black, panda-like rings under her eyes, and then Bunny realises she is not a junkie chick at all but a famous supermodel at the peak of her success whose name he can't remember, which makes Bunny's hard-on leap in his briefs, and then on closer inspection he realises that she is a junkie chick after all and Bunny cruises on, even though everybody who is into this kind of thing knows, more than anything in the world, that junkies give the best head (crack whores, the worst). Bunny turns on the radio and Kylie Minogue's hit 'Spinning Around' comes on, and Bunny can't believe his luck and feels a surge of almost limitless joy as the squelching, teasing synth starts and Kylie belts out her orgiastic paean to buggery and he thinks of Kylie's gold hotpants, those magnificent gilded orbs, which makes him think of riding River the waitress's large, blanched backside, his belly full of sausages and eggs back up in the hotel room, and he begins singing along, 'I'm spinning around, move out of my way, I know you're feeling me 'cause you like it like this', and the song seems to be coming out of all the windows of all the cars in all the world, and the beat is pounding like a motherfucker. Then he sees a group of pudgy mall-trawlers with their smirking midriffs and frosted lipstick, a potentially hot Arab chick in full burka (oh, man, labia from Arabia), and then a billboard advertising fucking Wonderbras or something and he says, 'Yes!' and takes a vicious, horn-blaring swerve, rerouting down Fourth Avenue, already screwing the top off a sample of hand cream. He parks and beats off, a big, happy smile on his face, and dispenses a gout of goo into a cum-encrusted sock he keeps under the car seat.

'Wo!' says Bunny and the deejay on the radio is saying 'Kylie Minogue, don't you love those hotpants!' and Bunny says, 'Oh, yeah!' and points the Punto into the traffic and drives the ten minutes it takes to get to his flat at Grayson Court in Portslade, still smiling and laughing and wondering if his wife Libby might be up for it when he gets home.

4

As Bunny turns into Church Road, the deejay is still talking about Kylie's gold lamé hotpants – how they are housed in a temperature-controlled vault in a museum in Australia and have reportedly been insured for eight million dollars (more than the Turin Shroud). Bunny feels his mobile vibrate and he flips it open, takes a deep breath and releases a measure of air and says, 'What?'

'I got one for you, Bunny.'

It is Geoffrey calling from the office. Geoffrey is Bunny's boss and he is also, in Bunny's view, something of a sad case, gone to fat in that mouse-sized office of his on Western Road, almost welded into a tortured swivel chair that he rarely seems to leave. A good-looking guy once upon a million years ago – there are framed photos of him on the back wall of his office, fit and almost handsome – but now an outsized, treacly-voiced pervert who sweats and sniffs and laughs into the handkerchief he forever waves theatrically in his fist. Geoffrey is a sad case, in Bunny's view, but he likes him all the same. Sometimes Geoffrey exudes a kind of paternal, Buddha-like wisdom that Bunny, on occasion, finds himself responding to.

'I'm listening, fat man,' says Bunny.

Geoffrey tells Bunny a joke about a guy who is having sex with his girlfriend and tells her to get down on her hands and knees because he wants to fuck her up the arse and the girl says that's a bit perverted and the guy says that's a big word for a six-year-old and Bunny says, 'I've heard it.'

Out of the radio comes a song that Bunny cannot identify and suddenly the whole thing is lost in a blast of static and Bunny rabbit-punches the radio, saying, 'Fuck!' whereupon heavy classical music blasts out. The music sounds like it is trumpeting the advent of something way beyond the bounds of terrible. Bunny looks askance at the car radio. He feels spooked by it – the way it seems to choose at random what it wants to hear – and he turns the volume down.

'Fucking radio,' says Bunny.

'What?' says Geoffrey

'My car radio is . . .' and Bunny hears the tortured squeal of the chair and Geoffrey open a can of lager on the other end of the line.

'. . . fucked.'

'You coming to the office, bwana?' says Geoffrey.

'Why would I do that?'

'Because your boss is lonely and I've got a fridge full of beer.'

'Got to check on the missus first, Geoffrey.'

'Well, send her my love,' says Geoffrey and he belches deeply.

'Yeah,' says Bunny.

'Listen, Bun, a woman called the office, says she's your dad's carer or something. She says you've got to go to your dad's place. It's urgent.'

'What now?'

'Hey, man, I'm just the messenger.'

Bunny turns the Punto into the forecourt of Grayson Court, snaps shut his phone and parks. He steps out of the car, with his sample case and his jacket slung over his shoulder. Hoops of sweat have formed under the arms of his canary yellow shirt (he'd put on a clean one after fucking River) and as he strides across the courtyard he feels a familiar and not unpleasant tightening in his groin.

'Maybe. Just maybe,' he singsongs to himself, thinking of his wife and patting at the pomaded curl that sits, coiled and cocky, on his forehead.

He enters the stairwell and launches himself up the concrete steps, passing on the first floor a young girl in a brief, penicillin-coloured mini-skirt and a white stretch cotton vest that says 'FCUK KIDS'. She has a pimply fourteen-year-old boy in grimy grey tracksuit trousers attached to her face. Bunny clocks her small, erect niplets jutting through the stretch weave of her vest and he leans in close to her throat as he moves past.

'Careful, Cynthia, that doggie looks infected,' he says.

The boy, his body fish-belly white and six-packed, with a mantle of acne across his shoulders, says, 'Fuck off, you cunt.'

Bunny lets out a series of dog barks.

'Arf! Arf! Arf!' he goes, leaning out over the stairwell and taking the steps two at a time.

'Come here, you wanker!' says the boy, clenching his face and making to go after him.

The young girl named Cynthia says to the boy, 'He's all right. Leave him alone,' then bares her long, braced teeth and, like a lunar probe or a lamprey, sinks down hungrily upon the boy's neck.

24

Bunny roots in his pocket for his key as he strides down the gangway to his door. The front door is painted the same canary yellow as Bunny's shirt and Bunny flashes for an unacknowledged instant an image of Libby, ten years ago, in Levis and yellow Marigolds, crouched by the door painting it, smiling up at him and wiping a strand of hair from her face with the back of her hand.

When he opens the door, the interior of the flat is dark and strange, and as he enters, he drops his sample case and attempts to hang his jacket on a metal peg that is no longer there. It has been snapped off. The jacket falls to the floor in a black heap. He flips the switch on the wall and nothing happens and he notices that the light bulb in the ceiling has been removed from its socket. He shuts the front door. He takes a step forward and, as his eyes adjust to the dark, he observes with a feeling of confusion a deeper disorder. A single bulb burns in a standard lamp, the tasselled shade cocked at an improbable angle, and in this pale uncertain light he sees that the furniture has been moved; his armchair, for instance, turned to face the wall like a naughty schoolboy and buried beneath a yoke of discarded clothes, the laminated dresser upended, its legs snapped off bar one from which a pair of Bunny's briefs hangs like a sorry flag.

'Jesus,' says Bunny.

On the coffee table is a towering stack of pizza boxes and about a dozen unopened two-litre bottles of Coke. Bunny understands, in slow motion, that it seems to be *his* clothes, in particular, that have been thrown about the place. There is a sour and cloying smell that Bunny remembers, on some level, but cannot identify.

'Hi, Dad,' comes a small voice, and a nine-year-old boy, in

blue shorts and bare feet, emerges suddenly out of the particled darkness.

'Fuck me, Bunny Boy! You scared the shit out of me!' says his father, spinning this way and that. 'What happened here?'

'I don't know, Dad.'

'What do you mean, "You don't know"? You bloody live here, don't you? Where's your mother?'

'She's locked herself in her room,' says Bunny Junior and rubs at his forehead, then scratches at the back of his leg. 'She won't come out, Dad.'

Bunny looks around him and is pole-axed by two parallel thoughts. First, that the state of the flat is personal to him, that it is a message – he sees now that some of his clothes have been slashed or torn apart – and that he is in some way responsible. An unspecified guilt, from out there on the boundaries of his psyche, pops its head over the fence, then ducks back down again. But this uneasiness is superseded by a second, more urgent, mood-altering realisation – that sex with his wife is almost certainly off the agenda and Bunny feels super-pissed off.

'What do you mean, "Won't come out"?!' he says, marching through the living room and down the hall and shouting 'Libby! Lib!'

In the hall, a box of Coco Pops has been evenly and deliberately emptied across the carpet and Bunny feels them exploding beneath his feet. He yells louder, incensed, 'Libby! For fuck's sake!'

Bunny Junior follows his father down the hall and says, 'There are Coco Pops everywhere, Dad,' and stomps about on them in his bare feet.

'Don't do that,' says Bunny to the boy. He rattles the door handle vigorously and yells, 'Libby! Open the door!'

His wife does not respond. Bunny presses his ear to the door and hears a peculiar high-toned vocal sound coming from inside the room.

'Libby?' he says quietly. There is something not unfamiliar about the weird, alien mewling and it affects Bunny in such a way that he lets his head loll back and sees that there are great lengths of Crazy String hanging from the empty light socket in the hall like the electric-blue entrails of an alien or something. He points, incredulously, and says, 'Wha-a-a?' and, after a time, drops in slow motion to his knees.

'Oh, that was me,' says Bunny Junior, pointing at the Crazy String. 'Sorry.'

Bunny presses his eye to the keyhole.

'Ha!' he exclaims, coming back to life.

Through the keyhole he can see his wife, Libby, standing by the window. Unbelievably, she is wearing the orange nightgown that she wore on their wedding night, which Bunny has not seen in years. In an instant, in a flash, he remembers, in dreamtime, his brand new wife walking towards him in their honeymoon hotel, the sheer near-invisible material of the nightgown hanging perilously from her swollen nipples, the phosphorescent skin beneath, the smudge of yellow pubic hair, veiled and dancing before his eyes.

Kneeling among the Coco Pops, his eye pressed to the keyhole, Bunny thinks, with an unannounced wave of euphoria, that the chances of a mid-afternoon fuck look decidedly better.

'Oh, come on, baby, it's your Bunnyman,' he says, but Libby still does not respond.

Bunny leaps to his feet, hammers at the door with his fists and screams, 'Open the fucking door!' as Bunny Junior says, 'I've got a key, Dad,' but Bunny pushes the boy to one side, takes a few steps back and slams himself into the door. The boy says, 'Dad, I've got a key!' and Bunny hisses, 'Get out of my way!' and this time flies at the door like a maniac, full force and grunting with the effort, and still the door does not open.

'Fuck!' he screams in frustration and drops to his knees, pressing a furious eye to the keyhole. 'Open the fucking door! You're scaring the kid!'

'Dad!'

'Stand clear, Bunny Boy!'

'*I've got a key*,' says the boy, holding the key out to his father.

'Well, why didn't you say so? Christ!'

Bunny takes the key, puts it in the keyhole and opens the bedroom door.

Bunny Junior follows his father in. He sees that *Teletubbies* is on the TV but the TV, small and portable, is on the floor over by the window. The red one named Po, with the circular antenna on its head, is saying something in a voice that the boy no longer has the ability to understand. Without taking his eyes off the TV, the boy senses his father has stopped moving and he perceives an orange smear of stillness in the corner of his vision. He hears his father say the word 'Fuck', but in a quiet, awestruck way, and decides not to lift his head. Instead, he looks at the carpet and keeps looking and notices a Coco Pop has lodged itself between the toes of his left foot.

Bunny curses quietly a second time and brings his hand up to his mouth. Libby Munro, in her orange nightdress, hangs from the security grille. Her feet rest on the floor and her knees are buckled. She has used her own crouched weight to strangle herself. Her face is the purple colour of an aubergine or something and Bunny thinks, for an instant, as he squeezes shut his eyes to expunge the thought, that her tits look good.

5

Bunny stands on the balcony outside his flat and leans out over the railing. He drinks from a can of lager and watches as two attendants push the gurney across the car park and deposit his wife into the back of the ambulance. There is no urgency to this act and it seems to Bunny, in an oblique way, eerily casual and routine. A summer breeze blows through the wind tunnels of the estate, collecting upon itself, growing stronger and flapping the edges of the sheet that hangs over the gurney. Bunny thinks he can see the side of his wife's foot but he is not sure. He draws on a cigarette and drinks from the can of lager.

As he leans out over the balcony railing and feels the pulse of his blood collecting in his face, he remembers by way of a gravitational swoon lying with Libby on a hotel bed in Eastbourne. He recalls her rising from the bed and walking to the bathroom, and somewhere between the retreat of those high blushing buttocks and the return of her yellow, freshly-douched bush, Bunny made a reckless and vertiginous decision and said, 'Libby Pennington, will you marry me?' and as he said these words the room spun wildly and he found himself gripping the sides of the bed, as if he may be jettisoned away.

Libby stood there, bold, naked, fists on hips and said, with a skewed smile, 'You're drunk.' (which was true) 'Ask me in the morning.' Bunny picked up his watch from the bedside table, made a show of holding it to his ear and tapping on the glass.

'It is morning,' he said, and Libby laughed in that wild, girlish way she had and sat down on the bed, next to Bunny.

'Will you honour and obey me?' (She was also drunk.)

'Um, yes,' said Bunny. He groped for a cigarette and put it in his mouth. Libby placed her hand between his legs and squeezed.

'In sickness and in health?'

'Um, OK,' said Bunny, lighting up and expelling a plume of grey smoke into the room. He closed his eyes. He heard her rustling about in her handbag and when he opened his eyes, she was writing something in lipstick on his chest.

'I got to take another pee,' she said and once again, through a veil of discharged smoke, he scoped that glorious, goodbye backside. Bunny stood up, the floor spongy and uncertain, looked at his image in the dressing-table mirror. Then the room tilted suddenly and blood rushed from his extremities and thundered in his face and his heart hammered in his chest and he held on to the dressing table as he read, in reverse, the single word, 'YES'.

As the spell retreated he looked up to see, standing in the doorway of the bathroom and smiling at him, his future wife.

Now, propped against the railing of the balcony, he feels, but does not cogitate, that this memory of his departed wife – her moving away from him through the haze of cigarette smoke in a down-at-heel hotel in Eastbourne – will forever dream-float in his consciousness. It will hang like a protective veil in front of the other memories, as the very happiest of them all and safeguard him from any hardboiled questions like how the fuck did it all come to this.

Bunny watches the unhurried ambulance drive away from the flats, followed by the police car.

They are taking my wife away, he thinks.

He drains the can of lager and crushes it in his fist, and hears his son ask, out of nowhere, 'Do you want another beer, Dad?'

He turns slowly and looks down at his son. (How long had he been there?) The boy seems diminished in stature and wears a pair of filthy complimentary hotel slippers about ten sizes too big for him that Bunny had brought home from a trip a million years ago. Bunny Junior presses his lips together in a wonky impression of a smile, making him look uncannily like his departed mother.

'I'll get you one, if you like.'

'Um, OK,' says Bunny and hands the crushed can to his son. 'You can put that in the bin.' The boy disappears.

Bunny holds on to the metal railing for a moment as he experiences a fresh attack of vertigo and wishes that everything would stop happening so fast. He feels as if his string has been severed and he is floating free beyond anything that would even vaguely resemble realness, without a single clue or idea or notion as to what on earth he is going to do now. What is he going to do?

He looks down at the forecourt below and sees a small contingent of residents who stand smoking in the great stretched slab of late afternoon shadow cast by the block. They have been drawn outside by the presence of the ambulance and the police car. They are, he realises, all women and they talk quietly amongst themselves but cast secret glances up at

Bunny every now and then. Bunny notices Cynthia, in her yellow mini-skirt and cotton vest, talking to a young mother who has a baby welded to one salient hip. Cynthia drops her cigarette on the ground and grinds it with a neat swivel of her flip-flop. Bunny notices the muscle leap in her young thigh. Cynthia looks up at Bunny and smiles with her long metallic teeth. Then she waves at Bunny by lifting her right hand and wiggling her fingers and from where Bunny is standing he can actually see the subtle rise of her young mound beneath the taut fabric of her mini-skirt. How old is she, anyway?

What is he going to do?

Bunny thinks, as he returns Cynthia's sad little wave and feels a gathering of manpower in his crotch, that maybe, in one way, he knows the answer. But he also thinks, on a wholly different level, that maybe, in another way, he does not know the answer at all. He thinks that he should work this question out, but he also thinks, with a sense of relief, that he can't be fucked. He feels a major decampment of stamina, of energy from his person, but notices paradoxically that his dick is hard, and as he turns and heads inside, he feels sad and lonely.

Bunny Junior sits on the sofa, tranced out in front of the television, a huge bottle of Coca-Cola clamped between his knees. He has a medical condition called blepharitis or granulated eyelids or something and he has run out of steroid eye drops. His eyes are puffy and sore and rimmed in red and he thinks at some point he should tell his father so that he can buy some more drops. He is glad all the people have cleared out. The police. The ambulance men. He was tired of the way they kept looking at him, whispering in the hallway like he couldn't hear or something. They kept making him think of his mum and every time he thought of his mum he felt like

33

he was going to drop through the middle of the world. They wouldn't stop asking him if he was all right, when all he was trying to do was watch the television. Can't anyone get any peace around here?

He notices his dad walk into the living room at approximately the same time as he remembers that he has forgotten to get him a beer from the fridge. How come he forgot to do that? His dad's face looks like grey felt. He walks differently, like he is not quite sure whose living room he is entering, like he's in a bit of a daze.

'What happened to my beer?' says Bunny, in slow motion, as he sits down next to Bunny Junior on the sofa.

'I forgot, Dad,' says Bunny Junior. 'The TV was on.'

The sleeve of a discarded sweater hangs over the top of the TV screen, partially obscuring what seems to be a news broadcast involving a giraffe that lies motionless, on its side, in its enclosure at the London Zoo. It is surrounded by a number of attendants and medical staff in Wellington boots and arabesques of smoke rise from its body.

'What are you watching that for?' asks Bunny, meaning the news, unable to think of anything else to say.

The boy rapid blinks to cool his eyes and wipes at his forehead with the back of his hand and says, 'The giraffe was struck by lightning, Dad, at the zoo. It's quite common on the veldts of Africa. They cop it all the time. They act like lightning rods. One minute they are minding their own business, the next minute they're jelly.'

Bunny hears his son, but his voice seems to come from a vast distance and his stomach makes a hollow, rumbling sound and he realises he hasn't eaten anything since breakfast and thinks he may be hungry. He takes one of the pizza boxes from

34

the stack on the coffee table and opens it. He waves it under his nose.

'How long have these been here?' says Bunny.

'I don't know, Dad,' says the boy. 'Maybe a million years?'

Bunny sniffs it.

'Smells all right,' he says and folds a slice in half and stuffs it in his mouth.

'Tastes all right, too,' he says, but it comes out sounding incomprehensible.

Bunny Junior reaches over and takes a slice.

'Very nice, Dad,' he says, and for a moment the fuzzed tones of the TV weld the boy to his father and they sit together on the sofa and say nothing. After some time Bunny points at the towering stack of pizza boxes on the coffee table in front of them, a cigarette burning between his fingers. His mouth is full of pizza and there is a questioning expression on his face and he is about to say something and he chews vigorously and continues to point at the pizza boxes.

Bunny Junior says, 'I think mum left them for us, Dad' and as he says this he feels the fiery centre of the world drag at his insides and he paddles his feet over the edge of the sofa so violently that his slippers fly off his feet. Bunny looks at his son and responds by nodding and swallowing and zoning in on the TV.

Later that night Bunny Junior says to his father, 'I better go to bed now, Dad.'

Bunny, zomboid, says, 'Ah, yeah', and a bit later on says, 'OK, then.'

The boy puts on his outsized slippers and says to his father,

'I'm usually in bed ages ago.' He rubs at his raw, bleared eyes with the back of his hands. 'My eyes are sore,' he says.

'OK, Bunny Boy, I'll just sit here then,' says his father and makes a vague, circular gesture with his hand, which Bunny Junior finds impossible to interpret.

'Well, I'll just go to bed then, now, Dad,' says the boy and stands and looks down at his father and sees he has returned to the thrall of the television. Two greased and roided gladiators, dressed in Lycra shock-absorbers, beat each other with Styrofoam-capped staves. They wear facemasks so there is nothing to suggest whether they are men or women as they bat and snarl at each other. Bunny Junior thinks he might sit down again and check this out but instead says, 'Goodnight, Dad.'

With exaggerated care, the boy steps over the piles of trashed clothes that lie about the living room like sleeping animals, as if they may, if he wrong-foots, awaken. He moves into the hall, the Coco Pops now ground into the carpet by the day's dismal traffic, and makes his way towards his room. He sees, in terror, from the corner of his eye, the closed door to the master bedroom and the key hanging from the lock like a reproach. Bunny Junior presses his lips together and squeezes shut his eyes. He decides he will not open them again until he is safe within the confines of his room. He makes the rest of the journey feeling along the hallway wall like a blind man until he arrives at the door to his room. He touches with his hand the poster of the cartoon rabbit flipping its middle finger that is Blu-tacked to the door and feels the plastic letters arranged along the top of it. They spell B-U-N-N-Y J-N-R. He pushes open his door and enters his bedroom and only then does he open his eyes.

Bunny Junior changes into his pyjamas, pulls back the sheet

36

on his bed, lies down, then reaches over and turns off his bedroom light. He is comforted by the canned applause that emanates from the living room and is happy his dad is close by. Above him a mobile of the nine planets of the solar system, painted in Day-Glo, rotates slowly, put into motion by the bedtime movements of the boy. As each planet turns and spins, Bunny Junior runs through the information he has collected about each one. For example – Saturn's interior is similar to Jupiter's, consisting of a rocky core, a liquid metallic hydrogen layer and a molecular hydrogen layer. Traces of various ices are present – stuff he has remembered from the encyclopaedia his mother gave him when he was seven. He wishes, vaguely, that his father would come in and sit with him while he tries to sleep. He feels like it will take two thousand light years before he will be able to get to sleep. He sleeps.

Back in the living room Bunny watches the TV without interest, without judgement or without any visible cognitive response whatsoever. Occasionally his head falls back and he drains a beer. He opens another. His eyes glaze over. He sucks a cigarette, like a machine. Like a robot, he does it all again. Yet, as the blue evening, framed in the window, darkens into nighttime, little pockets of emotion twitch at the corners of his eyes and his forehead creases and his hands begin to tremble.

Then without warning Bunny leaps to his feet, and as if he has been girding himself for this moment all evening, moves to the sideboard (procured by Libby from a garage sale in Lewes) and opens its frosted glass front. Bunny reaches inside and returns to the sofa with a bottle of malt whisky and a short, heavy glass.

He pours himself a drink, and then up-ends it down his throat. He gags and throws his body forward, shakes his head and repeats the action with the bottle and the glass again. Then with little stabs of his index finger punches a number into his mobile phone. The line engages and before there is even time for the purr of the ringtone, he hears an awful, protracted bout of coughing, deep and wet, that forces Bunny to hold the phone at arm's length from his ear.

In time, Bunny, clearly disturbed, says, 'Dad?' with an un-intended and violent emphasis on the initial letter − not a stammer as such, but the beginnings of one, as if the word has been wrenched from his mouth like a stinking tooth.

'Dad?' he says again, jamming the phone under his chin and firing up another fag.

The coughing stops and Bunny hears a vicious intake of air sucked through oversized dentures that actually sounds like a nest of aggrieved snakes. Then the seething, bilious enquiry, 'What?'

'Dad? It's me,' says Bunny as he reaches for the bottle and slops another shot into the glass, his hand jumping about in agitation.

'Who?' shouts his father.

'Dad, I've got something to tell you.'

'Who the fuck is this?' says his father and Bunny hears him chopping his dentures. His voice sounds murderous and mad.

'It's me.' Bunny's hand is jumping around on the end of his wrist so much he appears like he is waving or has epilepsy or he's just washed his hands and found there is no towel to dry them or something. He throws down the whisky, grimaces, shudders, sucks on his cigarette and finds that his whole body has started to shake.

'Who the fuck are you?' says the old man and the coughing starts up again, raking deep into the lungs.

'D-dad?' says Bunny, and he hears himself stutter and curses under his breath and tongs shut the phone. He tries to stick a fresh cigarette in his mouth but his head and his hand are jumping so much he finds it near-impossible. He lights it by steadying one hand with the other, then falls back against the sofa, expels the smoke violently and says, 'Fuck!'

He pictures his father, momentarily, as a medical skeleton sitting in an ancient leather armchair, tubercular lungs sucking at white powdery ribs, fag in hand, snarling into the telephone. The image terrifies him and he squeezes shut his eyes but the dread skull of his father continues to dance before his eyes. I'll try him again some other time – he thinks.

Later on, and a bottle of whisky gone and nothing else going down, Bunny lurches along the hallway and leans against the door to the master bedroom. He takes a breath and opens the door, his face tensed and inclined to the side, the way an amateur may defuse a large bomb.

With every intention of entering the room cautiously, Bunny stumbles and half-falls and staggers across the room and sits down on the unmade marital bed. He undresses down to his briefs. He turns and sees the curled inscription of his wife's body still trapped within the sheets and considers reaching out and placing his hand on it. He feels he would do this but is still spooked from having just visited the bathroom where he was confronted with the sight of his wife's collection of 'special' Ann Summers underwear hanging like lace bunting from the retractable clothesline above the bath. He had not seen these particular panties in years and he understood that they had been hung there as a kind of clue to something he was too drunk to fully fathom. Was his wife trying to tell him something? When he reached out and touched them with his fingers, the room swooned dramatically and the walls turned to Silly Putty and the next thing he knew he was lying on his back between the toilet and the bath. He let himself rest there for a moment and looked up at the line of pastel-coloured underwear that waved and danced above him, their gussets open wide like mouths, and Bunny was struck with a sudden and almost palpable sense of his wife's presence there in the bathroom. The room felt chilled and Bunny thought he could see query marks of vapour rising from his lips. He stood up and got the hell out of there.

Now, sitting in his briefs on the edge of the bed, Bunny pulls the drawer out of Libby's bedside table and dumps the contents – half-a-dozen little brown medicine bottles and pill packets – on the bed. Bunny locates the trusty Rohypnol, those pretty purple dissectible diamonds, and pops one, and then another, from their foil pockets and swallows them.

Bunny falls, in slow motion, backward and lies upon the bed. He closes his eyes and squeezes his genitals and tries to bring to mind a celebrity vagina but finds that his brain keeps bringing forth images of the day's horror – the empurpled face of his wife, the imagined death's head of his father, the screaming crotches of his wife's *ouvert* panties. He opens his eyes and finds his attention drifting to the security grille on the window and the room dervishes and Bunny, with an impressive display of both self-control and alcoholic paralysis, remains where he is, on this fucked-up magic carpet ride.

He does this until he can do it no more, whereupon he rises from the bed and returns, bombed-out, to the living room.

He stumbles over the dumped piles of his clothes. Is that ink? Has ink been poured over his clothes? He falls heavily on the sofa and fumbles with the remote and zaps at the TV. He finds the Adult Channel and a televised phone-in sex-line and he allows an East European girl named Evana, who has a tight, hot, wet pussy and the bedside manner of a mallet or something, to coax Bunny through the most forlorn wank, he thinks, in the history of the world.

Then Bunny falls back against the sofa, and before he can surrender to his drugged sleep he manages with a near-super-human act of will to press the 'OFF' button on the remote and see, for an instant, the TV go dead, so that for a few short hours the Munro home seems peaceful — no phantoms or ghosts, no clanking of chains, no voices calling from beyond the grave — just a father and his son sleeping, the night hushed and respectful, in a manner fitting a man who will quite soon be dead.

6

When Bunny Junior enters the living room, he squints into the light that pours through the window. A mop of bed-hair crowns his sleep-seamed face, and his pyjamas are runkled and a Spiderman web-blaster is attached to his forearm. He screws up his nose at the cloying odour and waves his hand in front of his face.

Then he sees, with a gasp and a rush of energised wind through his body, his father sprawled motionless on the sofa, grey as a kitchen glove and coated in a patina of cold grease. The metallic, outsized TV remote is still cradled banally in his dead hand like an anachronism. It looks antique and obsolete and somehow responsible for Bunny's condition, as if it had failed in its sole responsibility of keeping Bunny alive.

'Dad?' says the boy, quietly, then louder, 'Dad!'

He begins to hop from one foot to the other in his complimentary bathroom slippers. Bunny does not respond, and if he is breathing, then it is too shallow and inconsequential to produce any noticeable movement in his body.

Bunny Junior actually jumps up and down and screams 'Dad!' with such force that his father rears wildly up, batting at himself with his hands.

'What?!' he says.

Bunny Junior says, 'You didn't move!'

'What?'

'You just didn't move!'

'Hey? No, I fell asleep,' says Bunny and tries to recognise his son.

Bunny Junior turns and jabs his finger angrily towards the hall and the master bedroom, still hopping weirdly from foot to foot.

'Didn't you want to sleep in there?!' he says, in a loud voice, rubbing at his forehead with the back of his hand. 'Didn't you want to go and sleep in there?!'

Bunny sits up and wipes at the slick of drool on his bristled cheek.

'No. What? No, I fell asleep. What time is it?' says Bunny.

The boy does not actually move closer to his father but when Bunny looks at him he seems to hard-zoom into focus, which gives the impression of an almost supernatural forward motion, and Bunny rears back reactively.

'I should have used the key,' says Bunny Junior, anxiously.

Bunny feels the events of the previous day collect about him, stealing the air. He is, on an abstract level, shocked by the realisation that his life is now different. It has become tragic and lamentable. He has become pitiable. A widower. But more explicably he also understands that the Rohypnol and the whisky he consumed the night before still course through his system and this makes him feel, in a very real way, pretty good.

'What?'

'The key, Dad, I should have used it!'

'When? What?'

Bunny Junior looks at his father, his face twisted in rage,

his granulated eyeballs raw and alive in their sockets, his little fists clenched at his sides, and shouts, 'I just should have used the fucking key!'

Bunny, who has no idea of what is going on, does a kind of cabaret grab with his arm and ducks and weaves to avoid a slice of sunlight that scythes the room in two.

Grimacing, he says, 'Christ, keep your voice down.'

Then he raises himself up, wavers on new legs and feels all the love thunder through his bloodstream.

'Jesus, I'm loaded,' he says, and he stands there in his briefs. 'Is there anything to eat?'

Bunny Junior opens and closes his mouth and throws his arms out to the sides in a gesture that means 'I don't know' and says, in a sad, grief-modulated voice, 'I don't know.'

'Well, let's take a look then!' says Bunny. 'I could eat a bloody cow!'

Bunny Junior, who loves his father, compresses his lips into a skew-whiff smile and says, 'Me too, Dad!' and follows him into the farragoed kitchen, where, like the living room, stuff has been up-ended, flung around and scattered about.

'Yeah, well, I could eat two bloody cows!'

Bunny opens the cupboard door and reels back in mock-horror.

'Jesus Christ, there's a fucking *monkey* in here!' and pulls out a box of Coco Pops and, rattling them to his ear, turns towards the fridge and opens it. He notices that the coloured magnetic alphabet that has decorated the fridge in a non-sensical scramble of letters for the last five years has been arranged to say 'FUCK YR PUSSY' and he wonders, as he snaps the seal on a pint of milk and sniffs it, who would have done that.

'Actually, Bunny Boy, I could eat the whole fucking flock,' he says.

'Herd,' says the boy.

'Yeah, and them too.'

They sit opposite each other, bent over their bowls, and with a much-exaggerated display of appreciation, they eat their cereal.

'What key?' asks Bunny.

Bunny spends the following days organising the funeral arrangements and taking calls of enquiry and commiseration from God knows whom, all with a zoned-out, robotic insentience.

The phone call to Libby's mother, Doris Pennington, was made with all the sweat-soaked stupor of a man standing on a trapdoor with a rope around his neck. The woman's complete contempt for her son-in-law went way back, almost nine years, to the first time Libby walked out on him and made her tearful way back home to mother – cum-stained knickers (not hers) in the back seat of Bunny's old Toyota. The roaring silence that greeted the tragic news broke upon Bunny like a great wave and he sat there, heavy-lidded with the phone pressed to his ear, listening to the phantoms and ghosts inside the phone long after the line had gone dead. Bunny became convinced that he could detect the faraway rhythms of his wife's voice deep in the phone lines. He felt she was trying to tell him something and a chill ran through his bones and he castaneted the phone and sat there, gulping lungs of air like a fish.

Through these days Bunny made increasingly frequent and

protracted visits to the bathroom, beating off with a single-minded savagery, intense even by Bunny's standards. Now, sitting on the sofa with a large Scotch, his cock feels and looks like something that has been involved in a terrible accident – a cartoon hotdog, maybe, that has made an unsuccessful attempt to cross a busy road.

The boy sits beside him and the two of them are locked in a parenthesis of mutual zonkedness. Bunny Junior stares blankly at the encyclopaedia open in his lap. His father watches the television, smokes his fag and drinks his whisky, like an automaton.

After a time, Bunny turns his head and looks at his son and clocks the way he stares at his weird encyclopaedia. He sees him but he can't really believe he is there. What did this kid want? What is he supposed to do with him? Who is he? Bunny feels like an extinct volcano, lifeless and paralysed. Yeah, he thinks, I feel like an extinct volcano – with a weird little kid to look after and a mangled sausage for a dick.

Bunny scopes the living room. He has made some attempt at clearing up the debris and bringing some order back to the flat. In doing so he has uncovered the extent of the damage his wife had brought down upon the house. For example, he had found his Avril Lavigne (drool) and Britney (drool) and Beyoncé (drool) CDs floating in the toilet cistern; the entrails of his bootleg Tommy and Pamela video (a gift from his boss, Geoffrey) had been torn out and gallooned around the ceiling light in the bedroom; several unsuccessful attempts had been made to fasten to the wall a headshot of himself, taken at a company bash in the bar of The Wick, by way of a fork through the face, the tines

46

leaving an hysterical Morse code on the woodchip of the bathroom – dot dot dot, dash dash dash, dot dot dot – fuck you.

Bunny feels this was all done in a private language of blame. He feels a surge of guilt, but he doesn't know why. He feels victimised. She had a medical condition, for Christ's sake. She was depressed. The doctors said so. It had to do with a misfiring of her synapses or something. Still, it all feels so fucking *personal* and then there is a knock on the front door.

Bunny opens the door and is greeted by two social workers – Graeme somebody and Jennifer somebody – making an unannounced and unsolicited visit to monitor how Bunny and his son are coping. Bunny is glad he has made some effort to put right his house. He wishes, though, that he were a little more sober.

'Hello, young man,' says Jennifer to Bunny Junior and the boy offers a tight, little smile. 'Do you think we could talk to your dad for a minute?'

Bunny Junior nods and picks up his encyclopaedia and disappears into his bedroom.

'He's adorable,' says the woman and takes a seat opposite Bunny. She brings with her the ghost of a scent that Bunny remembers with absolute familiarity but cannot identify.

'We don't want to take up too much of your time,' says Graeme, but something in his tone makes this statement seem unsympathetic and accusatory.

Graeme is a tall man with a huge, round, aggressive head and a seriously sunburned face – a human stop sign – and he places himself behind Jennifer, stiff-legged, feet apart, in a sad parody of a Stasi thug. He says he is there as a moderator or a mediator or something, but Bunny is not really listening. He is looking at Jennifer, who is, no matter how you cut it, seriously hot. Barelegged and new on the job, she has dressed herself in a linen skirt and cotton blouse in an attempt to demonstrate a sort of conservative and professional remove – but who is she kidding? Bunny knows, almost psychically, that the bra she is wearing is anything but standard issue, and her panties, well, who knows, but by the way she is sitting in the chair in front of him, and wiggling her knee, he wonders if she is wearing any at all. He considers this for a protracted period of time and comes to believe that her glistening and moisturised lower leg is, as anyone who is into this sort of thing knows, suggestive of a waxed pussy. Bunny feels his eyes closing and realises, from a million miles away, that Jennifer is recommending he seek some emotional support and is running through a list of grief councillors, local twelve-step meetings and support groups. He remembers with a dreadful spasm what has happened to his wife and then he catches the social worker squeezing her thighs together. Jennifer kind of peters out and dries up.

Bunny offers little but monosyllabic responses. He becomes increasingly wary of Graeme, who keeps eyeballing him in an ultra-threatening way, like he was doing something wrong. His crimson face pulses with an aura of something malign and barely suppressed, and Bunny notices a sprinkling of dandruff, like ash, on his dark blue jacket. He tries to concentrate on the possibilities of Jennifer's vagina by defabricating her outfit. Then Bunny surprises himself by letting forth an ancient groan, a roar torn from the depths, and falling to his knees and flinging his face into Jennifer's lap.

'What am I going to do now? *What am I going to do now?*'
he bellows and fills his lungs with her salty, summer smell.
He feels, in an indirect way, that he has not smelt a woman
for what seems like an eternity. He presses his face
deeper into her lap and thinks – What is that smell? Opium?
Poison?

Jennifer rears back and says, 'Mr Munro!' and Bunny
wraps his arms around her cool, bare legs and sobs into her
dress.

Graeme, her gallant protector, steps forward and says, all
business but clearly unnerved, 'Mr Munro, I must ask you
to sit back in your seat!'

Bunny releases Jennifer, and says, quietly, 'What am I going
to do?' and in saying that, reaches up and, to his surprise,
finds his face is wet with real tears. And although he has to
arrange himself to disguise the advent of a full-blown hard-
on that has tented in his trousers, the question still hangs
in the air, just the same. What is he going to do?

He hangs his head and wipes his face and says, 'I'm so
sorry. Please excuse me.'

Jennifer roots around in her handbag and hands Bunny a
Kleenex.

'It may not seem like it now, Mr Munro, but things will
get better,' she says.

'Do you always carry these?' asks Bunny, waving the tissue.

Jennifer smiles and says, 'They are a much-needed tool
of the trade, I'm afraid.'

She straightens her skirt and makes to stand.

'Is there anything else you would like to discuss, Mr Munro?'
she says.

'Yes,' says Bunny, and he feels a bead of perspiration collect in the hollow beneath his Adam's apple. 'Do you believe in ghosts?'

Jennifer instinctively looks to Graeme for the official line on this question. Bunny thinks he can feel the heat coming off Graeme's barbecued face and he turns his head to look at him and glimpses Graeme rolling his eyes.

'What if you are not sure whether your wife has actually completely died?' asks Bunny, balling the tissue in his fist and flicking it across the room.

The social workers leave and Bunny takes his place on the sofa and watches the television.

'Can I come back in now?' asks Bunny Junior, appearing at the door.

'Well, yeah,' says Bunny, opening a beer.

The boy sits down next to his father and starts flip-flopping his feet.

'What is it with you and your feet?' says Bunny.

'Sorry, Dad.'

Bunny points at the television.

'Have you seen that?' he says.

'I didn't think you liked watching the news,' says the boy.

On the TV there is more CCTV footage of the devil guy who paints himself red, wears plastic joke-shop horns and attacks women. He has struck again. This time fatally. He has followed a young office worker named Beverly Hamilton into an underground car park and murdered her with a garden fork. He stabbed her hundreds of times. The car park is in Leeds, which, thinks Bunny, is further south. The public are in a state of shock. Later that day the Horned Killer, as the press have tagged him, had paraded in front of CCTV cameras at a nearby mall, panicking the shoppers. Then he disappeared. The police are 'baffled'.

'Do you believe this guy?' says Bunny.

'No, Dad, I don't!' says the boy.

7

There is a simple service for Libby Munro at St Nicolas Church in Portslade. Bunny and Bunny Junior stand in the church, heads bowed. They are dressed in the brand new black suits Bunny had found hanging, side by side, in the otherwise empty closet in his bedroom. A receipt he discovered in the jacket pocket showed that Libby had bought the suits from Top Shop in Churchill Square, two days before her suicide. What was that about?

Every day a newer, weirder and sadder aspect to Libby's demise reveals itself. A neighbour had said that she had seen Libby burning pieces of paper and dropping them over the balcony a couple of days before her death. They had turned out to be the love letters Bunny had written her before they were married. He found little burnt pieces of them under the stairwell with the syringes and the condoms. What had got into her? She must have been crazy.

The whey-faced and effeminate Father Miles, with a cumulus of white hair banked around his skull, delivers his eulogy in a pneumatic whisper that Bunny has to crane his head to fully hear. He refers to Libby as 'full of life and loved by all' and later 'selfless and generous beyond measure', not once mentioning her medical condition and her subsequent mode of departure, Bunny notices, other than to say 'she had joined the angels prematurely'.

Bunny gives a cursory scope of the congregation and sees, squeezed into the same pew, on the other side of the church, a small number of Libby's friends.

Patsy 'Bad Vibes' Parker throws Bunny incriminatory looks every so often, but Bunny expects nothing less. Patsy Parker has never liked Bunny and at every opportunity she can find alerts him to the fact. Patsy is short, with an over-developed backside, and to compensate for her low stature wears high heels much of the time on her tiny undersized feet. When she would come to visit Libby, she would walk down the gangway in an obscene and purposeful trot, reminding Bunny of one of the three little pigs, probably the one who made its house out of bricks. This is particularly pertinent, as she had once, in a fit of pique over some porny comment she had overheard him make about the walking fuck-fest Sonia Barnes from No. 12, called Bunny a wolf. Bunny assumed she meant the cartoon wolf, all drooling tongue and bulging eyeballs, and had actually taken this remark as a compliment. Each time he'd see her he would do his 'I'll huff and I'll puff and I'll blow your house down' routine. Bunny considers rolling out his tongue and bugging his eyeballs at her but realises with a certain satisfaction that he can't be fucked.

Next to Patsy Parker, Bunny sees, is Rebecca Beresford, who Libby would refer to at any given time as 'the older sister she never had', 'her soul mate' and 'her best friend in the world'. Rebecca Beresford stopped talking to Bunny years ago after an incident at a barbecue on Rottingdean beach that involved a half bottle of Blue Label Smirnoff, an uncooked chipolata, her fifteen-year-old daughter and a serious misreading of the signs. This led to a furore that a year of contrition could not defuse. Eventually an unspoken agreement was forged that mutual disdain was the only way forward. Whatever. Rebecca Beresford shoots scowling broadside glances at Bunny from the other side of the church.

Next to her is the seriously sexy Helen Claymore, who also gives Bunny nasty little looks, but Bunny can see that her heart isn't in them and that she is clearly up for it. This is not an opinion but a statement of fact. Helen Claymore is dressed in a tight, black tweed suit that does something insane to her breasts, militarises them, torpedoes them, and something out of this world to her depth-charged rear end. Helen Claymore has been transmitting signals to Bunny in this way for years and Bunny takes a deep breath and allows himself to open up to her vibes like a medium or spiritualist or something. He gives vent to his imagination and realises for the millionth time that he has none and so he pictures her vagina. Bunny marvels at this for an unspecified moment. He sees it hovering before his eyes like a holy apparition and intuits the wonder of it and feels his dick harden like a bent fork or a divining rod or a cistern lever – he can't decide which.

Then he hears a release of hissed gas and turns to see Libby's mother, Mrs Pennington, staring straight at him with a look of horror and sheer hatred on her face. She actually bares her teeth at him. Caught in the act – thinks Bunny – and bends his head in prayer.

The boy looks up at his father and then over at Mrs Pennington and smiles at her and raises his hand in a sad, little wave. His grandmother looks at him and shakes her head in rage and grief, and a great sob breaks from her chest. Her husband, a good-looking guy who had a stroke a year ago and is now consigned to a wheelchair, lifts a convulsive hand and places it over that of his despairing wife.

Suddenly, Father Miles is talking about 'those left behind', and when he mentions Libby's 'loving husband', Bunny thinks he can hear an audible groan from the congregation – a boo and a hiss for the bad guy. He thinks he may well be imagining this but, just in case, he repositions himself, giving them his back, as if to shield himself from their collective disdain by facing the wall.

When he opens his eyes his attention is grabbed by a painting of the Virgin Mary with the infant Jesus cradled in her arms. Underneath there is a lacquered plaque that reads *Madonna and Child*, which makes him close his eyes and incline his head again and think about Madonna and her waxed pussy (probably) and how he'd read in some interview that she liked having her yoga-toned bottom spanked.

Behind all this imagining he can hear the low whisper of his wife's eulogy and suddenly he feels a kind of imminent sense of her presence and, weirdly, his own doom. He can stand it no longer.

'Wait here,' he whispers to his son.

Bunny sidles from the pew and, head bent, sneaks out of the church. He ducks across the green square of lawn and, in a little public toilet made out of bricks, shaded by an implausible palm tree, he rests his head against the graffitied wall of the cubicle and beats off. He remains in this position for a time, then gloomily bats at a toilet paper dispenser, cleans himself up and exits the cubicle.

With eyes downcast, he stands before the reflective square of stainless steel screwed to the wall above the sink. After a while Bunny finds the courage to raise his head and look at himself. He half expects some drooling, slack-jawed ogre to greet him there in the smeared mirror and is pleasantly surprised to see that he recognises the face that stares back at him – warm, loveable and dimpled. He pats at his pomaded forelock and smiles at himself. He leans in closer. Yeah, there it is – that irresistible and unnameable allure – a little bashed and battered, to be sure, but who wouldn't be?

Then, on closer inspection, he sees something else there, looking back at him. He leans in nearer still. Something grievous has resided in his face that he is amazed to see adds to his general magnetism. There is an intensity to his eyes that was not there before – a tragic light – that he feels has untold potential and he shoots the mirror a sad, emotive smile and is aghast at his new-found pulling power. He tries to think of a papped celebrity who has been visited by some great tragedy and come out the other side looking better as a result, but can't think of one. This makes him feel mega-potent, ultra-capable and super-human, all at the same time.

But most of all, Bunny feels vindicated. Despite everything, he's got his mojo back. He feels he is ready to face the scowling disdain of this church full of uptight women. He even contemplates knocking out another one there at the sink. He sticks a Lambert & Butler in his mouth and lights it and blows a trumpet of smoke at his own reflected image.

Then he notices that the shadows behind him have begun to bleed and smudge and reposition themselves. They seem to be growing longer and taking on personalities that would not normally be attributed to them, as if they were advancing upon him from the spirit world. Bunny has the unforeseen feeling that he is going to die – not today, necessarily, but soon – and is puzzled to realise that he experiences a certain comfort in that. He feels, in an intuitive way, that the shadows are those of the dead, rearranging themselves, rolling over and making room for him.

He finds himself going weak at the knees and he rolls his head back and looks at the ceiling. He notices a white clump of perforated mud in the upper corner of the toilet block, the size and shape of a human heart. In time, Bunny realises he is looking at a wasps' nest and that it is alive and humming with malign industry. The wasps are preparing themselves – he thinks. He remembers the burning West Pier and his blood runs cold and he thinks – the starlings are circling. He closes his eyes and imagines for a split second a rush of perilous and apocalyptic visions – planes falling from the sky; a cow giving birth to a snake; red snow; an avalanche of iron maidens; a vagina with its mouth stapled shut; a phallus shaped like a mushroom cloud – and Bunny shudders, checks his teeth in the mirror and thinks – Man, where did that come from?

He centres his quiff, with a light tapping of the hands, then flicks his cigarette at the wasps' nest and, in a shower of sparks, exits the toilet block.

As he crosses the green and dandilioned lawn he sees Bunny Junior sitting on the steps of the church. The boy has taken his jacket off and draped it over his head.

'Is that you in there, Bunny Boy?' asks Bunny, looking this way and that.

'Yes,' says the boy, flatly.

'Why aren't you inside?' asks Bunny.

'Everybody left ages ago. They've gone to the cemetery. What happened to you?'

Bunny looks at his watch and, with a rush of blood to the head, wonders how long he has been in the toilet.

'Nature called,' says Bunny. 'Come on. Let's go.'

'What?' says the boy.

'If you took the bloody jacket off your head, you might be able to hear me,' says Bunny. 'I feel like I'm talking to a mushroom.'

Bunny Junior removes his jacket and squints up at his father. His eyes are shot with blood and rimmed in a pink crust.

'The sun hurts my eyes, Dad.'

'Come on, you'll be all right. Get in the car. We're late,' says Bunny, already moving across the lawn towards the Punto. Bunny Junior follows his father.

They climb into the dazzling yellow Punto, with its polka dots of seagull shit, and Bunny starts it up and swings into the mid-afternoon traffic.

'Christ, it's hot,' says Bunny, and father and son roll down the windows.

Bunny hits the radio and a super-authoritative female voice comes out.

'Cool,' he says.

'What?' asks the boy.

'*Woman's Hour.*'

'Is it, Dad?'

'It's educational,' says Bunny, turning up the volume.

The boy allows the air gusting through the window to blow across his face.

'I don't feel so great,' he says and closes his eyes.

Bunny Junior hears his dad say, 'You'll be all right, Bunny Boy,' and that makes him feel better because everybody knows that not knowing whether you are going to be all right is often the worst part of when you don't feel all right. He keeps his eyes closed and he listens to the radio. He hears a lady talking

58

about the sexualising or something of children through advertising. She starts talking about Barbie dolls and in particular a new doll called Bratz that looks like it has just had sex or taken a whole lot of drugs or something. When she says, 'Our children are having their childhoods stolen from them,' he hears his father repeat the line and then say it again as if he is storing it away in his memory. He feels the car slow and grind and squeal to a stop.

'We're here,' says Bunny. 'Are you all right?' He hears a tremor of irritation in his father's voice – not at him, probably, but at the whole world.

Bunny Junior opens his eyes and gives his dad a tight little smile and together they climb out of the Punto and make their way down the gravel path to the small collection of people that has gathered around what will be his mother's final resting place. Bunny and Bunny Junior ease their way in and, with muttered apologies, make their way to the graveside.

8

Bunny Junior hops from foot to foot and tries to listen to the vicar, but can't really hear him and anyway it is hard to concentrate because two squabbling seagulls that seem to be in the throes of some mating dance or something are becoming a major distraction. Bunny Junior hates seagulls. He always has and he always will. He keeps his head inclined but can see out of the corner of his eye that the seagulls are getting dangerously close. He read in the *Argus* only recently that a seagull attacked an old age pensioner in Hove. The man had a heart attack and died, and if his wife hadn't chased it away it would have definitely pecked the old man's eyes out and probably his guts as well.

Bunny Junior notices that Poodle, a friend of his father's from work, is standing at the back of the crowd, tapping his foot and wiggling his hips and secretly puffing on a cigarette that is cupped in his right hand. He notices that Poodle is wearing headphones. Bunny Junior smiles at Poodle and Poodle gives him the secret thumbs-up sign. Poodle is skinny, wears tight stonewashed jeans (even to a funeral) and sports a yellow, lacquered quiff. This makes him look a bit like, well, an evil poodle and Bunny Junior wonders which came first – the name or the 'do. The boy sees Poodle eyeball the seagulls, then flick his cigarette butt and, with an uncanny accuracy, hit one of them in the side of the head. Poodle punches the air and says, 'Yes!' loud enough for other people to turn around and look at him. His girlfriend, who has something grape-coloured on her top lip, elbows Poodle in the ribs. Poodle hangs his head in prayer. Then he winks at Bunny Junior and rolls his eyes, and when he smiles, he looks like a grinning dog. Of all his father's friends, Bunny Junior likes Poodle best. No contest.

The seagull, meanwhile, squawks horribly and snaps up the cigarette in its beak and flies off. Bunny Junior feels it was probably an incident like this that caused the West Pier to burn down – man drops cigarette butt, seagull picks it up thinking that it is food, takes it to the West Pier and drops it in a nest full of baby seagulls. The nest, built in the roof of the old, disused ballroom, bursts into flame, the pier catches alight and the pier burns down. Bunny Junior loves the West Pier because his mother took him on a special guided tour of the pier for his eighth birthday, then they walked all the way to Marrocco's for an ice cream. Bunny Junior loves the West Pier and he hates seagulls. He thinks they are bastards. In the world famous Booth Museum in Dyke Road there are a couple of stuffed ones and Bunny Junior remembers reading somewhere that the seagulls on the south coast of England are particularly large, perhaps the largest in the world. They are also amongst the most aggressive. Another thing he remembers about seagulls is that when they crap they actually target humans. This is a proven fact. They also attack light-reflecting colours like yellow, and this is why the Punto is always such a mess. His father hates seagulls almost as much as Bunny Junior does. They are big, aggro bastards. This is a proven fact.

He can see his mother's coffin being lowered into a hole in the ground. The casket seems much too small. He thinks for a moment that maybe there has been a terrible mistake and that they are burying the wrong person – a child, maybe, or a midget, or even an animal, like a German Shepherd or a Red Setter or something.

He half expects his mother to roll up and say to him, 'What are you doing here, dressed up in that fine suit?'

Bunny Junior would shake his head incredulously and say, 'I don't know, Mum.'

'Well, let's go home then, Bunny Boy,' she would say.

The boy senses a heat coming from his father, who stands next to him. His father looks down and says out of the corner of his mouth, loud enough for everyone to hear, 'Jesus Christ, Bunny Boy, what's wrong with you? Stop jiggling around!' Bunny Junior stops moving and hangs his head once more and closes his eyes.

Bunny looks across the crowd and notices, with a certain relief, that Poodle, Raymond and Geoffrey have all turned up to the burial. He sees that Poodle and Raymond have brought their current girlfriends with them. He is not quite sure why. He vaguely recalls suggesting, in a brain-fried phone call with his boss, Geoffrey, that they come back to his house for a few drinks after the funeral. He had forgotten about this.

Bunny notices that Poodle's girlfriend, tall and leggy in a dress the colour of weedkiller, is, by Poodle's usual standards, pretty fucking hot. Bunny can see, even from where he is positioned at the grave, that Poodle's girlfriend has a small, florid birthmark on her upper lip that makes her look as though she has been licking a blueberry ice cream. Bunny is surprised to find that this arouses him, because anything out of the ordinary usually turns him right off.

At the opposite end of the spectrum is Raymond's girlfriend. Raymond's girlfriend is definitely not hot. Raymond's girlfriend is called Barbara or something, and has been Raymond's girlfriend for about ten years and is, well, Raymond's girlfriend. Her body and her face are so completely uneventful that if it weren't for the fact that she is wearing a T-shirt that reads 'I'm not 40, I'm 18 with 22 years experience', she would be more or less invisible. Raymond and Barbara make a good couple, though, as Raymond also has no real personality to speak of.

Geoffrey, Bunny's boss, is travelling solo. He has parked his enormous rear end on a canvas faldstool and dabs at his face with his white handkerchief. Bunny thinks for a moment that he can see real tears on Geoffrey's bloated cheeks, but is not sure. Bunny feels a swell of emotion rise inside him and this makes him want to cry or something. He looks back to the burial and realises that the business of intoning over the grave is done and that Father Miles is looking at him with a perplexed expression on his face. Father Miles wants Bunny to do something. Bunny moves to the grave, picks up a handful of earth and drops it onto the lid of the simple, mahogany coffin. As he does this, he feels a kind of darkness spread over him.

Bunny sits on a bench under a little oak tree.

'Are you OK, Dad?' says the boy.

Bunny looks around him and sees the world slip back into focus.

He notices Poodle, Raymond and Geoffrey making their way towards him. Bunny motions to them with a flick of his head in the general direction of home and the three men and the girlfriends turn and head for the car park. Then he clocks Libby's mother, Mrs Pennington, pushing her wheelchair-bound husband along the gravel path with an air of steely determination.

'Wait here,' says Bunny to his son. 'Go and . . . um . . . play.'

'OK, Dad,' says the boy, looking up at his father with concern. He walks off, giving the remaining seagull, with its horrible yellow eye, a wide berth.

Bunny stands and follows Mrs Pennington down the path, and as he does so an abutment of cumuli tumble across the sun and an ominous shadow, accompanied by a cold breeze, moves visibly across the graveyard. Bunny sees Mrs Pennington's gloved hand reach down and turn up the collar of her husband's jacket. Bunny's pomaded forelock unravels and whips around his eyes as he calls out, 'Mrs Pennington! I need to speak to you!'

Mrs Pennington stops suddenly, then spins her husband around and Bunny is almost blown off his feet by the force field of hatred that envelops her. Her body visibly shakes, her black-gloved hands grip the handles of the wheelchair.

'Um . . . Mrs Pennington,' says Bunny.

'Have you any idea how much I despise you?' spits the woman.

'Mrs Pennington, I wanted to speak to you,' says Bunny, thinking – Man, this woman is *angry*.

'What?' she hisses. Her voice is educated, cultured and distorted with malice. 'Can you even comprehend the depth of my contempt?' She releases the wheelchair, screws her hands into small, black fists and pounds emphatically at her own grieving bosom. 'It runs to the *core*,' she snarls.

64

'I need your help,' says Bunny and knows, there and then, that he has made a fundamental mistake. The plan he had conceived last night on the sofa (he still could not bring himself to sleep in the master bedroom) seemed at the time nothing short of brilliant but now seems to have gone to sea in a sieve. This was not a good idea.

'My baby lies dead in her grave and you want something from me?!'

But Bunny perseveres.

'It's about your grandson, Mrs Pennington,' he says, and even though the temperature has dropped dramatically a trickle of perspiration runs down the side of Bunny's face and dark wet rings form in the armpits of his shirt.

Mrs Pennington stamps on the brake of the wheelchair and, in a freakish contra-zoom, moves towards Bunny and gets right up into his face.

'You tore her heart out. You wrung the life right out of her. My sweet, smiling baby girl . . . you killed her everyday . . . you and your *whores* . . . killed her like you throttled her in her sleep . . .'

Bunny takes a faltering step back and catches his heel on the pebbled border of the path and stumbles backward and the world tips and he thinks – This was not a good idea at all.

'She would call me and weep her little heart out. That happy, happy girl, look at what you did to her!' hisses Mrs Pennington, tears running unchecked down her face.

Her husband, with a surprising fleetness, shoots out his hand and grabs Bunny by the wrist with a rigid, cramped claw. The skin of his hand is red and silken and Bunny looks at it in horror.

'You were no kind . . . of . . . husband,' he says, and his

once-handsome face judders frantically on the tired spring of his collapsed and wattled neck.

Bunny rights himself, leans down and addresses Mr Pennington. 'You can talk,' he says.

'What?' screeches Mrs Pennington. 'What did you say?'

'I'm sorry,' says Bunny, raising his hands in a gesture of surrender and shaking his head. 'Mrs Pennington, I just thought that you could look after Bunny Junior, your grandson, for a while.' He takes a step forward and says something that has been playing out there on the farthest reaches of his consciousness for days and that now sends a vague signal of alarm through his body. 'I can't do it. I'm not capable. I don't know how.'

Mrs Pennington shakes he head. 'That poor, poor boy,' she says with real feeling. 'All he has is you . . . the great Bunny Munro . . .'

'That may be so, Mrs Pennington, but . . .'

Mrs Pennington takes a small tartan lap rug from a leather accessory bag that hangs from the back of the wheelchair and drapes it over her husband's knees. She rests her gloved fingers lightly on his shoulder and Mr Pennington places his hand, jumping and twitching, on top of hers.

'The problem is, *Bunny*, I look at him and all I see is you,' says Mrs Pennington, spitting Bunny's name out of her mouth like it was something putrid.

A worming headache has lodged itself directly over Bunny's right eye.

'Mrs Pennington, I implore you,' he says, but knows he is wasting his time.

The woman points at Bunny, her eyes as cold and as hard as flint, and says, 'You pig . . . you disgusting, fucking pig,' then turns her face away as if she can no longer bring herself to look upon him a moment longer.

Bunny is suddenly sick of all this – the sideways glances, the accusatory looks, the open hostility – the great tidal wave of blame that he has been forced to endure on this of all days and he says to Mrs Pennington, super-pissed-off. 'Well, thanks a lot, *Grandma*.' Then he turns to the chair-bound Mr Pennington, who is in the process of raising an outraged finger in Bunny's direction, and says, 'So long, Romeo.'

'You are a disgrace,' says Mr Pennington, from the corner of his mouth.

'At least I can wipe my own arse,' says Bunny, and turns and makes his way back down the gravel path, dabbing at the chilled sweat on his face with the sleeve of his jacket.

He sees Bunny Junior attempting unsuccessfully to squirt a seagull with water from a drinking fountain. The boy stops when he sees his father lurching towards him. Bunny Junior looks down the path at Mrs Pennington, a black hump of grief folded over her husband, and gives her a little wave.

'Don't waste your time,' says Bunny, sticking a cigarette in his mouth and furiously patting his pockets for his Zippo.

'What's wrong with Grandma?' says the boy.

'You want the truth?'

'OK, Dad,' says the boy. He follows his father down the path towards the Punto.

'She's a fucking bitch,' says Bunny, and torches his cigarette.

Bunny Junior wishes he had sunglasses like his dad, black wraparounds that made him look 'insectile'. His granulated eyelids cause him to blink more than other people do and he thinks he should remind his father that he needs to get the special eye drops before he goes completely blind or something. The boy can see the pulsing, scarlet band across his father's neck and the violence with which he is puffing his fag and blowing the smoke out of his nose. He looks like an animated Looney Toons bull or Mexican Toro or something – thinks the boy – and understands that now is not the time to ask him about such things as eye drops.

Bunny pulls open the door of the Punto and drops into the driver's seat and slams the door shut with such finality that it feels almost premonitory – like it's the end of things. He starts up the Punto and takes a blind and near-suicidal swerve into the traffic and the six-axle concrete mixer that bears down on him, horn blaring, could have been the very event that ruptured Bunny's mortal coil and sent him to his death – but it is not. The concrete mixer, oxblood-coloured with 'DUDMAN' painted in capitals across the front, blasts past with a tanned and tattooed arm hanging out the window as it makes its way to the depot at Fishersgate. Bunny doesn't even blink.

Instead Bunny punches the radio and a bombast of classical music pours out and Bunny hits it again – this radio with a mind of its own – and lucks out on a commercial station and wondrously, miraculously, there, pouring from the speakers in all its thrilling optimism and sexual emancipation and gold hotpants comes *that song* – and all the aggrieving rage hisses out of Bunny like a leaky valve, the boiling heat drains from his face and he turns to his son, knuckles his head and says, 'Whoever said that there isn't a God is full of shit!'

'Full of craperoo!' says the boy, smiling, and rubbing his eyes.

'Full of about ten tons of steaming manure!' says Bunny. 'I mean, what a song!'

'Full of a big bucket of faeces!' says the boy.

Bunny thrusts his hips forward in the seat and jerks back and forth to that joyous techno beat and feels the music reach purposefully down to the base of his spine and then mushroom outwards with a warmth that makes him feel like he has pissed himself or given birth or come in his pants or something.

'Oh, man,' says Bunny, and he presses the heel of his hand into his crotch and the day's images of murderous grandmothers and scornful cripples and poncey vicars and gaggles of sneering fucking bitches evaporate into the ether and he says, 'It's a bloody wonder this song is legal!'

9

Bunny opens the front door. He has removed his jacket and now wears a cornflower blue shirt with a design that looks like polka dots but is actually, on more careful inspection, antique Roman coins that have, if you get right up close, tiny and varied vignettes of copulating couples printed on them. By some miracle Libby missed this item of clothing when she decided to redesign Bunny's wardrobe with a kitchen knife and a bottle of Indian ink. She did, however, do irrevocable damage to the famous 'Greek' shirt that Poodle had given Bunny for his wedding anniversary. Poodle had picked this up on the Internet on a site for modern-day Lotharios, cocksmen and bedroom-hoppers called seducer.com. It had a not-so-discreet pattern involving a Grecian sex god or something – a dude with an olive wreath around his head and an appendage so impressive it had to be supported in a sling by two plump-cheeked cherubim. Bunny found this particular shirt stuffed down the waste-disposal unit and he had sat down on the floor of the kitchen and wept into its shredded remains.

'Hey, fuck-face,' said Poodle, entering the flat with a canine grin and a drugged sheen to his eyes.

'Jesus, Poo. Mind your manners,' says the leggy blonde hanging on to Poodle's arm, and kicks him in the shin.

'Wo! Steady, girl!' says Poodle, and hops up and down on one stonewashed leg while Bunny notices, with an electrical libidinous stirring, that the purple birthmark on the blonde's top lip is shaped a bit like a rabbit.

Raymond, jacketless, moves around Poodle with a carton of lager cradled in his arms and an imitation smile on his face. Through a miasma of alcohol fumes that Bunny finds vaguely comforting, Raymond says, blandly, 'All right, Bun?'

Raymond's girlfriend, who is almost certainly called Barbara, pops her head up from behind Raymond like an idea-free think-bubble and says, 'Hi, Bun.'

Bunny says, 'Hi . . . um . . .' and thinks maybe her name isn't Barbara after all and Raymond says, in a stage whisper, 'Barbara' and Bunny says, 'OK, yeah, Barbara . . . sorry, Barbara.'

Whatever Barbara says by way of a reply is lost in the clamorous and stentorian advent of Geoffrey, who bursts through the door, a litre of Scotch poking from each pocket of his vast linen jacket. Wheezing frighteningly from his trip up the stairs, he waves his ever-present handkerchief in the air and bellows, 'Bunny . . . Bunny . . . Bunny' and follows this with a perfect landslide of sweating flesh and not so much embraces Bunny as digests him.

'That was a lovely service, Bun,' says Geoffrey and everyone agrees.

The blonde with the birthmark moves forward and says to Bunny, 'It really was special.'

Bunny turns to Poodle and says, 'And Poodle, your friend is . . .' but Poodle is nowhere to be seen. Bunny looks down the hall in time to see the surreptitious closing of the bathroom door. Things are looking up, thinks Bunny.

The leggy blonde smiles at Bunny and introduces herself. 'My name is River,' she says.

Bunny looks momentarily confused and then is hit by a brief but intense moment of vertigo, where the floor buckles and the walls tilt and Bunny is forced to hold on to Geoffrey's shoulder for support.

'You all right, Bun?' asks Geoffrey, throwing a wing of pillowed flesh across Bunny's shoulder.

'Shit, that's weird, I just met . . .' says Bunny, and then he flashes on the dumpy waitress from the Grenville Hotel – her plump, white buttocks, the pounding headboard, her mantra of attenuated moans – and the whole scenario threatens to overwhelm him.

'I just wish everything would slow down,' says Bunny, 'I wish everything would just level out,' and immediately wonders why he said this.

'Um,' says Raymond, embarrassed.

'Of course you do, Bun,' says Geoffrey, patting Bunny on the back, sympathetically.

'I'm sorry for your loss,' says River, extending her hand, the tips of her long, thin fingers painted in coral pink varnish. Bunny, who has pulled himself together, takes her hand and feels an electro-magnetic exchange of such force that he jumps back and shakes his hand vigorously and says, 'Did you feel that?!' He looks aghast at River, whose head is tilted to the side, her brow furrowed. '*Did you feel that?*' he says. 'Oh, baby, I am the Duracell Bunny!' and he does a fair imitation of the pink, battery-powered, drumming rabbit, up and down the hall.

River looks at Bunny with her large, liquid eyes and unconsciously touches the birthmark on her lip.

Bunny says, blowing on his hand, 'Next you're going to tell

me you were born near a river!' and starts laughing and patting at the creases on the front of his trousers. There is general bafflement at this remark and everyone looks at the floor and Bunny hopes Poodle hasn't vacuumed up all the whiz.

'And who is this?' says River.

Bunny Junior has appeared like a little wraith in the hall and stands with his fists jammed up under his armpits. River reaches down and messes his hair and when she has finished the boy tries to rearrange it as it was.

'That's Bunny Junior,' says Bunny. 'He's my son.'

The boy points a thumb at his father and, with a narrow smile, says, 'And he's my dad.'

Everyone laughs at this, which confounds Bunny Junior because what he says is true. This is how it essentially is for Bunny Junior. He loves his dad. He thinks there is no dad better, cleverer or more capable, and he stands there beside him with a sense of pride – he's my *dad* – and he also, of course, stands beside him because he has nowhere else to go.

'Oh, my God, he is so cute,' says River and messes up his hair again. 'If you were just a few years older . . .'

The door to the bathroom bursts open and Poodle barrels out, teeth bared and eyes glittering. He rubs at his nose with the back of his hand and says, 'Jesus Christ, River, the kid is nine years old.'

River pinches the boy's cheek and says, 'I know. I was just saying . . .'

'Well, don't,' says Poodle. His yellow quiff has somehow taken on an even more lustrous sheen – it actually sparkles, as he swivels around and says, 'Check this out, River! Think of a country . . . any country . . .'

'What?' says River.

73

'Just think of a bloody country. Jesus . . .' says Poodle and winks at Bunny Junior.

'OK,' says River, 'Mongolia.'

'OK, Bunny Boy, don't let your Uncle Poodle down. What's the capital of Mongolia?'

Bunny Junior screws up his face in mock concentration, looks at the ceiling, strokes his chin and scratches his head.

'Ulaanbaadar,' says the boy and the guests all applaud.

'And he's got brains,' says River and places her hand on the back of the boy's neck and he feels an oily and unfamiliar heat pulsing from it.

'It used to be called Urga,' says Bunny Junior, quietly.

'Brains?' says Poodle. 'The boy's a fucking genius!'

River claps her hot hands over Bunny Junior's ears and says, 'Wo! Language!'

'Shall we go in then?' says Bunny.

As the grown-ups move into the living room, Bunny Junior hears Poodle whisper to River, 'Christ, it's fucking dark in here. Where are all the light bulbs?'

He sees River elbow Poodle in the ribs and whisper back, 'Jesus, Poo, the guy just lost his wife. What do you expect, a fucking disco ball?'

Later that night Bunny Junior lies on his bed and stares at the ceiling and watches the green glow of the planets revolve above his head. He trances on the spectral refractions of light that move across the ceiling and journey down the wall. He runs through the things he knows about Pluto – for example, how it is composed primarily of rock and ice and is relatively small, approximately a fifth the mass of the Earth's moon and a third its volume – and after he has done that for a while, he brings his wristwatch up to his ear and listens to the ticking, loud and unstoppable, of time passing. It occurs to him that with each tick of the clock the memory of his mother fades, and she slips away. He feels, with a rush of iced wind across his heart, that even by just lying there he is losing her, little by little. He closes his eyes and attempts with reasonable success to ransack his memory and conjure up images of her. He hopes by doing this that he will prevent her from melting away completely. He wants, deep down, to remember her back into existence.

He remembers her picking him up from school in her pink velour tracksuit, the prettiest of the mums, he remembers her attending, with much sympathetic cooing, to a bloody nose, and further back he thinks he can remember her applauding him when he rode his bike no-hands. He recalls receiving his encyclopaedia for no other reason than 'she loved him to bits', and further back he has a distant, colour-bleached memory of crawling across the kitchen floor and attaching himself to her long, smooth leg and feeling a surprising strength as she dragged him around the kitchen floor. He pictures himself – is this a memory? – lying newly born and swaddled in a blanket with his mother's cool hand on his forehead and the dark proximity of what must have been his father.

In time, the boy feels his mother return to him, and becomes aware of her presence in the room with him. He feels a general stirring of the air and he notices that the glow-in-the-dark planets are spinning with a renewed energy and the fairy refractions of light move down the walls with the speed of ghostly, green rain.

'Can't a guy get some sleep around here?' says Bunny Junior, out loud.

Then he hears a raucous burst of laughter coming from the living room, so he says it again, leaving three second gaps between the words.

'Can't . . . a . . . guy . . . get . . . some . . . sleep . . . around . . . here?'

Then he smiles because he knows deep in his bones that his dad has gone and said something really funny probably. He kicks off his sheet and slides his feet into his slippers.

10

Bunny sits in the living room, slumped low on the sofa, full of Geoffrey's Scotch and Poodle's cocaine. His mood has soured and he is not sure why. He has been trying to imagine Poodle's River's pussy but is having great difficulty doing so. River sits opposite him and every time she laughs at Poodle – who is wearing a plastic Viking helmet on his head that most likely belongs to Bunny Junior – the knee of her left leg swings open like old Farmer John's broken gate and Bunny can see the bright flag of her canary yellow panties. This would usually be enough to send Bunny into a near religious state of rapture but his ever-faithful one-track mind keeps taking unsolicited detours down the dread length of memory lane. This means that even though he is gazing heavy-lidded and slack-jawed between River's tanned, toned legs and clocking the embossed stereotype of her pussy displayed on the crotch of her panties, his mind takes him to, say, the time he sat with his new and heavily pregnant wife, Libby, on the pebbled beach at Hove. Under a full and yellow moon, and leaning against a concrete groyne, she lifts up her blouse and exposes the taut, neat bump of her condition and the heel of the unborn child sliding eerily across its purple-veined and pearly surface.

'Jesus, Bun, are you ready for this?' asked Libby.

Bunny pinched the foetal heel between thumb and fore-finger and said, 'You're talking to Bunny Munro, babe, you haven't seen me when I get going!'

Maybe it is because of the Libby-centric nature of the day but this memory leaves Bunny feeling sad and deflated.

He becomes conscious of the fact that Barbara, who is well into her second bottle of Spumante, is saying something to Raymond, who is completely shit-faced and quite possibly asleep.

'A boy needs his father. Jesus Christ, Raymond, it's more than some kids have got,' she says, slurring her words.

Raymond, with mouth open and eyes closed, unexpectedly raises an index finger as if to make some crucial point and rotates it enigmatically and then possibly obscenely and continues to rotate it as Barbara diverts her attention to Bunny and says, 'At least he's got you, Bunny.'

River nods in agreement, licks the purple birthmark on her upper lip, looks directly at Bunny and lets her gate swing wide.

'You poor man,' she says.

Bunny feels his eyes tear up and hears himself say, in a dreamy, disconnected way, 'My dad raised me pretty much on his own. Taught me everything I know.'

Poodle starts to stand, a near-empty bottle of Scotch in his hand, and then freezes in a comic semi-crouch as he forgets why he has stood up. He looks about him suspiciously, then flops back onto the sofa beside Bunny.

'Yeah, and look how you turned out,' he says, and exposes his needle-like teeth in a sub-human grin.

Bunny, in slow motion, registers this remark and says with a sudden influx of meaning, 'Say another thing about my dad, Poodle, and I'll fucking slap you.'

Poodle's head has fallen over the arm of the sofa, the Viking helmet cleaving miraculously to his yellow hairdo, and does not hear this. His eyes have rolled back into their orbits and his lids flutter weirdly.

'Bum coke,' he mutters.

River says, 'You poor man' again, and does the thing with her left knee and Bunny resumes his gaze and again his mind takes him elsewhere.

He remembers Libby lying in bed in the maternity ward of the Royal Sussex County Hospital, the newborn infant in her arms. He remembers her looking down at the child and holding the bundle to her breast with a love that involved the whole of her heart. She looked up at Bunny with a question in her eyes. Bunny registered a single, cold bead of perspiration journey down the side of his face and soak into his collar. He knew, at that moment, that everything had changed. Nothing would be the same again. He couldn't think of anything to say to his wife except maybe goodbye as he stared down at the tiny being in her arms. There was just too much love. He felt that the infant had secretly flipped the switch on an ejector seat that had flung him, unmanned, into the outer limits of his marriage. He didn't say goodbye, of course, but rather, 'God, babe, I need a cigarette,' and approximated a smile and slipped out of the hospital into the rain-filled street.

Bunny responds to this memory by rearing forward, slapping the table and shaking his head to release the thought.

'I got one!' he says, with a sudden, unaccountable enthusiasm.

Raymond's eyes pop open and he produces an insipid smile and Barbara giggles and River cleavages forward. Geoffrey, who is sitting alone and wedged into Bunny's armchair, like he has been there all his life, rubs his hands together (he loves a joke) and says, 'OK, here we go!' His little round eyes glisten in anticipation.

Bunny says, 'Excuse me, ladies, if this may be a little . . .'

'Offensive,' says Geoffrey, with a low chuckle.

'Yeah . . . offensive,' says Bunny and snaps open his Zippo and torches a cigarette.

'Well . . .' he says and Bunny tells a joke about a guy who decides to have a 'mood' party. He gets everything ready, the decorations, the nibbles, the booze, makes everything real nice, and there is a knock on the door and the first guy arrives and he's all dressed in green and the host says, 'What are you?' and the guy in green says, 'I'm jealousy.' Then there is another knock on the door and the next guy arrives and he is dressed in pink. The guy in pink sticks one hand on his hip, minces in, saying, 'I'm pretty in pink.' A few minutes later there is a loud knock on the door and our host opens it and sees two huge black guys standing there, buck-naked, and one of them has his dick in a bowl of custard and the other one has his dick shoved in a stewed pear. The guy having the party says, 'What have you two come as?' and the first black guy says, 'Ah'm fucking dis custard!' and then the other black guy says, 'An ah cum in dis pear!'

The room erupts into laughter, Barbara and Raymond almost clutching each other in glee, Geoffrey chuckling into his handkerchief and looking at Bunny with what amounts to a kind of paternal pride, and River's leg is banging back and forth so hard and fast that it appears like she is trying to send out some sort of super-urgent semaphore signal with the crotch of her canary-coloured panties. Even Poodle manages what may be interpreted as a thumbs-up sign. Bunny has come back to us!

'That's my dad!' says a small voice and the laughter dies out.

Bunny Junior stands in the doorway in his pyjamas and his oversized slippers, tiny blue shadows under his red-rimmed eyes.

'All right, Bunny Boy, back to bed,' says his father.

'That was a funny one, Dad!' says Bunny Junior, hopping up and down.

River, whose hair has become unpinned and hangs over one eye, flattens her skirt and stands unsteadily, and in doing so knocks the coffee table, sending cans and bottles flying.

'Oops. Sorry,' says River and Bunny sees the outline of her long, taut thigh and a blur of tanned flesh between the top of her skirt and her blouse. She turns and bends over and reveals to Bunny the golden arches of her exposed thong, rising from between her buttocks like the McDonald's logo.

'She knocked the cans off the table, Dad!' says the boy, in a big, loud voice, pointing at River.

Bunny tries to stand but cannot and falls back into the sofa.

'And Poodle's got my Viking helmet on!'

River weaves across the living room and Bunny feels the last kinetic twinge of cocaine behind his right eye. His guts feel tight and overdriven and he sees with a palpable sense of horror the possibility of daylight through the window.

'Oh, you poor little darling. Come on, sweetheart, let's get you back to bed,' says River and takes the boy by the hand.

'Dad?' says Bunny Junior as River leads him away. 'Dad?' he says.

Poodle, whose head still hangs over the edge of the sofa, opens one eye in time to witness their upside-down departure.

'Good kid,' he says, as the Viking helmet tumbles from his head. 'And a real nice arse.'

'In you go,' says River, and the boy crawls into bed. He lies there in the dark, rigid and covered with a sheet. River smells smoky and sickly sweet and forbidden and not a bit like his mother. He sees the outline of her giant-sized breasts rising above him and is aware of the proximity of her bottom to his hand. He is afraid to move it. He experiences an acute physical stirring and, as a consequence, feels a flush of shamed blood to his face and he squeezes shut his eyes in anguish.

'That's right, sweetheart, close your eyes,' she says and the boy feels her hot, damp hand on his forehead and he wants to cry so much that he secretly bites into his lower lip.

'Everything will be all right,' says River, her voice slurred and booze-modulated. 'Try to think of nice things – only nice things. Don't worry about your mummy. She will be fine now. She is in heaven with the angels. Everybody is happy there and they smile all the time because they don't have to worry any more. They just float around and play and have fun and be happy.'

Bunny Junior feels a suffocating heat emanating from River's body and thinks he can hear her bones rolling inside her flesh. He feels sick with it.

'First she will meet Saint Peter, and Saint Peter is a beautiful, wise old man, with a big white beard, and he is the keeper of the gates of heaven, and when he sees your mummy coming he will take out his big golden key and open up the door for her . . .'

Bunny Junior feels the bed fall away and a sudden darkness close on him and he thinks he hears his mother appear at the door and say, 'Who is this person sitting next to you on the bed?'

Bunny Junior will shrug his shoulders and say, 'I don't know, Mum.'

And his mother will say, 'Well, maybe we should tell her to just go away?'

And he will say, 'Yeah, maybe we should just do that, Mum.'

Bunny Junior smiles and tastes the salt of his blood and, in time, sleeps.

11

River enters the kitchen and finds Bunny standing in the middle of the floor, wavering from side to side with a box of Coco Pops in his hand. His shirt hangs open and he is looking out the window in terror at the granulated light of morning. Somewhere, in one of the adjoining flats, a dog yaps and above him there is the unsettling sound of someone dragging furniture around.

'He's asleep now. He's such a sweet kid. He sure loves his dad, that boy.'

Bunny turns towards her, and then looks bewildered at the cereal box in his hand as if seeing it for the first time. He puts it on the counter.

'Where are the others?' asks Bunny, his voice sounding far away, like it is coming from the room where the yapping dog is.

River looks at the magnetic alphabet on the door of the fridge and says, 'They've all gone. They said to say goodbye.'

'How's Poodle?'

'They had to carry him out.'

'That's our Poo,' says Bunny, weakly.

'Did you write this?' says River, pointing at the obscene message in coloured letters on the fridge.

'I think maybe my wife did,' says Bunny.

River turns her back to Bunny and he spies a blue varicose vein, like a reptile's tongue, behind her knee. River takes a yellow plastic 'M' and makes a small amendment to the phrase so that it says 'FUCK MY PUSSY', then turns back to Bunny, her hair hanging over one eye, her large, round breasts rising and falling. Bunny leans forward and inspects the letters on the fridge, moving back and forth in an unsuccessful attempt to bring the letters into focus. The phrase warps and blurs before his eyes and it looks to Bunny like some abecedary from Arabia or Mars or somewhere and he says, 'What?'

Then he stands up straight and throws his arms out to the side and the air in the kitchen kaleidoscopes and fragments and Bunny opens his mouth like a fish and says, 'What?' again, only this time rhetorically.

River puts her arms out in front of her, zombie-style, and glides towards Bunny, as if she is on a travelator with no apparent evidence of any ambulatory action whatsoever. She says, with a great swell of feeling, 'Oh, you poor man.' And before Bunny can say 'What?' a third time, she throws her long, athletic arms around his neck and pulls him to her and he cries genuine tears into her great, heaving, augmented breasts.

Bunny lies on his back on the sofa. He is naked and his clothes sit in sad, little heaps on the living room floor. River, also naked, straddles him and with enormous verve moves piston-like over his unresponsive body. Bunny's considerable member retains a certain curiosity – it must be said – but the rest of him feels wholly disembodied, as if it attaches no intrinsic value to the matter at hand. He feels like the flenched blubber a butcher may trim from a choice fillet of prime English beef and, as the song says, he has never felt this way before. This is completely new territory for him. He can see that the hard globes of River's breasts are perfect and better than the real thing and he attempts to lift his arm in order to pinch her nipples, which are the size and texture of liquorice Jelly Spogs, or stick his finger in her arsehole or something, but realises with a certain amount of satisfaction that he can't be fucked and he lets his arm drop to the side.

River squeezes Bunny's cock with her muscular vagina.

'Wow,' says Bunny, from the depths of space.

'Pilates,' says River.

'Huh?' grunts Bunny.

'Cunt crunches,' says River, and contracts her pelvic floor again.

The remote is lodged under Bunny's left buttock and as he shifts his weight the television turns on. Bunny's head lolls off the edge of the sofa and he sees (upside-down) CCTV footage of the Horned Killer with his trident terrorising shoppers in a Tesco car park in Birmingham. The bad-news ribbon that runs along the bottom of the screen informs Bunny that the guy has struck again. Earlier that day he had walked into a shared accommodation in Bordesley Green and butchered two young nurses asleep in their beds, with a garden fork. There is general panic in the Midlands. The police continue to be baffled.

'He's just getting started,' mutters Bunny, the flicker of the TV reflecting in his upside-down eyes. 'And he's coming this way.'

River, however, is lost to her gesture of altruism and does not hear. Bunny lifts his head and looks at her and sees that River's visage has changed somehow – there is a pout of hubris and self-admiration as she picks up the rhythm of what she would consider to be, come morning's sober light, basically a sympathy fuck.

'Oh,' she says, as she pounds her bullet-proof pussy down.

'You,' she says, her pistons firing,

'Poor,' (down)

'Poor,' (yum)

'Man.'

Bunny is about to close his eyes when he sees, by the window, hidden in the folds of the rose-coloured chenille curtains, what appears to be his deceased wife, Libby. She is dressed in her orange nightdress and she is waving at him. Spooked, Bunny makes a hopeless, wounded sound and opens his mouth and releases a hiss of gas as if his very soul was escaping and then bucks frantically at River in an attempt to dislodge her, which is just what River needs to send her over the edge. Bunny, trapped in the vice of her climaxing haunches, squeezes shut his eyes. River screams and digs her nails into his chest. Bunny opens his eyes again, looks wildly around, but Libby has gone.

'My wife was there,' he says to River or somebody. 'She was watching.'

'Oh, yeah?' says River, disimpaling herself. 'You might want to see somebody about that. I know a guy in Kemp Town you could talk to.'

Bunny jabs his finger at the news bulletin on the TV. 'And *he* is coming down!'

'Uh huh? Look, I've got to go,' says River and raises the perfect orbs of her rear end, slick with her various juices, into the early morning air and looks under the sofa for her canary yellow panties.

*   *   *

River leaves soon after, closing the front door behind her as Bunny feigns sleep on the sofa. But his mind is alert to all manner of things. He thinks, for instance, that he should get up and put on a pair of trousers or something before his son wakes up. He wonders also what his wife wants from him and hopes that he will not be the subject of any further hauntings and supernatural visitations. He wonders, with a shudder, if the disconnectedness he felt while screwing River is a permanent condition and he considers the idea that perhaps he is all washed-up as a world-class cocksman. Maybe Libby's suicide has jinxed him. Cursed him, maybe. It is certainly possible. Stories abound about people being put off their game by seemingly innocuous and unconnected events. Poodle told Bunny only recently about a local pussy-hound from Portslade who went from stud to dud after attending a Celine Dion concert. He just couldn't get it up any more. He told Poodle it was like trying to stuff a dead canary in a cash dispenser. In the end he hung up his tackle and became a landscape gardener in Walberswick. Chilling stuff. Whatever. Bunny knows that there are things going on in this world – great mysteries – that he will never be able to work out. He wonders, also, with a gnawing, abdominal anxiety, whether he will ever get it together enough to go and visit his ailing father. And then he starts thinking, in an abstract kind of way, about his son, Bunny Junior, and what the fuck he is going to do with him. What do you do with a kid who can barely locate his own backside? But most of all he wonders how he is going to spend another night in this spooked-out, three-roomed council flat, with its crummy vibe and its deeply fucked-up juju. Bunny realises, lying there on the sofa, that he can't fucking handle it.

But even though these questions whirl around Bunny's mind like rooftops and tractors and farm animals in a tornado or twister or something, another part of Bunny's mind – the plotter, the designer, the maker-of-plans, works quietly away, sifting through the data to find a way forward.

And in time it comes to him, not in a blinding flash, but rather in a shift of the gears of the heart, or perhaps a release of dread from his body, or a stabilising of his internal chemistry. He feels, in that instant, that he knows what he has to do, and with that knowledge comes an enormous sense of relief. The answer, as is so often the way, has been staring him in the face all along.

Bunny smiles, then drapes River's canary yellow panties over his face and sucks on the crotch and happily jerks off, then falls into a deep and uncluttered sleep, thinking – Easy, no problem, vagina, vagina.

PART TWO

SALESMAN

12

Bunny Junior lies on the floor of his bedroom reading his encyclopaedia. The carpet is thin and his knees and elbows and hip-bones hurt from lying in the same position for so long and he keeps thinking he should get up off the floor and lie on his bed but he knows that the discomfort he feels keeps him awake and alert and his memory keen. He is in the process of storing information. He is well into the letter 'M' and is reading about Merlin, who was a wizard or sage in the Arthurian legends, whose magic was used to help King Arthur. His mother bought the encyclopaedia for him, just because 'she loved him to bits', the boy likes to remember. Bunny Junior thinks it is an elegant-looking book with a jacket the exact colour of one of those citronella-impregnated mosquito candles. Merlin was the son of an incubus and a mortal woman, and the boy looks up 'incubus' and finds that an incubus is a malevolent spirit who has intercourse with women in their sleep, then he looks up 'intercourse' and thinks – Wow, imagine that – as he gradually intuits the presence of his father standing in the doorway of his room.

His father has showered and shaved and his ornamental curl that sits in the middle of his forehead has been artfully arranged into something musical, like a treble clef or a fiddlehead, and even though his eyes are a shocking scarlet colour and his hands tremble so much that he has had to keep them in his pockets, he looks, on the face of it, dynamic and handsome. He is wearing a navy blue suit and a shirt that is covered in little maroon diamonds and he is wearing his favourite tie – the one with the cartoon rabbits on it. He is staring down at Bunny Junior and smiling. Bunny Junior thinks – Well, what's going on? He thinks – Boy, something good must be coming down!

'Hi, Dad!' says the boy.

'You got a suitcase?' says Bunny.

'I don't know, Dad.'

'Well, find one!' says Bunny, flinging his arms out to the sides in mock-exasperation. 'Jesus! Haven't I taught you anything?'

'What for, Dad?'

'What do you mean, "What for?"'

'What do I need a suitcase for?' says the boy, thinking – *He's sending me away* – and he feels the wind rush out of him.

'Well, what do you think you need a bloody suitcase for?' says Bunny.

'Am I going somewhere?' says the boy, jumping from foot to foot and wiping at his forehead with the back of his hand.

'Not *I*,' says Bunny, '*We* . . .'

'We?'

'Yeah.'

'Where are we going, Dad?'

Bunny Junior is dressed in a pair of shorts and flip-flops. He wears a faded T-shirt that has a picture of an orange crazy-paved mutant called The Thing printed on it. The T-shirt is a couple of sizes too small for Bunny Junior and is covered in holes, but the boy wears it for reasons of nostalgia that only he can understand.

'We are hitting the road!' says Bunny, cocking a thumb and jerking it over his shoulder in the general direction of the outside world.

'Really?' says the boy, smiling so much that his teeth show.

'Really,' says Bunny. 'But you can't go looking like a bloody hobo. It's the first rule of salesmanship. Be presentable.'

'Just you and me, Dad?' says the boy, peeling off the T-shirt, balling it up and pitching it across the room.

'Just you and me, Bunny Boy.'

Outside the morning sun is resplendent, the sky is blue, and white clouds scud optimistically overhead. A breeze, with the faintest of Arctic memories riding on it, blows from the north-east. Bunny and Bunny Junior launch themselves down the stairwell and haul their suitcases across the terrace of the estate. Bunny feels, just by stepping out of the flat, a renewed optimism and strength. He smiles. He whistles.

Bunny sees Cynthia sitting like an omen on the swing in the tiny children's play area. She wears white-cuffed sailor's shorts, a white vest and her frosted-white toenails glow opal-like against the black, rubberised tarmac.

'Where are you going?' she says and smiles at Bunny and her orthodontic braces flash in the sun.

'We're so outta here,' says Bunny Junior, who has found himself a pair of shades. He cocks his thumb at the Punto sitting in the car park. 'Like, gone,' he says.

Bunny, who has tranced out on the bunched intersection of Cynthia's shorts, says, 'Yeah, we're out of here.'

'Shame,' says Cynthia and leans forward to reveal a pure white thong rising from the sweet arcuation of her creamy buttocks.

'Fuck me,' says Bunny, under his breath. He looks up to the third floor and sees the yellow front door of his flat like a hex or a curse or something. He feels a cold whirl in his intestines. 'Yeah, Cynthia, we are definitely out of here.'

'Hitting the road,' says Bunny Junior.

'Shame,' says Cynthia, unnecessarily, and snaps her gum. She lifts her legs and leans back on the swing, setting it in motion.

'Come on, Dad,' says Bunny Junior and together they walk across to the car park. Bunny thinks – That wasn't so hard – as he pops the boot on the Punto and they throw in their bags. They climb into the car and Bunny inserts the ignition key and the engine coughs and strains and in time turns.

Bunny Junior puts his head out the window and makes an unsolicited observation. 'The sky looks like a giant swimming pool, Dad,' he says.

'Oh, yeah?' says Bunny, decommissioning Cynthia's shorts and imagining the hello and goodbye of her oscillating, play-ground pussy.

'Olympic-sized,' says the boy.

Bunny drives out of the estate and a boy with dirty yellow hair sticking out from under a bright red baseball cap and various chrome labrets inserted into his sensory organs appears out of nowhere, riding a skateboard. He wears a green T-shirt that says 'Lick My Kunst' and cuts recklessly in front of the Punto. Bunny hits the horn and the boy responds with a sharp upward movement of the middle finger. Bunny rolls down the window and yells, 'Sk8ter boi,' and immediately thinks of Avril

Lavigne and then Avril Lavigne's vagina. He recalls Poodle saying that he had seen on the Internet that Avril Lavigne was 'a real crazy chick'. She must be, with that zany black eyeliner, thinks Bunny.

He hits the traffic on the roundabout and blasts his horn again, this time at a maroon 'DUDMAN' concrete mixer truck that bears down heavily on the Punto. It roars past, a tattooed arm hanging from the driver's window, its middle finger extended.

'Man,' says Bunny, 'everyone's gone crazy!' and he pulls into a petrol station and fills the Punto. Then he heads for the offices of Eternity Enterprises that operates out of a cramped room on Western Road, above a video store that doubles as a cut-rate off-licence. Bunny pulls into a disabled parking bay and kills the motor.

'Wait here, Bunny Boy, I'll be back in a minute,' he says and he hauls himself out of the car. Bunny thinks his dad looks like a real go-getter, with his sample case and his suit.

'OK, Dad,' says Bunny Junior and he adjust his sunglasses. 'I'll wait here.'

Bunny makes to cross the road, then turns back and sticks his head through the driver's seat window.

'If a traffic warden comes by, pretend you're a spastic or something.'

'OK, Dad.'

The boy watches his father cross the road and thinks there is something about the way his dad moves through the world that is truly impressive. Cars screech to a halt, drivers shake their fists and stick their heads out the windows and curse and blow their horns and Bunny walks on as if radiating some super-human force field, like he has walked off the pages of a comic book. The world can't touch him. He seems to be the grand generator of some hyper-powerful electricity.

'It's clobbering time!' says Bunny Junior, completely to himself.

Bunny crosses the road and sees a young mother or an au pair or something looking trance-like at a poster for the movie *Seabiscuit* in the video shop window. In a buggy a little girl, her face smeared in something chemical-green, holds a Barbie doll or a Bratz doll or something and writhes in her safety harness.

'Excellent,' says Bunny.

The woman has a sprinkling of freckles on the back of her neck and a prominent ridge of cartilage along the top of her nose. She wears a logo-free T-shirt and black Havaianas and her toenails are painted the colour of plums. She turns and looks at Bunny, dark smudges under her eyes.

'Eh?' she says.

Bunny nods at the poster.

'The film,' he says.

'Yeah?' says the woman.

Then Bunny looks at the child, squirming in her loculus of havoc, the Bratz doll clutched in her podgy little fist.

'These children are having their childhoods stolen from them,' he says. He leans down and touches the little girl on the top of her head with his fingers and smiles at the woman. 'Poor things.'

The woman bends over the buggy and moves away and Bunny clocks her hunched and hurried retreat.

'Definitely a mummy,' he says to himself.

He presses the intercom of 'Eternity Enterprises'.

'Who is it?' says a distorted, robot voice through the

intercom and Bunny looks up at the video cam mounted above the doorway and flips it the finger. The monitor squawks and Bunny enters. He bounds up the stairs two at a time and continues down a dank, low-ceilinged hall until he comes to a door that says, in a Gothic demi-bold font, 'ETERNITY ENTERPRISES'. Without knocking, he opens it and enters.

Geoffrey sits in his swivel chair like some infernal cyber-experiment gone horribly wrong – the unholy welding of too much man with too little machine. He is a circus elephant on roller-skates or a semi-deflated Michelin Man in a Hawaiian shirt. He looks up at Bunny with his implausibly wise, button-like eyes and says, 'What's green and smells like bacon?'

Bunny rolls his eyes at Geoffrey, faux-bored.

'Kermit's finger,' says Geoffrey.

There is a painful screech of tortured springs as Geoffrey leans back in his chair. Then, with an air of satisfaction, he steeples his fingers over his riotous girth and smiles.

'I've heard it,' says Bunny.

'Yeah, but it's a stone classic.'

'If you say so, Geoffrey.'

'Always worth reviving, I say, lest we forget,' says Geoffrey.

Geoffrey seems supremely at home in this environment, as if everything he needs is here in this pinched and cut-rate room – and indeed it is – his fridge full of lager, his Swedish porn collection, his telephone and his little swivel chair; but the office is hot and airless and Bunny feels, almost immediately, a rivulet of perspiration wind its way between his shoulder blades. With a watery redistribution of weight, Geoffrey leans his garish bulk forward and all the little grass-

99

skirted hula dancers slip and slide. His face is laddered by the sunlight that pours through the half-open Venetian blinds and he is forced to squint and his bright, little eyes sink into his face.

'I've got a question for you, Bun,' he says. 'What are you doing here?'

Bunny hooks one finger into his collar and says, 'I'm ready to go.'

Geoffrey gestures to the single wooden chair in the corner and says, 'Take a seat, bwana, you're making me nervous.'

Bunny drags the chair to the desk and sits down and is about to say something but Geoffrey raises one massive paw in the air.

'Are you sure, my man? There is no pressure here. Shouldn't you take a little time just to, you know, sort some things out?'

'I'm all right, Geoffrey. Just give me the list and some samples. I'm all out of samples.'

'When I lost my Hilda, Bun, you know, it took a while.'

Bunny feels a wobble in the room's atmospherics and a vague acceleration of his blood. This is pissing him off. He slaps his palm down on the desktop.

'What am I gonna do? Sit around the house all day, tugging at my dick? Now, Geoffrey, give me the fucking list.'

Bunny entertains the idea of asking his boss if he was ever visited by his wife after she died, but thinks better of it. That is all behind him now.

'OK, Bunny, you're the boss,' says Geoffrey, handing Bunny a list of names and addresses that he folds in two and slips into the inside pocket of his jacket. Bunny realises he has been sweating so heavily that drops of perspiration have soaked into the fabric of his tie.

'No, Geoffrey, you're the boss. I just happen to be the only guy in this two-bit operation that has the faintest fucking idea how to sell anything.'

The door flies open and Poodle enters with his leering grin, his stonewashed jeans and his yellow, architectural 'do. His booze-blown eyes are a terrifying Virgin red.

'I rest my case,' says Bunny, standing.

'Christ!' says Poodle, 'What happened last night?'

'I think you may have been a little excessive in your libations,' says Geoffrey. 'You brought shame upon the house of Eternity Enterprises.'

Then Geoffrey looks at Bunny and says, 'What do you want?'

'The lot. Hand shit. Face shit. Body shit. Hair shit.'

Geoffrey reaches down under the desk and produces a collection of various sachets, tubes and miniature bottles of lotions and creams, and Bunny sweeps them into his sample case.

Then Bunny turns to Poodle, who is looking sideways at Bunny, his eyes glinting, his needle-like teeth bared in a peerless impression of a happy velociraptor. He moves the flat of his hand slowly across the considerable bulge in his stonewashed jeans and raises an eyebrow.

'I fucked your lady friend last night,' said Bunny.

'I know. She told me. She said it was a little . . . sad,' says Poodle.

'Oh, yeah? Can you ask her for my dick back?'

Poodle emits a low chuckle and with the tips of his manicured fingers tugs at the gold sleeper in his ear.

'I know. Incredible, eh? She's a yoga-nut. She's training to become an instructor.' Poodle rubs his hands together then performs a Jackoesque swivel of his hips. 'Fun and games!' He squeezes his genitals. 'Coming down to The Wick for a drinky-poo?'

'No,' says Bunny, 'I've got my kid in the car.'

Poodle moves to the window in a lewd creep. He wears tight jeans and a clean, white Polo shirt that accentuate his broad shoulders and small, compact buttocks but give him the proportions of a hyena. He peers through the slatted blinds, the sunlight jazzing the pale irises of his eyes.

'Fuck, Bun, some cunt's giving you a ticket!'

'Shit,' says Bunny, and he snaps shut his sample case.

'Hey, Bun,' says Poodle, squinting in the light as though he can't believe what he sees.

Bunny, who is halfway out the door, turns.

'Your kid looks like he is having some kind of fit!'

Bunny slams the door and Geoffrey moves his great weight to the fridge and tosses Poodle a beer.

'I'm worried about that guy,' he says.

Bunny grabs the parking ticket that is taped to the windscreen of the Punto and for the benefit of the traffic warden, who is walking down the street, tapping away at his electronic ticket dispenser, his hat angled ironically on his head, Bunny performs an impressive porno-panto of a man fucking a traffic warden up the arse. The traffic warden watches Bunny expression-free for a moment, which inspires Bunny to do his famous imper-sonation of a traffic warden sucking his own dick. Then he watches the traffic warden curse under his breath and start marching down the street towards the Punto, whereupon

Bunny performs a basic risk-assessment exercise – he is big and he is black – and climbs in the Punto and starts the car. The traffic warden stops, shakes his head and walks away.

'The nerve of that guy,' says Bunny, looking over his shoulder. 'And with a retard in the car and everything!'

'He was a bit of a bastard, wasn't he, Dad?' says Bunny Junior.

Bunny looks at his son and smiles.

'You said it, Bunny Boy.'

There is a loud and sudden knock on the roof of the Punto and Bunny jumps and looks everywhere at once. Poodle's face appears in the window and he mimics rolling it down.

'It's Poodle,' says the boy.

'I can see that,' says Bunny and winds down the window.

Poodle slips two fingers into the breast pocket of his Polo shirt and extracts a small piece of notepaper and hands it to Bunny.

'My gift to you. She lives in Newhaven,' he says out of the corner of his mouth, running a buffed fingernail along his cheekbone. He licks his lips and says, 'Ouch!'

Bunny rolls his eyes towards the boy and then back to Poodle, who is unconsciously dabbing at the raw and flaky entrance to his right nostril with his finger.

'Oh, yeah,' says Poodle. He crouches down and says to the boy, 'Hey, Bunny Boy. Nice shades.'

'Hi,' says the boy.

'No school today?' says Poodle, clamping a Mayfair Ultra Light between his teeth and torching it.

The boy shakes his head.

'Lucky you,' says Poodle.

Then he looks at Bunny, and his face elongates into something sleek and lupine, and the transformation is so convincing that Bunny can almost hear the bones snap in his face.

'You'll find her a most accommodating customer,' says Poodle in a stage whisper, and then leans through the window. Bunny can feel his breath, hot and excited, against his ear. 'It will help with the grieving process,' he says.

Bunny stares blankly at Poodle, the nerve under his right eye contracting. Poodle stiffens and tiny beads of sweat appear on his upper lip. He tries to smile but cannot, overrun by a kind of rigor.

'Sorry, Bun, that was out of line.'

Bunny reaches up and pinches Poodle's shaved and polished cheek and says quietly, 'You're a cunt, Poodle. Did you know that?'

Poodle grins sheepishly and draws on his fag, his hand betraying the faintest of tremors, 'Ah . . . yes, actually I do.'

Bunny pats Poodle's cheek gently, almost strokes it.

'But I love you,' he says.

'And I love you,' says Poodle.

'Now, fuck off,' says Bunny and rolls up the window.

Bunny screws up the piece of paper that Poodle has given him and tosses it on the floor at Bunny Junior's feet. Poodle stands on the pavement, hand raised in a sardonic goodbye, and then fucks the air lewdly, the shape of his penis curled and visible against the inside leg of his jeans. Bunny guns the engine and veers blindly into the traffic on Western Road.

'He's a funny one, isn't he, Dad?' says Bunny Junior.

'Poodle, my boy, is a bloody idiot,' says Bunny.

'What are we going to do now, Dad?'

But Bunny barely registers his son's question because suddenly, and completely unexpectedly, Bunny is experiencing something beyond the realms of anything he has experienced before. The simple act of crumpling up Poodle's 'gift' and casting it aside has filled Bunny with a belief that he is in command of his life. He is also registering, in an unprecedented way, a feeling of virtuousness. He feels a momentary wave of euphoria course through his system, a cup of love in his bowels, and he turns left at Adelaide Crescent and heads down towards the sea.

'I am in control of my appetites,' says Bunny, quietly, to himself.

'Me, too, Dad,' says Bunny Junior.

They pass the majestic downward sweep of Regency terraces along Adelaide Crescent and watch in silence as a father tosses a Frisbee to his young son in the public gardens, while the mother lays down a tartan rug, then bends over a wicker picnic basket. Ouch – thinks Bunny.

'What are we going to do now, Dad?' says the boy.

'Now, we are going to shake the old money tree, that's what we're going to do,' says Bunny.

Bunny Junior takes off his shades and screws up his face.

'What?' he says.

'We are going to relieve a few boobs of their cabbage.'

The boy smiles at Bunny, but the smile is the kind of smile that looks like it has fallen off the child's face, shattered on the ground and then been glued back together at random – it's a zigzag smile, a seesaw smile, a wonky little broken smile. Bunny registers this but also the look of unknowing on the child's face, the total lack of comprehension, the giant cartoon question mark floating over his head, and thinks – This kid doesn't understand a fucking thing. And what's with that smile?

'We're gonna sell some stuff!' says Bunny, exasperated.

'You're good at that, aren't you, Dad?' says the boy, shifting in his seat and spinning his sunglasses around like a propeller.

Bunny leans in close to him and says, with a flush of awe and wonder, 'Bunny Boy, I am the best!'

Bunny hears the boy say, 'Everybody thinks you're the best, don't they, Dad?!' but they are passing a bus shelter, advertising Kylie Minogue's brand new range of lingerie for Selfridges called 'Love Kylie', and Bunny tries to remember what Poodle told him he had seen on the Internet about Kylie but draws a blank. Instead he feels a rush of blood, viral and urgent, throb in his extremities, his fingers pulsing on the steering wheel. He looks at the boy.

'I could sell a bicycle to a barracuda!' says Bunny, and the boy laughs.

'No . . . no . . . I could sell *two* bicycles to a barracuda!'

The boy looks up at his father and, seeing the ease with which he moves in and out of the traffic, one hand on the wheel, his elbow out the window and his brilliant sense of humour and how he can make everybody like him, even complete strangers, his world-class smile, his wraparound shades, his tie with the cartoon rabbits on it, his amazing curl, his fags and the whole thing with his sample case, he shouts, 'You're fantastic, Dad!'

Bunny throws back his head and shouts back, 'Shit, Bunny Boy, I could sell the whole bloody bike shed!' and laughs and then remembers what it was that Poodle had said about Kylie Minogue – how he had read a blog somewhere saying that Kylie went off like a fucking firecracker in the sack and that there was, like, nothing she wouldn't do! She was *insatiable!*

Bunny glances at the crumpled piece of paper that rolls

around Bunny Junior's feet and bares his teeth and wrenches his eyes away and makes an emphatic change of gear and presses on, and says, 'You've got a lot to learn.'

'I know, Dad,' says the boy.

13

'It's like this, Bunny Boy, if you walk up to an oak tree or a bloody elm or something – you know, one of those big bastards – one with a thick, heavy trunk with giant roots that grow deep in the soil and great branches that are covered in leaves, right, and you walk up to it and give the tree a shake, well, what happens?'

Bunny drives the Punto super-slow through the Wellborne estate in Portslade and looks at the customer list Geoffrey has given him. The towers cast long, dark shadows across the courtyard and Bunny hunches down in the Punto and peers up through the front windscreen searching for the flat with the corresponding number.

'I really don't know, Dad,' says Bunny Junior, listening intently, retaining the information and knowing, in time, he will probably understand.

'Well, nothing bloody happens, of course!' says Bunny and slows the Punto to a halt. 'You can stand there shaking it till the cows come home and all that will happen is your arms will get tired. Right?'

The boy's attention is diverted momentarily by three youths that perch on the back of a wooden bench, smoking. Depersonalised in their massive jeans and their oversized sneakers, the ends of their cigarettes flare from deep within the dark recesses of their hoods and Bunny Junior slips on his shades and shrinks down in his seat.

'Right, Dad,' he says.

Bunny rolls down the window, sticks his head out and looks up at the flats.

'Jesus! They could put fucking numbers on the doors, at least,' he says.

Then he adjusts the rear-view mirror and looks at his reflection and manipulates the waxed curlicue of hair that sits on his forehead like the horn of some mythological beast.

'But if you go up to a skinny, dry, fucked-up little tree, with a withered trunk and a few leaves clinging on for dear life, and you put your hands around it and shake the shit out of it – as we say in the trade – those bloody leaves will come flying off! Yeah?'

'OK, Dad,' says the boy, and he watches as one of the youths pulls back the edge of his hood and reveals a white hockey mask with a human skull printed on it.

'Now, the big oak tree is the rich bastard, right, and the skinny tree is the poor cunt who hasn't got any money. Are you with me?'

Bunny Junior nods.

'Now, that sounds easier than it actually is, Bunny Boy. Do you want to know why?'

'OK, Dad.'

'Because every fucking bastard and his dog has got hold of the little tree and is shaking it for all that it's worth – the government, the bloody landlord, the lottery they don't have a chance in hell of winning, the council, their bloody exes, their hundred snotty-nosed brats running around because they are too bloody stupid to exercise a bit of self-control, all the useless shit they see on TV, fucking Tesco, parking fines, insurance on this and insurance on that, the boozer, the fruit machines, the bookies – every bastard and his three-legged, one-eyed, pox-ridden dog are shaking this little tree,' says Bunny, clamping his hands together and making like he is throttling someone.

'So what do you go and do, Dad?' says Bunny Junior.

'Well, you've got to have something they think they need, you know, above all else.'

'And what's that, Dad?'

'Hope . . . you know . . . *the dream*. You've got to sell them the dream.'

'And what's the dream, Dad?'

'What's the dream?'

Bunny Junior sees his father adjust his tie, then reach into the back seat of the Punto and grab his sample case. He unlocks it, checks its contents, and closes it again. He looks at Bunny Junior, squares his shoulders, opens the door to the Punto, points his thumb at his chest and says, 'Me.'

Bunny climbs out of the car then leans back in through the open door.

'I won't be long. Stay in the car,' he says, and closes the door.

Bunny Junior looks around nervously, then thinks – Well, nobody is going to hurt a nine-year-old, especially one who is wearing shades – but as a precautionary measure slides down a little further in his seat and, over the top of the window, watches his father approach the juveniles – who are probably responsible for about one hundred heinous murders between them and have *intercourse* all the time – sitting on the bench.

'Any of you guys know which is flat ninety-five?' asks Bunny.

The youth in the middle – although Bunny is not completely sure – says 'Fuck off', then executes an unconscious variation on the Mos Def Wave but with the middle finger extended.

Bunny smiles deferentially and says, 'Well, yes, OK, but do you think number ninety-five is in this block?' He points west. 'Or in this block?' He points east.

The young men suck on their cigarettes, jets of nostril smoke issuing from the obscurity of their hoods. No one says anything, but there is a general ratcheting-up of the potential for violence as the youths realign their bodies inside their giant, comic-book clothes. The youth in the middle propels a bead of spittle into the air and it lands at Bunny's feet.

Bunny takes a step closer and addresses him.

'You know what you remind me of, son?'

'What's that, granddad?'

'A clitoris.'

'A what?'

'I think it's the hood.'

Bunny turns and walks towards the first of the buildings. The lit butt of a cigarette flies past his ear and Bunny calls out, without looking back, 'They'll kill you, those things! You'll get cancer and die!'

He reaches the stairwell of the building and waves his arms theatrically, as if addressing the world, and yells, 'Think of the great loss to humanity that would be!'

Then Bunny disappears into the sunless vestibule of the stairwell. He hop-skips over a condom full of dead teenage spunk that lies among the debris that has collected around the steps. He heads up the stairs, the acrid chemical tang of bleach and urine hitting him in the face like a slap, and for no particular reason at all he thinks of the sexy-surreal dichotomy between Pamela Anderson's furry Ugg boots and her (almost) shaved pussy. By the time he reaches the top of the staircase, there is a radical teepeeing of the front of his trousers. To his surprise he finds, as if by some miracle, that he is standing outside No. 95. He turns and looks over the balcony and concentrates on the galactic pattern of seagull shit that decorates the roof of the Punto until his erection subsides.

He notices that the youths have left the wooden bench and in their place is a fat guy in a floral dress growling like a beast and pulling the price tag off what looks like a large potted orchid.

Bunny hopes, in a peripheral way, that Bunny Junior has locked the car door. Then he turns around and knocks on the door of No. 95.

Bunny Junior opens his encyclopaedia at the letter 'M' and reads about the mantis, an insect with a well-camouflaged body, mobile head and large eyes. He reads that the female eats the male head-first during copulation, then looks up 'copulation' and thinks – Wow, imagine that. He commits this to memory by putting it in a virtual colour-coded box and storing it in the shelved data bank of his mind. He has hundreds of these boxes that relate and interrelate and can be drawn upon at will, in an instant. Ask him about the Battle of Britain or about the deathwatch beetle and he can tell you. If you want to know about Galapagos Islands or the Heimlich manoeuvre, then Bunny Junior is your man. It's a talent he has.

But two things worry Bunny Junior as he sits slumped in the front seat of the Punto.

First, when he tries to call to mind his mother he finds her image is still disappearing. He can remember the year they started building the Eiffel Tower but he finds it increasingly difficult to recall what his mother looked like. This makes him feel bad. He tries to arrange his memories of the things they did together in the form of exhibits, frozen in time, like the stuffed birds in the glass cases in the world-famous Booth Museum. He arranges them in his memory as if they were waxwork statues or something. But the image of his mother is vanishing, so that when he goes to look at the scene of, say, the day his mother pushed him on the swing in the playground of St Ann's Well Gardens, he can see himself vaulted high into the air, his legs kicking out, his face alive with laughter – but who is doing the pushing? A slowly dissolving ghost-lady as incomplete as a hologram. He feels, in this instance, forever suspended on the swing, high in the air, never to descend, beyond human touch and consequence, motherless, and after he has stopped crying and dabbing at his tears with the sleeve of his shirt, he worries about the other thing.

On the bench where the juvenile delinquents were sitting is a fat guy in a dress, playing with a pot plant. He wears a lilac wig. Every now and then he looks up at the boy and makes a noise like some kind of monster – maybe a werewolf or a hellhound or something. This scares Bunny Junior and very secretly he reaches across and pushes down the lock on the car door. As he does this, he looks over at the entrance to the stairwell where his father disappeared and standing there, with her back turned towards him and partially lost in shadow, is a woman with blonde hair, dressed in an orange nightdress. Bunny Junior puts his hands up to his face and before his eyes he sees her step deeper into the shadows and disappear or dematerialise or atomise or something, he can't decide which.

14

'Now, let's see what we've got here,' says Bunny, the oiled spiral of his hair — his lovelock — relaxing attractively on his forehead. 'Zoë, I've got you down for the Replenishing Hand Cream, the Elastin Extra Relief Hand and Body Lotion, the Almond, Honey, Milk and Aloe Mask, the Phytocitrus Hair Masque, the Re-Nutriv Lifting Cream and Morrocan Rose Otto Bath Oil, very nice, that one, the ladies tell me . . .'

Bunny sits at a circular table in a neat kitchen with three women in their mid-thirties. Zoë is dressed in chocolate-brown velour tracksuit bottoms and a T-shirt from LA Fitness on North Road. She is tall, with auburn hair and dark brown eyes and a little pink butterfly tattooed on the inside of her right wrist. Crazy — thinks Bunny — as he leans towards her and reads from his order form. He notices, momentarily, that the miniature crystal snowflakes that dangle from her ears refract diamonds of light unflatteringly on the underside of her jaw.

Amanda, on the other hand, is small and reminds Bunny of Kylie Minogue, except that she is goblinned by a mass of candy-coloured hair extensions and has enormous breasts, tiny hips and practically no rear-end at all. She also wears the same chocolate-brown velour tracksuit bottoms as Zoë and jiggles an infant on her lap that gurgles and points at things that are not there or that are there but only it can see.

Georgia, whose home it is, wears a peach-coloured T-shirt with what appears to be a metallic-silver representation of a mushroom printed on the front. She wears blue jeans and matching denim espadrilles, has violet eyes and is overweight, and although each of the women has the high-hearted but baby-blasted look of new mothers, there is an air of jeopardy about Georgia that produces a nervous, tinkling giggle.

Zoë gestures at the order form and says, 'If that doesn't sort me out, nothing will!'

Tiny Amanda has a large and guttural laugh while big Georgia's laugh sounds like the ringing of little bells and, in an oblique way, this weird mismatch amuses Bunny and his cheeks dimple. He turns his attention to Amanda and touches her briefly on the wrist with his index finger. The infant lets forth a wail of protest at this intrusion and, without taking her eyes off Bunny, Amanda works a dummy into the child's mouth.

Bunny consults his order form.

'Now, Amanda, I've got you down for the same as Zoë but not the Hair Masque because of your . . .'

'Hair extensions!' say Zoë and Amanda, craning forward. They are on their second bottle of red and Amanda, in particular, appears a little flushed. On the table in front of them sits Bunny's open sample case, displaying the little bottles and sachets of lotions and creams.

'. . . Hair extensions. And very nice they are too. Plus, you wanted the Dermo-expertise Eye Solace,' says Bunny. 'And . . . a bottle of Scotch and a good night's sleep.'

The women laugh and Amanda says, 'Oh, for a good night's sleep!' and mock-throttles her baby.

Bunny clocks the way Georgia tugs at her T-shirt and squirms in her chair as he turns to her and says, in a playful voice, 'Now, *Georgia*, I am *very* disappointed in you.' He takes note of the flush of colour that rises at her throat.

'Ooh, Georgia, the man is disappointed!' says Zoë and reprimands Georgia with a gentle slap to the back of the hand. Georgia bows her head, sips her wine and tugs at her T-shirt, all at the same time.

'You've ordered the hand cream, the body lotion, the Almond and Aloe Mask, the Hair Masque and the Lifting Cream but you have not . . . and it hurts me to say this . . . you have *not* ordered the Moroccan Rose Otto Bath Oil.'

'Georgia!' scolds Zoë. 'You complete fiend!'

'Now what baffles me is why a woman as fine as yourself feels it justifiable to deny her body the very thing it aches for . . . liquid heaven . . . one hundred per cent plant oils and natural fragrance . . . romantic, old-fashioned, sensuous . . . Barry White in a bottle, this stuff . . . with a hint of the East. Slip into this at the end of the day and it will waft you to paradise . . .'

Bunny places his hand on the underside of Georgia's wrist and presses on the soft dough of her flesh and believes he can feel her pulse quicken. He leans in close and whispers, 'I am very, very disappointed.'

'Georgia, buy the bloody bath oil!' screams Amanda or Zoë, and once again they shriek with laughter. The baby on Amanda's lap jettisons the dummy from its mouth and bares the glazed ridges of its gums and makes a noise impossible to interpret.

Minute beads of perspiration have formed under Georgia's eyes, as she says, 'All right. I'll have the bath oil!' and then releases her fraught and silvery giggle.

Bunny shoots his cuffs and writes on the order form.

'One bottle of Moroccan Rose Oil for the lovely Georgia.'

Bunny smiles at Georgia and Georgia, in time, meets his eyes, and smiles back at him and Bunny knows, without arrogance or hubris, more than he knows anything in this world, that he could fuck Georgia in a heartbeat. Amanda too, he thinks. Zoë would need a little more work but it was Georgia that would give out and give out all the fucking way.

'Now, ladies, I have some rather special Men's products. A gift for the hubby, perhaps?'

The three women look at each other and then collapse into laughter.

Zoë says, 'Got any facial scrub with ground glass in it?!'

Amanda says, 'How about a Moroccan Acid Bath!'

'Do I detect a little husband trouble?' he says.

'Not any more!' says Amanda or Zoë, and they hi-five each other in solidarity.

Bunny looks at Georgia and says, 'Not you too?'

Georgia nods. 'Gone,' she says.

'What? *Gone*, gone?' says Bunny.

'Yep. Gone, gone,' says Georgia.

Bunny leans forward and the lubricated forelock snakes on his brow as though it possesses its own heartbeat. He says, conspiratorially, 'If you don't mind me saying so, ladies, they must be out of their fucking minds.'

At this point two small girls waddle into the kitchen, something incomprehensible having severed the hypnotic pull of the vast plasma-screen TV in the living room. With zombied eyes, they stop and look up at the adults and one of the children reaches around and pulls her bikini bottom out of the crack in her arse. Then she turns and disappears back into the living room, the other child following close behind.

'Charming,' says Bunny, and the women laugh their different laughs, then lapse into a weighted silence as if the course of their lives were altering before their eyes – old skins falling away, weeping wounds healing, new and hopeful horizons opening.

Zoë picks a piece of lint from the leg of her chocolate velour tracksuit.

'You got any kids, Mr Munro?'

Bunny realises he was wrong about Zoë and he could fuck her too and a small, grey kitten enters the kitchen through a cat-flap and walks nonchalantly through the room.

'Call me Bunny,' he says and puts his hands behind his head and waggles them like rabbits' ears. He creases his nose and makes a snuffling sound.

'You got any kids, Bunny?' says Zoë.

'One. A boy,' he says and experiences an uncomfortable intestinal spasm as he remembers his son waiting in the car. He looks at his watch.

'What's his name?' asks Georgia.

'Bunny Junior,' says Bunny with a disarming pathos that fills the room with a gentle heartfelt ache. 'He's the light of my life, that little guy. The sun rises and sets with him.'

'And Mrs Munro?' says Zoë, craning forward and breathing deep into her lungs. Bunny notices, with a specialist's eye, that Zoë's breasts make no concessions to any gravitational bias whatsoever, as if they were hewn from granite or flint or something.

'Gone,' says Bunny, feeling an unexpected constriction of the throat.

'How?'

Georgia bats Zoë on the arm and says, 'Don't be so nosey.'

'She passed away,' says Bunny. 'Recently.'

'No,' says the chorus of mothers.

Georgia's hand goes to her mouth and she says, 'Oh, you poor man,' and wants to put her hand over Bunny's but resists the impulse.

'I'm not going to tell you it's been easy,' says Bunny, looking over his shoulder.

'No,' say the women, 'of course not.'

Bunny raises his glass of wine and has the eerie feeling that this scenario is not his alone, or even that of the three women, but rather they are players in somebody else's observance and he looks over his shoulder again to see if anybody is there.

'Do you feel that?' says Bunny, bringing his shoulders up around his ears.

The women look at him questioningly.

'A kind of chill in the room?' he says and looks over his shoulder again, but then lifts his glass and says, 'To life!' His hand trembles and the wine slops from the glass and seeps into the cuff of his shirt.

'To life,' say the women, looking at each other.

'And all the crap that goes with it,' says Bunny and empties the glass down his throat, then says, 'Are you sure you don't feel that?'

Bunny shudders and looks behind him. He checks his watch but the numbers blur. He pulls on his jacket.

'I've got to go, ladies,' he says and this remark is greeted with a clamour of protest. 'Now, now, girls, I'm a working man,' says Bunny and pulls up the collar of his jacket.

He notices a whorl of fog curl from his lips like a question mark.

'Did you see that?' he says, looking this way and that.

He reaches into the top pocket of his jacket and produces some business cards. He hands one each to Zoë and Amanda.

'Your products will be with you within ten working days. If there is anything you need, don't . . . um . . . hesitate to call. OK? It's been . . . um . . . an absolute pleasure,' he says.

Bunny turns to Georgia and he sees her through a bleared film. Georgia looks at Bunny, her violet eyes, wells of sympathy.

'Are you all right?' she says.

'Um . . . here is my card. Now, please don't lose it . . . ah . . . and if there is anything and I . . . um . . . mean *anything* I can . . . ah . . . do for you, please don't hesitate to call. Night or . . . um . . . you know . . . day.'

Georgia puts her hand over Bunny's and says, 'What is it?' then reaches into her purse and hands Bunny a Kleenex. Bunny realises, with a shiver, that the metallic mushroom on the front of Georgia's T-shirt is not a mushroom at all but a mushroom cloud.

'You have the most . . . ah . . . extraordinary eyes, Georgia,' says Bunny and dabs at his cheeks. 'Um . . . they go way . . . um . . . down.'

'Oh, you poor man,' whispers Georgia to herself.

'To the depths . . . um . . .'

Zoë puts her hand to her mouth and blows a tiny sprite of vapour across the pink butterfly tattooed on her wrist. She looks at Amanda and, with an intake of breath, says, 'Oh, my God.'

Bunny snaps shut his sample case and scrapes back his chair and he stands and says, 'Goodbye, ladies.'

He looks all around him, opens the door and disappears, leaving behind him an atmosphere of incredulity and sadness.

'Wow,' says Zoë.

Bunny stands on the gangway, then leans out over the balcony and realises, in a tentative way, that some sort of demand is being made of him from the other side – the dead side – but has no idea what. He descends the stairs and marches across the windblown courtyard of the estate, through its boxy, black shadows and towards the Punto.

The fat man in the dress and the lavender wig sees Bunny and rears up from the bench and, with the pot-plant held out in front of him like he's holding a child who had fouled its nappy or a pack of nitro-glycerine or something, lurches towards Bunny, a low growl rising from his throat.

Bunny stops, plants his feet on the ground and says, 'Don't come near me, you fucking nut-job!'

The guy looks at Bunny and sees something in him sufficiently impressive to inspire an urgent rethink as to the wisdom of his current course of action. He performs a comic, under-cranked retreat and sits back down in his hunched and plaguey position on the bench.

'Fucking wacko,' says Bunny and crosses the courtyard to the Punto and climbs in.

'Are you all right, Dad?' says Bunny Junior.

'What?' says Bunny. 'Fucking what?'

The boy closes his encyclopaedia and says to his father, 'I don't really like it here, Dad.'

Bunny starts the Punto and says, more to himself than to his son, 'Well, let's get the f-u-c-k out of here, then.'

'Where to, Dad?'

Bunny reaches into the pocket of his jacket and produces the client list and shoves it into Bunny Junior's hand.

'This is the client list,' says Bunny.

'OK,' says Bunny Junior.

Then Bunny reaches across the boy and punches the glove compartment and it springs open. He pulls out a street directory.

'This is an A to Z,' he says.

'OK,' says the boy.

'OK. Now, you're the navigator,' says Bunny, and the Punto lurches into the street.

'The navigator?' says the boy.

'The navigator!' says Bunny.

Bunny Junior looks at the list and executes a flourish of his hand that he hopes will impress his father and make him like him, or at least not be angry with him. He points at the names.

'Next stop, Shoreham!' he says, optimistically.

15

Bunny Junior sits in the Punto and watches a little Sun beetle land on the windscreen and, from his unique vantage point, admires its black jewel-like underbelly as it moves about the glass. He marvels too at its mysterious, coppery sheen and wonders how anything so common could be so beautiful. He reaches into his pocket and removes a black marker and places it against the windscreen and traces the meandering trajectory of the Sun beetle on the glass. He wonders if there is any order or system to it. Bunny Junior loves beetles — always has and always will. When he was smaller he had a cigarette box full of dead beetles and he tries to remember what he did with it. He had all sorts of beetles — Devil's Coach-horses, Black Clocks and Brown Chafers, Whirligigs, Sun beetles (like this one), Malachites, Red Soldiers and Sextons, Red Cardinals and Stag Beetles and his favourite, the Rhino Beetle. The Rhino Beetle is the strongest creature in the world and has three horns on its head and can lift 850 times its own weight. If a human could do this, it would mean he could lift 65 tons. He runs through all the beetles he knows quietly and to himself, and as he does so, he traces the now clearly random wanderings of this most ordinary of beetles, making the patch of windscreen look like the outer surface of a slowly expanding human brain. He is managing the job as navigator really well, he thinks – he has a knack for reading the maps and giving clear instructions and his dad, who can be a tough customer to please if you aren't up to scratch, says he is doing really well. Part of him wonders what he is actually *doing*, though, sitting in the car all day and missing school. 'Learning the ropes,' he guesses.

The air is turning a coral pink and candy-coloured clouds have been hung about the sky like shredded banners and the sun is falling behind the houses and he can hear the starlings creating their late-afternoon racket. His father has promised that this is the last job of the day, and the Sun beetle crawls its anarchic and pointless beat and before his raw and crusted eyes, the great black brain expands.

'The Replenishing Cream with Rose Flower has almost magical restorative powers,' says Bunny.

He is sitting on a calico-covered sofa in the living room of a modest but well kept home in Ovingdean. He feels exhausted, wrung out and, above all, spooked. He is coming to believe that there are forces at work, within and around him, over which he has little or no control. He feels, obliquely, as though he is playing second banana in somebody else's movie and that the dialogue is in asynchronous Martian and the subtitles are in Mongolian or something. He is finding it exceedingly diffi-cult to ascertain who the *first* banana is. The optimism of the morning has given way to the notion that he is, in short, basi-cally all over the fucking shop. On top of this, he is finding it hard to come to terms with the fact that there is a very real possibility his wife is observing him from the dead side and that he should, in some way, behave himself. This is close to impossible when the woman sitting in front of him, a Miss Charlotte Parnovar, is a bone fide, died-in-the-wool melon farmer who is giving off such serious and incontestable signals that Bunny can practically see the sparks leaping back and forth between them. Bunny, it should be said, has always considered himself a prize conductor of electricity and, as he massages lotion into staticky Charlotte's hands, he begins the process of erecting a finial or air terminal or strike-termination device in his zebra-skin briefs.

'This collagen- and elastin-rich cream can improve moisture up to two hundred per cent,' says Bunny.

'Oh, yeah?' says Charlotte.

Charlotte has an interestingly high forehead that is, in a sexy way, completely void of expression except for the fact that there is a strange dry cyst, like a white whelk, in the centre of it. She has a soft powdering of near-invisible down on her upper jaw and her stiff, peroxide-ravaged hair is pulled back and clamped to the back of her head with a metal clip. This is done with such severity that it actually elongates her subtly derisive eyes. Charlotte sits across from Bunny on a matching calico sofa, wearing loose-fitting towelling shorts and a pink cotton vest stretched across large, pillowy breasts. She wears a tiny diamanté charm on a silver chain around her neck, like a glittering treasure washed up on a coral shelf.

On the far wall hangs a framed picture from a West End musical and on the opposite wall a poster of a self-portrait by Frida Kahlo, dressed as a gypsy and holding a little brown monkey. On the coffee table in front of him – a homemade affair of stressed brick and smoke-grey Perspex – sits Bunny's sample case beside an incongruous bowl of stale potpourri.

Bunny squeezes more lotion into Charlotte's hands, kneading them and tugging on her fingers.

'Its unique healing powers penetrate deep into the skin, leaving your hands feeling supple and . . . blissed out,' he says, and he can see, if he adjusts his sight line fractionally, Charlotte's inner thigh muscle jump and spasm in the gaping leg of her shorts. Her fingers are bony and strong and lubricated and, as he squeezes and unsqueezes them, he imagines her vagina barely an arm's length away.

'It's . . . um . . . miraculous,' says Bunny.

'I don't doubt it for a second,' says Charlotte.

Her voice has a super-sexy masculinity to it, and Bunny frets for a second but shortly after realises the folly in this — if she were a dyke, she wouldn't be sitting here letting him do his thing with her hands, and he relaxes and presses his thumb into her open palm and slowly rotates it.

'They've done actual tests,' says Bunny, emphasising the last word, elongating it, softening it.

'What kind of tests?' says Charlotte, imitating him, gently mocking him.

'Scientific ones,' says Bunny.

'Hmmm,' says Charlotte and Bunny can see a secret and slightly sardonic smile find its way into the corner of her mouth.

'Yeah, does wonders for the wrists too,' he says, moving up and feeling hard, ribbed muscle in her forearms.

Charlotte closes her eyes. 'Hmmm,' she says again.

'Sexy lady,' says Bunny, under his breath.

'What did you say?'

Bunny nods at the poster of Frida Kahlo, who looks down at them from under her one bizarre and conjoined eyebrow with flat expressionless eyes.

'In the picture,' says Bunny.

Bunny registers the hint of condescension in Charlotte's smile.

'Oh, Frida Kahlo. Yes, she's beautiful, isn't she? I think that was painted in the 1940s,' she says, looking up at the picture.

Bunny thinks he feels a surge of electricity pass through Charlotte's fingers into his, moving through his bones and straight into the base of his spine. He is overwhelmed by a multitude of tantalising things he can say but for some reason he says, 'Didn't they have tweezers back then?'

Charlotte's features shift infinitesimally, but in doing so her face becomes angular and severe.

'I'm sorry,' she says. 'What do you mean?'

Bunny holds a finger up to his forehead, and even as he does so, he feels a sense of things unravelling and of having lost control.

'The mono-brow,' he says, regretting it instantly.

'The what?' says Charlotte.

'Makes you wonder what her legs looked like,' he says before he can stop himself.

'I'm sorry, I don't follow you,' says Charlotte, extracting her hand from Bunny's and staring at him with a fierce disbelief.

'I can see why the monkey likes her,' he says, jamming a knuckle into his mouth.

Charlotte leans forward and connects with Bunny's eyes.

'I don't know if you can follow this, but Frida Kahlo was involved in a terrible accident that left her severely handicapped. I think she was hit by a truck, if you must know!'

Bunny picks up a towel and wipes the excess moisturiser from his hands. He feels disorientated and he can almost see the words as they tumble from his mouth, as if someone else was filling in his speech bubbles – someone with a deviant love of catastrophe.

'Really? To be perfectly honest, I find the picture a little depressing. But what would I know? Still, if she painted it with her foot . . .'

Then, effortlessly and seamlessly, Bunny says, 'Speaking of which, I have a sensational balm that is just heaven for the tootsies . . . Miss . . . may I call you Charlotte?'

Charlotte looks at Bunny, her head angled as though she were trying to decode the anarchic scribblings of a child.

'You can call me Bunny,' says Bunny, and he waggles his hands behind his head like rabbits' ears.

A low, unpleasant chuckle escapes Charlotte's throat and she picks at the cyst on her forehead and says, 'You're kidding, right?'

Bunny feels, suddenly, that although all evidence points to the contrary, he may have a chance of pulling this exchange back from the abyss and says, 'I'm deadly serious, Charlotte.'

'That's the kind of name I'd give to my . . .'

'Rabbit?'

Charlotte softens and, despite herself, smiles and says, 'Yeah . . . Rabbit.'

Bunny sees the super-toned muscle in Charlotte's thigh twitch and thinks he sees, carried on the happy, ozonic air, golden sparks of love jumping out of the legs of her pink towelling shorts. Emboldened, Bunny leans in and wiggles his eyebrows and says, suggestively, 'Well, Charlotte, you know what they say about rabbits?'

'No, I don't. What?'

'Well, they're . . . um . . . well, you know . . .' says Bunny.

'No, I don't know what they say,' and then Charlotte adds something that sees this entire episode slip through Bunny's fingers like the string of a child's fly-away balloon.

'Does this routine actually work on the ladies, Bunny?'

Charlotte waggles her hands behind her head, mocking him, and Bunny feels a spike of umbrage worm its way through his bowels.

'You'd be surprised,' he says and, before he can check himself, winks at her.

Charlotte shrieks with laughter and says, 'Did you just *wink* at me?'

Bunny thinks – Did I? – then feels her laughter scrape its fingers down his spine.

'I might have,' he says, 'or I might have had something in my eye.'

What the fuck? – he thinks. *What the fuck!*

Charlotte howls and cups her hands over her mouth, then points at Bunny and shouts, 'You are beyond belief!'

'So I've been told,' says Bunny.

'Where have you crawled from? The tar pits?'

'The *what* pits?'

'You should be embalmed and have a sign hung around your neck saying, "extinct".'

'I resent that,' says Bunny. 'I take personal hygiene very seriously,' but even as he says this he can sense the faintest odour of flophouse sweat rising from his armpits.

'Not stink . . . *Ex-tinct* . . . like a dodo.'

'Wo, steady on,' says Bunny, and with a kind of wounded awe watches Charlotte's features vulcanise before his eyes; the dry blonde hair take on the appearance of a steel helmet and her eyes, a fierce, warring, metallic sheen.

'You ridiculous man.'

'Hey, I'm just trying to do my job here.'

'You sad, ridiculous little man,' she says.

'What is this? Jesus!' says Bunny as he grabs handfuls of beauty samples and throws them into his case. A shadow falls across his face and he looks devastated and injured. 'Jesus,' he repeats to himself.

Then Charlotte's face changes again, and without warning she puts her soft, greased fingers over Bunny's hand and says, with a fair approximation of genuine concern, 'Oh, I'm sorry, Mr Munro. I've gone too far. I've wounded you. That wasn't fair.'

Bunny feels a sudden and excruciating pressure on his bladder. He holds up his hand and shakes it as if to ward off further comment.

'No, it's all right, I just need to use your bathroom.'

'What?' says Charlotte.

'Yeah,' says Bunny, 'I've been on the road all day. I need to go so much I can taste it!'

Charlotte shrieks with laughter and a nerve twitches under Bunny's right eye.

'Oh, man, you're a class act! It's down the hall!' she says and cocks a thumb in the direction of the bathroom.

Charlotte's laughter follows Bunny as he quick-marches towards the bathroom. He feels a violent and boiling rage towards her but is not completely surprised to see visions of her sparky vagina strobe before his eyes. He enters the bathroom in a fury, scrabbles at his flies and passes a stream of urine with such puissance that it makes the bones in his face ache. A glaze of sweat covers Bunny's brow and his quiff lies on his forehead as limp and insentient as roadkill. Bunny hears a renewed shriek of laughter come from the living room and he bares his teeth.

'Fucking bitch,' he says and he pisses on her carpet. Then he pisses on her lilac-coloured walls, then on the rack full of magazines, then on the hand towels and with a grand flourish he rises up on his toes and pisses on her electric toothbrush that sits in a glass next to the basin. Then he zips himself up, opens the door and strides back down the hall, full of a renewed and unobstructed purpose, and says, 'All right, do you want to buy any of this shit or not?'

'I detect a note of hostility, Mr Munro,' says Charlotte, standing up from the sofa and rolling her head around on her neck in order to release some pent-up tension. Bunny notices that she is tall and broad across the shoulders, and the shell-like furuncle on her forehead seems to have morphed into a tiny tusk or horn or something.

'Well, we fucking *dodos* get like that sometimes,' says Bunny, and the corner of his eye flutters.

Charlotte stands firm, hands clasped benignly in front of her, and says, as if imparting a simple, incontrovertible fact, 'For your information, Mr Munro, I am a black belt in Tae Kwon Do.'

'Oh, yeah?' says Bunny, 'Well, I just pissed all over your bathroom . . .'

'You what?' says Charlotte, taking a step closer.

'That's right. The walls, the carpet, your *Hello* magazines.'

'You what?!'

'Your fucking toothbrush!' says Bunny, showing his straight, white teeth.

Suddenly, and without discussion, Charlotte begins to jump up and down on the balls of her feet, her muscular arms relaxed and loose at her sides. Bunny is immediately and completely transfixed by the sight of the diamanté charm being tossed around on its happy pink bolster like a child on a trampoline. He notices that Charlotte is not wearing a bra and that, before his very eyes, her nipples are stiffening and now jut through the thin cotton of her T-shirt, hard and fierce and unusually protracted. He sees, incredibly, what appear to be tiny cartoon sparks shooting from them and he thinks, for a sweet moment, that maybe, just maybe, all is not lost. He feels his cock roar awake. Meanwhile, Charlotte Parnovar steps forward, and with a solitary rabbit-punch, busts Bunny's nose. There is an audible crack, a supernova of light, a geyser of blood, and Bunny tumbles backwards over the calico sofa and lands in a stunned heap on the floor by the front door.

'Hai!' says Charlotte.

There is a great pumping of blood from Bunny's nose that splashes down his tie and his jaw yawns open and he makes a sucking noise like a fish. In slow motion, he allows his head to fall forward and watches the bright blood pool in his cupped hands and says, not loudly but with the purest kind of outrage, 'Fuck!'

Charlotte continues to hop up and down, her nipples as hard as bone.

'The foundations of Tae Kwon Do are built on integrity, peace and respect. You ought to try some, *Rabbit Man*.'

Painfully, Bunny climbs to his feet, points one trembling finger at her and says, 'You horrible, fucking slag.' He says, 'You mad . . . ugly . . . diseased . . .' and Charlotte Parnovar grins and swivels and tilts her hip to the side.

* * *

Bunny Junior looks at his watch and wonders what is taking his father so long. He looks towards the small semi-detached house that Bunny entered and sees, but does not hear, the front door burst open and his father launched backwards through the air, arms by his sides, like he has been shot from a cannon. The boy watches his father crash land on the garden path and lie there. He sees, but does not hear, the door slam shut. Then, before he has even considered what he should do, the door opens again and his father's sample case flies out approximating much the same trajectory as its owner, exploding on the path and disgorging its cargo of tiny bottles and sachets all over the tattered lawn.

The boy sees his father lift his head, then roll over and raise himself up on his hands and knees and grasp wildly at the scattered samples, tossing them in his case. He tries unsuccessfully to close it.

Then his father stands, sample case clutched to his chest, but the time it takes to perform this relatively simple act is horrible in its despairing retardation. The boy watches his father stumble down the footpath, pulling a handkerchief from the pocket of his trousers and clamping it to what appears to be a very bloody nose.

Then the door to the Punto flies open and, with a muffled moan, Bunny drops into the driver's seat. The boy looks on in horror but then has a sudden and overwhelming urge to laugh – the crazy crimson face, the handkerchief, the busted sample case – until he sees that his father's rabbit tie is spotted with blood. The urge to laugh vanishes and the boy feels a cold grief roar through his chest. He rubs at his forehead with the back of his hand and paddles the air frantically beneath his feet, even though he doesn't really know why.

'Dad,' he says, pointing at the tie.

'Just don't ask,' says Bunny and hurls the sample case into the back seat, but as he does so the case springs open and its contents fly all over the inside of the car. He grabs at them futilely and makes the word 'fuck' sound like the worst word in the world.

'*Fuck*,' he roars.

Then Bunny looks at himself in the rear-view mirror and actually screams.

'That muff-munching dyke broke my fucking nose!'

'Dad,' says the boy, still pointing his finger at his father's tie.

Bunny notices that the inside of the windscreen has been decorated with a strange and intricate web of black markings. They draw him in like a spell.

'What the fuck,' he says, but his voice has turned breathy and remote.

His outraged body achieves, in that instant, a kind of drugged laxity and he sinks back into his seat, hypnotised. A fresh ribbon of blood unravels from his nose.

Bunny says, again, 'What the fuck.'

Then Bunny Junior realises what it is about his father's tie that makes him feel so unhappy and he starts thinking about Rhino beetles and how they are part of the Scarab family and that the males use their horns in mating battles against other males and that they are among the largest beetles in the whole *fucking* world.

'Pick up that piece of paper, down there, on the floor,' says Bunny, after a while. The boy thinks his father sounds like a robot or Cyberman or something.

'Are we going home now, Dad?' says the boy.

'Do as you're told.'

The boy reaches down and picks up the piece of crumpled paper.

'Here it is, Dad,' says the boy.

'Read what it says,' says Bunny.

Bunny Junior makes a great show of straightening out the piece of paper by flattening it on his knee and then, with a certain ostentation, says, 'Pamela Stokes, Meeching Road, Newhaven.' Then the boy looks at his father with a clamped and idiot-sweet smile.

Bunny reaches over and snaps a tissue from the glove box and rolls it into twin plugs and inserts them up his nose. With the sleeve of his jacket he rubs at the dark tracery on the windscreen. Then he stops and looks at the boy.

'Well?' he says.

'Well, what, Dad?' says Bunny Junior.

'Well, are you the bloody navigator or what?'

Bunny Junior opens the A–Z.

'Is Newhaven a nice place, Dad?'

Bunny rotates the plugs in his nostrils, pats at his bloodstained tie, smoothes down his hair and enacts a bizarre performance with his fingers that the boy is unable to interpret.

'Bunny Boy, you're gonna love it.'

16

On an enormous plasma-screen TV that sits in the far corner of a living room in a small maisonette in Newhaven, Bunny thinks he can see, at the very edge of his vision, new CCTV footage of the Horned Killer careening through a stampede of shoppers with his trademark trident. But Bunny cannot be completely sure as a wedge of late-afternoon sunlight has moved across the screen and obliterated the image. He can detect, however, in the colour-bleached pixels, a now familiar sense of terror – he recognises the crowd's horrified screams – and he wonders, for a split second, how close to Brighton this crazy fucker actually is, as he says to Pamela Stokes, 'We offer a line of highly indulgent, high-performance skin care that combines the best of over a century of achievements in dermatological research with sensually pleasing, luxury formulations.'

Bunny thinks that Pamela Stokes looks like she has walked out of the all-time fucking Mr Whippy of one of Poodle's wet dreams. She wears a blood-coloured halter-neck top stretched over a boob job from Mars and a black denim skirt with an arabesque of emerald glitter on each thigh. Her eyebrows are fine and perfectly arched. The look on her face suggests that there is nothing she hasn't seen, her eyes, bottomless wells of experience. On her left cheek she has a tiny V-shaped scar, as if a small bird had pecked her there.

'What happened to your nose?' she says.

'You don't want to know,' says Bunny, and he touches gently the plugs of blood-soaked toilet paper. 'Suffice to say the other guy looks a lot worse,' he says and waves away further comment except to say, 'at least I still *have* a nose.'

Bunny leans forward in his armchair and continues his pitch.

'This comprehensive collection works in synergy with the skin's natural rhythms to help defend against signs of premature aging and provides unprecedented skincare benefits . . .'

'Are you all named after cute little animals at . . .' and Pamela points at the logo on Bunny's sample case with a hot pink Day-Glo fingernail, '. . . Eternity Enterprises?'

'Hey?' says Bunny.

'He told you where I lived, didn't he?' says Pamela, looking directly at Bunny.

'Well . . .'

'What was his name?'

'Um . . . Poodle,' says Bunny, as he twists the cap off a miniature tube of hand cream. He sighs. What a fucked-up day, he thinks. Had all of womankind had the painters in on the same fucking day?

'What did he say about me?' says Pamela.

'He said that you were a most accommodating customer.'

'Did he now?' says Pamela, and Bunny's eyes mist at the drama of her lungs filling with weary air and releasing a compunctious sigh.

'Most obliging, he said. Generous, even.'

Bunny notices a giant baby-blue rabbit wrapped in cellophane perched on the mantelpiece, but before he has even had time to contemplate the extraordinary synchronicity of this, Pamela, who looks as though she has been forced to make some unpleasant and ill-fated decision, sinks back into the sofa and says, 'Tell me more about the hand lotion.'

'Well, Pamela, this rich, hydrating, age-targeting lotion softens the skin and exfoliates surface cells for a smoother . . .'

Pamela reaches under her skirt and with a subtle upward shift of her hips slips off her panties. They are as white and blank as a snowflake.

'. . . Um . . . younger look. It is formulated with a relaxing fragrance . . .'

Pamela hitches up her skirt and opens her legs.

'. . . that inspires feelings of . . . comfort and . . . calm,' says Bunny and he notices a sculpted domino of black fuzz balanced on top of her gash like a pirate flag or a Jolly Roger or something. He closes his eyes for a moment and imagines Avril Lavigne's vagina and tears run down his cheeks.

'Are you all right?' asks Pamela.

'It's been a hard day,' says Bunny, wiping his face with the back of his hand.

'I've got a feeling about you,' she says, not unkindly.

'Yeah,' says Bunny.

'I think things are going to get a whole lot worse.'

'I know,' he says, with a sudden and dizzying awareness. 'That's what scares me.'

Pamela pushes her hips forward.

'Do you like pussy, Bunny?'

There is a soft, sucking sound as Bunny's bottom lip drops open. He experiences a great, cinematic rushing-away of the years.

'I do,' he says.

'How much do you like it?'

'I love it.' He feels the evaporating of a massive psychic weight as his life tunnels backwards.

'How much do you love it?'

'I love it beyond all things. I love it more than life itself.'

Pamela readjusts the position of her hips.

'Do you love my pussy?' she says

She slips a long curled finger into her vagina.

'Yes, I do. I love it beyond measure,' says Bunny, in a tiny, uncomplicated voice. 'I love it till the cows come home.'

Pamela chides him gently.

'You wouldn't lie to me, Bunny?' she says, her left hand splayed and circling like a pink, amputated starfish.

'Never. It is the truth, the whole truth and nothing but the truth. Cross my heart and hope to die.'

Pamela slips her finger out and it glistens as she beckons to Bunny and says from deep in her throat, 'Well, come and get it.'

Bunny slides from the armchair and drops to his hands and knees and with movements that seem newborn and unpractised he crawls across the worn carpet of her maisonette – a tube of hand cream clamped in his fist, a fucking rocket in his briefs and a little trail of plashed tears behind him.

Quasar – a distant compact body far beyond our galaxy, which looks star-like on a photograph but has a red shift character- istic of an extremely remote object. The distinctive features of quasars are an extremely compact structure and high red shift velocity corresponding to velocities approaching the speed of light. They are the most luminous objects in the universe – thinks Bunny Junior – and he brings his knees up to his chest. The boy believes that if he remains where he is, in the Punto on Meeching Road, Newhaven, his mother will eventually find him, and even as he thinks this he becomes aware of a shift in the air and the smell of his mother's hand cream. He feels the feathery touch of her hand on his brow. He can feel her trace his profile with an index finger, down his forehead, between his sleeping eyes, along the length of his nose and onto his lips, where she presses her finger down in the approximation of a kiss. Bunny Junior hears a voice – either his or hers, he is not sure which – that says, 'You . . . are . . . the . . . most . . . luminous . . . object . . . in . . . the . . . universe,' and he feels a gentle folding of the air around him.

'What's the capital of China!?'

Bunny Junior awakes to the smell of hand cream and the retracting flutter of his mother's fingers. His father sits beside him, panting and super-charged, his jacket off, his shirt open, his powerful pomaded hair crazy and all over the shop. White foam has collected in the corners of his mouth, his nose looks like a small, injured tomato and his eyes are energised with a wild joy.

Bunny Junior sits up and grabs at the empty air in front of his face.

'Mummy?' he says. 'Mummy?'

'Eh?' says Bunny.

The boy rubs the sleep from his face. 'Beijing,' he says.

Bunny enacts a little stunt with his index fingers.

'What's the capital of Mongolia?'

The boy opens and closes boxes in his mind, but he is groggy with sleep and this takes time.

'Come on! The clock's ticking,' says Bunny, who is now frantically combing his hair in the rear-view mirror.

'Ulaanbaadar,' he says, 'formerly Urga.'

Bunny stops combing his hair and for some reason does an impersonation of Frankenstein's monster, then mimes electricity coming out his ears and exclaims, 'Ulaanbaa . . . what?!'

'Ulaanbaadar, Dad,' says Bunny Junior.

Bunny lets forth a great infectious laugh and slaps his thighs and lurches over, grabs his son in a headlock and knuckles the top of his skull.

'My son, the bloody genius! You ought to be on the telly!' shouts Bunny as he twists the key in the ignition and veers into the road. There is a blare of car horns and Bunny says, pulling at the crotch of his trousers, 'Fuck, it's good to be back on the road!'

'That took a really long time, Dad,' says the boy.

'What?'

'You were in there a really long time.'

Bunny turns into the Brighton Road and says, 'Yeah, I know, but if you want to come on the road with me, the first thing you got to learn is *patience*. That is the first and fundamental law of salesmanship, Bunny Boy. Patience.'

Bunny guns the engine and overtakes a maroon cement truck.

'It's like those bloody Zulu warriors in Africa or wherever.'

'Natal,' says the boy.

'What?'

'South Africa.'

'Yeah, fuck, whatever. The thing is – if a Zulu warrior wants to spear an antelope or a zebra or something, he doesn't go stomping through the bush with his boots on and hope the antelope is gonna stay put. Right? He has to employ, what is known in the trade as stealth. Stealth and . . .'

'Patience,' says Bunny Junior and compresses a smile.

Bunny begins to beat on his chest a solemn tattoo with his fist and his face gathers in intensity.

'You become one with your prey . . . and move quietly, stealthily, towards it and then . . . *Wham!* . . . you stick your spear right through its bloody heart!'

Bunny slams his hand on the dashboard for dramatic emphasis, and then he looks at the boy and says, 'Why are you doing that loopy thing with your feet?'

'You left your tie behind, Dad.'

Bunny's hand rises to his throat.

'Shit,' he says, softly.

'You left it back at the last house,' says the boy.

Bunny punches his son playfully on the arm.

'Ah, well, Bunny Boy, you tell me a Zulu warrior that ever wore a bloody tie!'

The Punto is now heading west along the coastal road and the boy watches the sun as it falls beyond the horizon and casts the sea in yellow gold, then pink gold, and then an ethereal, sorrowing blue.

'Aren't you going to go back and get it?'

'Shit, no, I've got a suitcase full of ties!'

'Mum gave you that tie,' says Bunny Junior.

Bunny scratches his head and turns to the boy.

'OK, son, this is serious. This is the real deal. This is one of those moments in life when you've really got to listen and, young as you are, try to understand. There is another law of salesmanship that I haven't told you about. It is the absolutely crucial law. It's even more important than the patience law. Any salesman worth his salt will tell you the same thing. Now, do you want to know what it is?'

'OK, Dad.'

'Well, stop flopping your feet around and I'll tell you.'

'OK, Dad.'

'Never go back. All right? Never, ever, go back. Now, do you want me to tell you why?'

'OK,' says the boy, and all down the coastal road the street-lights come on and the boy sees an awesome, mystical majesty in it.

Bunny looks gravely at the boy and says, 'They may renege on the order.'

'Might they?' says the boy.

'Yes, believe me, it happens,' says Bunny. 'OK?'

'OK, Dad,' and they smile at each other.

Bunny turns his headlights on and they pass a billboard — a topless Kate Moss, in a pair of Calvin Klein jeans — and he recalls a conversation between Poodle, Geoffrey and himself, down The Wick. Poodle, who kept throwing back tequilas, sucking a lemon and licking the armpit of the girl sitting next to him, said, 'Well, if you include the haunches, I am defi-nitely a leg man.' Geoffrey, who was sitting there like King Tut or Buddha or somebody, cupped his own considerable breasts and said, 'Tit man, no contest.' Then they looked at Bunny, who pretended to give it some thought, but didn't really need to. 'Vagina man,' said Bunny, and his two colleagues went quiet and nodded in silent agreement. Bunny loves Kate Moss, thinks she's cool, vanishes her Calvin Kleins, hammers the car horn and thinks, 'I'm fucking back.'

'I know where she bought that tie, if you want to get another one,' says the boy.

Bunny slams his hands on the wheel of the Punto and looks all around him and says, 'Close your eyes. Go on, close your eyes and don't open them till I tell you.'

The boy puts his hands in his lap and closes his eyes.

The Punto takes a sudden, violent swerve into a roadside McDonald's and screeches to a halt.

'Now open them,' says Bunny, and the boy can hear the trembling madness in his father's voice. The light from the giant McDonald's sign illuminates the boy's face, coating it in gold, and Bunny can see a little yellow 'M' reflected in each of his son's eyes as he throws open the door of the Punto and steps monstrously out and into the early evening light.

'Now, tell me you don't love your dad!' he roars.

17

Bunny sits in McDonald's with a defibrillated hard-on due to the fact that underneath the cashier's red and yellow uniform she hardly has any clothes on. The cashier wears a nametag that says 'Emily' and she keeps glancing across at Bunny with huge vacant eyes and wiggling all around. She has a black lacquered beehive, a conga-line of raw acne across her forehead and a vagina. Bunny thinks she is similar to Kate Moss, only shorter, fatter and more ugly. He bites deep into his Big Mac and says to his son, 'I fucking love McDonald's.'

He knows fundamentally, as if it is carved into his very bones, that he could fuck Emily the cashier without any real resistance, but he also understands, in a sorrowful way, that there is a time issue, a problem with the venue (although it wouldn't be the first time he had slipped it to a waitress in the ladies') and, of course, he has his nine-year-old son sitting opposite him, flip-flopping his feet, smiling his wonky smile and playing with a plastic Darth Vader figurine that came free with his Happy Meal.

'Me too,' says Bunny Junior.

Bunny takes another bite of his Big Mac and knows what everybody knows who is into this sort of thing – that with its flaccid bun, its spongy meat, the cheese, the slimy little pickle and, of course, the briny special sauce, biting into a Big Mac was as close to eating pussy as, well, eating pussy. Bunny put this to Poodle down The Wick one lunchtime, and Poodle, self-proclaimed sexpert and barracuda, argued that eating a tuna carpaccio was actually a lot more like eating pussy than a Big Mac, and this argument raged all through the afternoon, becoming increasingly hostile as the pints went down. Finally Geoffrey, in his near-Godlike wisdom, decided that eating a Big Mac was like eating a fat chick's pussy and eating a tuna carpaccio was like eating a skinny chick's pussy, and they left it that. Whatever. Bunny wipes at a blob of special sauce that runs down his chin with the back of his hand. He licks his lips as Emily the cashier throws Bunny another look and scratches at her acne. Bunny can see her nipples actually harden under her uniform, and the effect this has on him is so monumental that Bunny hardly registers that his son is asking him a question.

'Are you all right, Dad?'

Bunny was thinking that if Emily the cashier took a ten-minute smoko and went downstairs to the toilet, and if he bought Bunny Boy another Coke or Sprite or something – well, who knows? – nothing ventured, nothing gained, as they say in the trade. Bunny starts making surreptitious signals, a subtle jerking of the cheekbone towards the customer bathrooms and a kind of egging of the eyeballs, and he hears the boy say, in an anxious little voice, 'Dad?'

He hopes that his son doesn't blow the whole thing for him, so he whispers, out of the corner of his mouth, 'Stay cool, Bunny Boy, just stay cool.' Then he says, in the voice of a replicant or something, his eyes glued to the waitress, 'Do you want another Coke or Sprite or something?'

Bunny Junior says, 'Um,' and then the manager, a fucking teenager with braces on his teeth and with a nametag that says 'Ashley', walks over and asks Bunny to leave. The skin on Ashley's face has actually turned a shade of green and is peppered with blackheads the size of confetti. He has grease spots on his company tie.

'I come here a lot. I'm a loyal customer,' says Bunny.

'Yeah . . . um . . . well, I know you do,' says Ashley the manager.

Outside, under the golden arches, Bunny opens the door of the Punto and flops into the driver's seat. The boy climbs in and Bunny says, 'I fucking hate McDonald's.'

Bunny Junior wants to ask his father why they had to leave the McDonald's in such a hurry, but way back in the sub-caverns of his mind, stirring like some hideous, hibernating beast, the answer is already taking shape.

The boy whispers, 'What are we going to do now, Dad?'

Bunny kicks over the engine of the Punto and the car comes reluctantly and cantankerously to life. He turns out of the McDonald's car park and merges into the night traffic on the coastal road and all the crouched cars move past.

'We are gonna get as far away from this place as possible,' he says.

The boy yawns deep and shudders.

'Are we going home now, Dad?'

'Shit, no!' says Bunny, checking his rear-view mirror. 'We're on the road!'

'What are we gonna do, Dad?'

'You, me and Darth Vader there are checking into a hotel!'

Bunny checks his mirror again – he's looking for any police action, the wail of a siren, the flashing blue light looming up behind him — but there is nothing but the somnambulant creep of the evening traffic. He turns off the seafront road, though, just in case, and disappears down a side street. The last thing he needs is to be nicked in breach of his Antisocial Behaviour Order. That would be a serious bummer. Bunny looks at his son, who for some reason has an extremely deranged smile on his face.

'Really, Dad?' he says. '*A hotel?*'

'That's right! And you know what we are going to do when we get there?' Blocks of yellow light move across the boy's face and his eyes are round and wild as Bunny adds, with due reverence, 'Room service.'

'What's room service, Dad?'

'Jesus Christ, Bunny Boy, you know the capital of Mongolia but you don't know what room service is?'

Bunny has been banned for life from three McDonald's, one Burger King and thrown out of the Kentucky Fried on Western Road with such force that he fractured two of his ribs. This was on a busy Saturday in the middle of the afternoon. Bunny also has four separate ASBOs in the Sussex area.

'Room service is when you lie on your bed in a hotel room, close your eyes and think of anything in the world that you want, and I mean anything, then you ring up reception, ask for it and some jobber in a bowtie brings it up for you.'

'Anything, Dad?' says the boy, twisting his Darth Vader and realising at the same time that he didn't actually have anything to worry about all along.

'Sandwiches, cup of tea, fish and chips, a bottle of vino . . . um . . . fags . . . a massage . . . anything. And another thing, Bunny Boy . . .'

The Punto passes a shadowy man with tattoos on his arms

changing the back tire on a maroon cement truck (with the word 'DUDMAN' painted across the bonnet in giant cream letters) parked in a lay-by at the side of the road. Bunny Junior notices with a jolt of panic that its windscreen wipers are moving back and forth at a tremendous rate, but it isn't raining.

'When we get to the hotel, I'm gonna show you the weirdest thing in the world!'

The boy looks up at his father and says, 'What, Dad?'

Bunny rolls his eyes and says, 'I'm talking fucking completely Wacko Jacko!'

'What's that, Dad?' says Bunny Junior again, stifling a yawn.

'I mean seriously off the planet, Janet!'

'Da-ad!' says the boy.

'I mean bananas in fucking pyjamas!'

The boy laughs and says, 'Da-a-ad!'

Bunny changes lanes, looks awed and leans in close to Bunny Junior for dramatic effect.

'The tiniest fucking soaps you've ever seen in your life.'

'Soaps?' says Bunny Junior.

'Yeah, smaller than a matchbox, they are.'

'Really,' says the boy and squeezes his lips together in a smile.

'And individually wrapped,' says Bunny.

Bunny Junior's face glows gold, then tarnishes, and then glows gold again, and goes on like that for a while. He holds out his hand, his thumb and forefinger extended to suggest the size of a matchbox.

'Really? This big?' he says, amazed.

'What?'

'The soaps,' says Bunny Junior.

'Smaller.'

Bunny holds his thumb and forefinger about an inch and a half apart and whispers to his son, 'They are *tiny*.'

Bunny Junior can smell the fish on the salted air blowing up from the sea. A mist rolls up from the dark waters and curls about the Punto, a ghostly white. He waggles his black plastic figurine.

'Soap for Darth Vader,' says Bunny Junior.

Bunny flips on his high beams and says, 'You got it, Bunny Boy.'

18

Bunny remembers the day he and Libby arrived home from the hospital with the baby. The tiny child's eyes, yet to find their colour, peered out of his scarlet, Claymation face as they laid him in the cot.

Bunny said to Libby, 'I don't know what to say to him.'

'It doesn't really matter, Bun. He is three days old.'

'Yeah, I guess.'

'Tell him he's beautiful,' said Libby.

'But he's not. He looks like somebody stepped on him.'

'Well, tell him that then,' she said. 'Only, in a nice voice.'

Bunny leaned into the crib. The child seemed to Bunny both terrifyingly present and a thousand light years away, all at the same time. There was something about him that he just couldn't handle, so full of his mother's love.

'You look like somebody put you through the mincer, little guy.'

Bunny Junior jerked his tiny bunched fingers in the air and changed the shape of his mouth.

'See? He likes it,' said Libby.

'You look like a bowl of Bolognese,' said Bunny. 'You look like a baboon's arse.'

Libby giggled and placed her raw and swollen fingers against the baby's head and the baby closed its eyes.

'Don't listen to him. He's jealous,' she said.

That was also the day that Sabrina Cantrell, Libby's work-mate and 'oldest friend', came to pay her a visit. While Libby nursed the baby in the living room, in their tiny kitchenette Sabrina made the exhausted new mother a cup of tea. Bunny, who offered to help her, was suddenly and unexpectedly visited by a venereal compulsion that involved Sabrina Cantrell's arse and both his hands — something midway between a slap and a full-blown squeeze. It came out of nowhere, this compulsion, and even as he groped up great handfuls of her backside he wondered — What the fuck am I doing? Nothing came of it, of course, and it was the last time he ever saw Sabrina Cantrell, but a chain of events was set in motion that Bunny felt was beyond his control. There was a voice and a command, there was an action and there was indeed a consequence — shock-waves reverberated through the Munro household for weeks. Why had he done it? Who knows? Whatever. Fuck you.

Bunny rarely thought about that first marital miscalcula-tion — what it was that guided his hands inexorably towards their forbidden resting place — but he did often think about the *feel* of Sabrina Cantrell's backside under the thin crepe skirt, that wonderful contracting of the buttocks, the jump of outraged muscle, before the shit and the fan had their fateful assignation.

As he lies on his back, in his zebra-striped briefs at the Queensbury Hotel in Regency Square, working his way through a bottle of Scotch and watching with ancient eyes the tiny TV that blithers in the corner of the room, Bunny places a finger gently on the bridge of his nose and two thin rivulets of new dark blood emerge and run down his chin and drop soundlessly onto his chest. He curses to himself, rolls a Kleenex into plugs and inserts them up each nostril.

The room is a riot of psychedelic wallpaper and blood-coloured paisley carpet that appears to be designed around the ghosted, Technicolor nightmares of an Australian backstreet abortionist. The scarlet curtains hang like strips of uncooked meat and a paper lightshade that hangs from the ceiling writhes with fierce, whiskered Chinese dragons. The room reeks of bad plumbing and bleach and there is no room service and there is no mini-bar.

Bunny Junior lies on the other bed, in his pyjamas, engaged in an epic battle with his tormented eyelids – nodding off, then jerking awake, then nodding off again – a little yawn, a little scratch, a little folding of the hands to sleep.

'Daddy?' he mutters, rhetorically, sadly, to himself.

Bunny stops thinking about Sabrina Cantrell's backside and starts thinking about her pussy instead and quite soon he is thinking about Avril Lavigne's vagina. He is almost positive that Avril Lavigne possesses the fucking Valhalla of all vaginas, and in response to this late-night meditation he carefully folds a copy of the *Daily Mail* over his semi-tumescent member. There is, after all, a child in the room.

Bunny lights a Lambert & Butler and focuses on the television. A woman on a 'confessional' talk show is admitting to being sex addict. This holds no special interest to Bunny except that he finds it difficult to see how this woman, with her triplicate chins, flabby arms and lardy rear-end, could find enough guys willing to indulge her rank appetites. But apparently this was not a problem, and she gives a lurid and detailed account of her nympho-sploits. In time they bring on her husband, beaten-down and camera-shy, and she asks him to forgive her. The camera does a slow zoom on her tear-sodden face as she says, 'Oh, Frank, I have done bad things. Terrible, terrible things. Could you please find it in your heart to forgive me?'

Bunny pours himself another Scotch and lights up a Lambert & Butler.

'Kill the bitch,' he mutters.

Bunny Junior opens his eyes and, in a faraway voice that rises up from the soft curds of sleep, says 'What did you say, Dad?'

'Kill the bitch,' answers Bunny, but the boy's eyes have closed again.

Then the sound seems to drop out of the television and the face of the host, a guy with a floppy yellow fringe and a salad-green suit, seems to morph into that of a braying cartoon horse or laughing hyena or something and Bunny, appalled, closes his eyes.

He recalls, with a shudder, Libby standing in their kitch-enette, red-eyed with confusion and disbelief, holding the baby and the telephone, and asking Bunny, point-blank, 'Is it true?'

She had been on the phone with Sabrina Cantrell, who had rung up to inform Libby that her husband had groped her in the kitchen and was, in all probability, a sexual pervert or something.

Bunny did not answer but hung his head and examined the monochromatic checkerboard linoleum on the floor of the kitchenette.

'Why?' she sobbed.

Bunny, in all honesty, had no fucking idea and he said this to her, shaking his head.

He remembered, quite distinctly, the baby, sitting like a little prince in his wife's arms, lift one well-sucked fist and uncurl his index finger and point it at Bunny. Bunny recalls looking at the child and having the overwhelming desire to go down to the Wick with Poodle. After half a dozen pints Poodle put a comforting arm around Bunny and bared his shark-like teeth and said, 'Don't worry, Bun, she'll get used to it.'

Bunny opens his eyes and sees the boy has raised himself up and is sitting on the edge of his bed, a look of concern on his face.

'Are you all right, Dad?' says the boy.

But before Bunny can think of what to answer, the TV comes alive with a urgent blast of music and a voice that cries, *'Wakey-wakey!'* and the boy and his father look at the screen and see an advertisement for Butlins Holiday Camp in Bognor Regis. Various photographs framed in yellow cartoon stars cartwheel across the screen, showing the range of activities offered at Butlins – the Tiki Bar with its simulated electrical storms, the Empress Ballroom with its crimson curtains and tuxedoed band, the indoor and outdoor swimming pools, the world-famous monorail, the putting green, the adult quiz nights, the giant fibreglass rabbit that stands sentry by the pool, the Apache Fort, the Gaiety Building and amusement arcade. Smiling staff members in their trademark red coats show smiling patrons to their individual chalets and finally, in pink neon, blinking hypnotically across the screen, the Butlin's Holiday Camp mission statement, 'Our true intent is all for your delight.'

Bunny's eyes grow wide, his mouth drops open and says with genuine feeling, 'Fuck me. Butlins.' He sits straight up and jams another Lambert & Butler in his mouth. 'Are you watching this, Bunny Boy? *Butlins!*'

'What's Butlins, Dad?'

Bunny Zippos his cigarette and points at the TV, expels a noisy trumpet of smoke and says, 'Butlins, my boy, is the best fucking place in the world!'

'What is it, Dad?'

'It's a holiday camp,' says Bunny. 'My father took me there when I was a kid,' and with the mention of his father, Bunny feels a butcher's hook twisting in his bowels. He looks at his watch and screws up his face and says to himself, 'Christ, my old dad.'

'Why is it the best place in the world?' asks the boy.

'Has anyone ever mentioned you ask a lot of fucking questions?'

'Yes.'

Bunny reaches across to the bedside table and grabs the Scotch and, waving the bottle with an extravagant flourish, says, 'Well, let me just pour a little drink and I'll tell you.'

Bunny slops whisky into his glass, then lies back against the headboard and says, with emphasis, 'But you've got to listen.'

Bunny Junior's head suddenly wobbles dramatically on his neck and he falls back on the bed, arms splayed. He closes his eyes.

'OK, Dad,' he says.

'Don't bloody ask me why Dad took me to Butlins. He no doubt had some raunchy tête-à-tête or some liaison kangaroo with some slapper or something, I don't know, he was a squire of the dames, my old man, and he loved a bit of the fluff. Not bad-looking either, in his day,' says Bunny.

'When we arrived he changed his shirt, had a shave, put pomade in his hair, you know, then sent me down the pool, for a swim. He said he'd come by and get me later on.'

The boy's breath deepens and he brings his little square knees up to his chest and appears to sleep. Bunny pours the Scotch down his throat, then attempts to place the glass back on the bedside table but he misses and the glass rolls around the shrieking paisley carpet. He retreats deep into his memory and he sees the throbbing terraced lawns and the turquoise water churning with screaming children. He sees the fifteen-foot bucktooth rabbit that stands by the swimming pool. His voice comes out tired and sad.

'So I went down to the pool, and I was doing this thing that I liked to do. I'd crouch down with just my eyes looking over the top of the water and glide around like a crocodile or a bloody alligator and watch all the kids jumping around and doing bombs and cavorting about. I used to feel like nobody could see me but, you know, I could see them.'

Bunny attempts to make some gesture with his hand to illustrate a point and for a brief moment he wonders how on earth he ever ended up this way.

'Anyway, on this particular occasion I started to get the feeling that someone was watching me and I turned around and there, sitting on the edge of the pool, was a girl . . . about my age . . . I was just a kid . . .'

Bunny sees, in his mind, the girl with her long wet hair and her nut-coloured limbs, and he finds that hot tears are running down his face, and once again he circles his hand in the air, his cigarette dead between his fingers.

'And she was smiling at me . . . watching me . . . and smiling at me and, Bunny Boy, I got to tell you, she had the most beautiful eyes I'd ever seen and she wore a tiny yellow polka-dot bikini and she was all caramel-coloured from the sun . . . with these violet eyes . . . and something came over me, I don't know what, but all the bloody emptiness I felt as a kid seemed to evaporate and I filled with something . . . a kind of power. I felt like a bloody machine.'

Bunny can see, in his mind's eye, the afternoon sun spinning in the sky and the glare of it as it touched the surface of the pool. He can see the water part as he floated slowly through it.

'So I kind of glided towards her and the closer I got the more she smiled . . . and I don't know what came over me, but I stood up and asked her what her name was . . . fucking *twelve years old* I was . . .'

The cigarette falls from Bunny's fingers and lands on the scarlet carpet.

'. . . and she said her name was Penny Charade . . . I kid you not. Penny Charade . . . I'll never forget it . . . and when I told her my name she laughed and I laughed and I knew that I had this power . . . this special thing that all the other bastards who were flopping around in the pool trying to impress the girls didn't have . . . I had this gift . . . a talent . . . and it was in that moment that I knew what I was put on this stupid fucking planet to do . . .'

Bunny Junior, incredibly, opens one raw eye and says, 'What happened then, Dad?' and closes it again.

'Well, it was getting late and her mum and dad came and got her and I stayed at the pool, happier than I'd ever been, just floating around . . . all full of this gift until I was the last person in the pool . . .'

Bunny could see, deep in his memory, the night fall over

Butlins and a spray of stars spritz across the sky, and he wiped the tears from his face with the back of his hand.

'Then it began to get dark and the stars came out and I started to get cold so I went back to our chalet.'

This time the boy keeps his eyes closed when he says, 'What happened to the girl, Dad?'

'Well, the next day my dad sent me down to the pool again and I looked for Penny Charade but she wasn't there, and I was moving through the water feeling sorry for myself when I noticed another girl who was smiling at me, then another one, and suddenly the whole pool was heaving with Penny Charades . . . on the side of the pool . . . swimming in the water, on the fucking diving board, waving and smiling and laying on their towels, playing with blow-up balls and there it was again . . . that feeling . . . that power . . . and me with *the gift* . . .'

Bunny gropes around on the bed until he finds the remote and, with a crack of static, it implodes into nothingness and he closes his eyes. A great wall of darkness moves towards him. He can see it coming, vast and imperious. It is unconsciousness and it is sleep. It moves like a great tidal wave but before it breaks over him and he is away, before he renders himself completely to that oblivious sleep, he thinks, with a sudden, terrible, bottomless dread, of Avril Lavigne's vagina.

19

'Is that your dad in my house?' says the little girl on the bicycle.

'Yeah, I guess,' says Bunny Junior, who has been trying to read about Mata Hari in his encyclopaedia, but can't concentrate on the words because he is so worried about his father. In the breakfast room at the Queensbury, his dad was jumping around like his pants were on fire. He'd eat a bit of sausage, get up and rabbit into his phone, then sit back down and spill his coffee everywhere. He'd disappear into the bathroom and not come out for ages, then follow the waitress around the breakfast room and talk to her a mile a minute about who knows what – Bunny Junior sure didn't know. The boy ate his breakfast quickly and, anxious to leave, pulled out the client list and said, 'Where to now, Dad?' but his dad told him they were going to visit a loyal customer in Rottingdean – one they could tap into at any time. She just loved that body cream! Then he was stuffing his mouth with eggs and toast and chasing the waitress around the breakfast room again, waggling his hands behind his head like a rabbit. He had put on a new shirt with brown and orange diagonal stripes and a tie with a little picture of a floppy-eared rabbit sticking his head out of a magician's hat, but he hadn't shaved and his hair was sticking up like nobody's business.

Bunny Junior was not used to worrying about his dad. He was more used to worrying about his mum. Once, when his father was away, she had come into the bedroom and sat on the bed and put her arms around him and cried her eyes out and he hadn't known what to do but wonder where the old mum had gone.

Now he is sitting in the Punto outside a large, newly built house in Rottingdean, and a girl who looked about the same age as him, maybe a little older, is asking him a question. She is straddling a bicycle and has a small brown mole on her cheek. She rings the bell three times before she speaks to him again.

'Your dad is giving my mum a fuck,' she says.

She wears a strawberry tankini with the word 'TOXIC' written in little silver studs across her chest. Bunny Junior notices, when she turns to look back at her house, that one side of her bikini bottom has ridden up the crack in her bum.

'He's my dad,' says Bunny Junior, screwing up one eye and sticking his head out the car window and looking up and down the street but not knowing what it was he was looking for.

'Yeah, I know,' says the girl. 'He's sticking his dick in her.'

The boy responds with a tilt of the chin but his feet start flip-flopping furiously.

'Yeah, well, he's the best salesman in the world,' he says.

The girl rocks back and forth on the bicycle and says, 'She makes me go out of the house. But you can hear her from miles away. She sounds like a strangled chicken. Cock-a-doodle-do!' The little girl flaps her elbows for emphasis.

'You mean a rooster,' says the boy.

'Yeah, whatever. You can hear her for miles.'

Bunny Junior points at the girl's bicycle and says, 'My dad could sell your bicycle to a barracuda.'

The girl pushes her fringe out of her eyes and says, 'A what?'

'It's a predatory fish,' he says. 'Its jaws are armed with hundreds of razor-like teeth.'

'Oh,' says the girl.

She rings the bell on her bicycle and says, 'My dad bought me this.'

'The bicycle?' says the boy.

'No, the bell.'

The little girls rocks some more and grimaces for no particular reason. Bunny Junior likes this girl. He thinks she is very pretty and he hasn't really spoken to a girl before. He paddles his feet for a while and thinks about something to say.

'My mum died,' he says without warning and he experiences a sudden thundering of his blood to his face and he pushes himself back into the seat of the Punto, mortified and ashamed.

'Yeah?' says the girl, then wheels her bicycle up to the window and Bunny Junior sees that she has crimson glitter nail polish on her fingers and a smear of blue shadow over each eye.

'I wish my mum would die,' she says. 'She's a fucking bitch-face.'

The surge of blood subsides and the roaring in his ears abates and Bunny Junior takes his sunglasses from the glove box and slips them on.

'I don't have to go to school,' he says.

The young girl smiles, realigns her bikini bottoms, pushes her fringe out of her eyes and says, 'Cool.'

'My dad says I don't have to.'

They say nothing for a minute and Bunny Junior adjusts his shades and the girl cocks her head and looks at the boy sitting in the car, and the sun beats down and she rings her bell twice. Bunny Junior reaches over to the driver's side and taps the car horn two times in response. They smile at each other and together they both look down the road somewhere. They see Bunny exit the house and march across the sun-scorched lawn, tucking his shirt into his trousers.

'Here he comes,' says Bunny Junior quietly, 'my dad.'

The boy wishes his dad would turn around and go back inside because he doesn't want to see his dad – although he looks a lot better coming out of the house than he did going in. On the way here, his dad kept turning the radio on and off and moving around in his seat and sounding the horn and swigging from his bottle and driving like a mental case, and when he arrived at the house he actually hopped across the lawn like a rabbit. Most of all, though, he wanted his dad to go back into the house because all of a sudden he could think of a million and one things he wanted to tell this girl on the bicycle – about outer space, the veldts of Africa or the microcosmic world of insects or something, and he didn't even know her name.

'Excuse me, young lady,' says Bunny as he marches up to the Punto.

Bunny is thinking that there is nothing like getting your pipes cleaned first thing in the morning to set you up for the rest of the day. He had woken gloomy and hungover and full of dirty water, and had probably hit the bottle a little heavy in recompense. He thought he may have set something up with the cute little waitress from the breakfast room at the

Queensbury Hotel, but he was not completely sure. Then he remembered Mylene Huq from Rottingdean, and a quick call to Poodle was enough to secure her address. The story goes that Mylene Huq's husband took off with someone half his age and that Mylene Huq has been involved in an epic revenge-fuck ever since. Meanwhile, the word has spread around the local studs and everyone was getting in while the going was good. This kind of opportunity is usually short-lived and always ends in tears, but there is no denying that in the throes of their particular brand of wild justice these bitches go off like fucking firecrackers.

'Excuse me, young lady,' he says again.

'Finished giving my mum a fuck?' says the young girl on the bicycle.

'Eh?' says Bunny, opening the door of the Punto.

'Finishing sticking your dick in my mum?'

Bunny leans in close to the girl and rings the bell on her bike and says, 'Actually, yes, I have, and it was very nice, thank you very much.' Then he folds himself up and drops with a contemptuous grunt into the driver's seat. He turns the key in the ignition and the Punto makes its noises and, insolently and unwilling, starts first time.

'Jesus, who's your girlfriend?' says Bunny. 'What a little ball-breaker.'

Wisps of sea mist curl around the Punto as Bunny moves onto the ocean road.

'She just came and talked to me, Dad.'

'Fancy you, did she?' said Bunny, popping a fag between his teeth and patting the pockets of his jacket for his Zippo.

Bunny Junior fingers his Darth Vader and says, 'Da-ad.' He feels a kind of rising heat.

'No, she did, I can tell. She had that special light in her eyes!'

'Da-ad!'

'I'm telling you, Bunny Boy, I can spot it a mile off!'

Bunny turns to his son and punches him on the arm. Bunny Junior is happy that his dad is happy and he is happy that his dad is not mental and he is also just happy and he says, in a loud voice, 'Maybe I should go back and give her a fuck!'

Bunny looks at his son as if for the first time and then throws out a great laugh. He knuckles the boy's skull.

'One day, Bunny Boy, one day!' he exclaims, and with the blue sea on one side, and green fields on the other, Bunny Junior waves the client list in the air and holds up the A–Z and laughs, 'Where to now, Dad?'

Soon Bunny Junior will sit back in his seat and stare out at the white, weather-bitten cliffs and the flocks of seagulls that feast on the newly turned earth in the fields that line the coastal road. He will think that even though his mother would come into his room and hold him and stroke his forehead and cry her eyes out, her hand was still the softest, sweetest, warmest thing he had ever felt, and he will look up and see a flock of starlings trace the angles of her face in the sky. He will think that if he could just feel that soft, warm hand on his forehead again then he would he didn't know what.

On the television mounted on the wall of a small café in Western Road there is a special report on the Horned Killer. A young mother has been murdered with a garden fork in her home in Maida Vale. The attack was so vicious that the authorities initially had difficulties identifying the sex of the victim. The same afternoon, the killer had done his diabolical streak for the CCTV cameras through a shopping complex in Queensway. Then, as always, he disappeared. On the TV, Bunny sees a stylised map of England that reminds him of a cartoon rabbit (without ears) and shows, with a red line, the dismal, southbound trajectory of the murderer's infernal journey. Some part of Bunny takes all this personally, but he is not sure why.

The guy serving behind the counter has shaved and oiled his head and leans towards Bunny and cocks his thumb at the TV and says, 'Can you believe this guy?' He wears a tight red T-shirt and Bunny, who sits eating a ketchup-smothered Cornish pasty and sucking a pink milkshake through a straw, notices the ringed contours of his nipple piercings through the fabric.

'He's working his way to Brighton,' says Bunny, ominously.

'What makes you say that, man?'

'I can feel it in my guts,' says Bunny. 'He is coming down.'

Bunny Junior looks around the café and sucks his milkshake and moves back and forth on his swivel-topped stool. He watches a couple nearby, hunched over bowls of spaghetti Bolognese and involved in some heated, whispered altercation. The woman throws furtive glances around the restaurant and the boy tries to decode the nature of their dispute by reading the man's lips but this proves impossible as he keeps covering his mouth with his hand. Then his attention is drawn to a lone man eating from a plate of chips. He wears a black shirt and has thick white hair and a silver zodiac symbol on a chain around his neck and he is looking directly at the boy. He dips a chip in mayonnaise, puts it in his mouth and smiles at the boy with genuine warmth.

'All the freaks wash down here,' says Bunny to the guy

behind the counter, but he has turned away and is now serving someone else, so Bunny directs his attention to his son.

'In this business, Bunny Boy, you meet all kinds of crazy people. It's the nature of the game. You get a certain understanding for them,' he says.

The man in the black shirt and the pendant counts some money into a tiny tin plate. He gives Bunny Junior a secret wave, licks the salt off the ends of his fingers, then picks up his jacket, turns his back and leaves.

'You've got to live by your wits. It's an instinct,' says Bunny. 'Always keep one eye open. You turn your back on someone for a second and the next minute they're boiling your head in a saucepan. It's something you learn over time, Bunny Boy . . .'

Through the lunchtime crowd Bunny Junior glimpses a woman in an orange dress with blonde hair standing in the queue across the café at the sandwich counter. Her head is inclined away from him, her face hidden in her hair, and sometimes he can see her and sometimes he can't.

'Be bloody prepared,' says Bunny.

'For the crazy guy,' says Bunny Junior, distractedly.

'You got it, Bunny Boy. One eye on the nutter.'

Bunny Junior stands and ducks and weaves and tries to get a glimpse of the woman who could well be his mother, but he can't see her any more and he hears his dad say, 'Once I did this job in Hastings and there was a little girl there that had tiny flippers for hands and her tongue was so long she had it pinned to the lapel of her jacket.'

Bunny Junior climbs back up on his stool and sits very still, hands folded in his lap. The blood has drained from his face and when Bunny looks at his son, he registers his haunted expression.

'Tell me about it, Bunny Boy! It gives me the creeps just thinking about it!'

Bunny takes out his wallet and the man behind the counter, with his lubricated dome and his erotic accoutrements, says to Bunny as he takes his money, 'You in town long?'

Bunny delivers a disdainful look and, with Bunny Junior close behind, leaves the café. Outside he stops, throws out his hands in outrage and says to the boy, 'Do I look like I've got a mangina? Do I look like I've got a *munt?*'

'Um,' says the boy.

'Tell me the truth. Do I look like a fucking *fag* to you?'

Bunny Junior, who realises he has forgotten to finish his pasty, looks up and down the street and forgets to answer his father as he sees what appears to be a triangle of orange fabric slip around a corner and disappear.

20

Bunny stands outside a ground-floor flat in Charles Street, Kemp Town, and wonders what he is doing. He turns and sees his son's face watching him through the window of the Punto – the boy squeezing out his jinked smile – and he wonders what he is doing. At the front door, he presses the buzzer and sees a dark shape wobble, mirage-like, on the other side of the frosted glass – icing sugar sunset with powdered palm trees – then rattle a series of locks and chains, and he wonders what he is doing. He looks at the name on the client list and it says Mrs Candice Brooks and he experiences in the base of his spine a thrill of sexual anticipation that brings clarity of purpose to his mind. But the door opens and a tiny, bent and impossibly ancient lady in dark glasses appears before him and says in a surprisingly youthful voice, 'Can I help you?'

Bunny sighs and wonders what he is doing. Then it comes to him – he is here to sell stuff. He closes his eyes and composes himself and approximates a person who has charm and who is in control. This is not as easy as it sounds because Bunny feels, in an oblique way, that a kind of lunacy has come to visit and decided to stay until all the lights go out. 'I'm looking for a Mrs Candice Brooks,' he says.

With an arthritic and bejewelled hand, the old lady adjusts her glasses and says, 'Yes, I'm Mrs Brooks. What can I do for you, young man?'

Bunny thinks — Young man? Jesus, is she blind? — then realises that actually she is. He silently cogitates whether this is, for him, an advantage or a disadvantage. He decides on the former due to his inherent optimism.

'Mrs Brooks, my name is Bunny Munro. I am a representative of Eternity Enterprises. You have contacted our central office and asked for a free demonstration of our range of beauty products.'

'I did?' says the old lady, her ringed fingers tapping and clacking around the edge of the door.

'Your name is on our list, Mrs Brooks.'

'Oh, I don't doubt it, Mr Munro. Daresay I will forget to turn up to my own funeral,' says the old lady, with a grim chuckle.

Mrs Brooks invites Bunny in and leads him through a small, sunless kitchen. Bunny thinks, as he checks out her swollen ankles and her support stockings, that chances are Mrs Candice Brooks will turn out to be a classic time-waster — a lonely old bird that just wants to talk. He remembers when he used to go out with his dad, who was in the antique business, and it was precisely this kind of good-natured biddy that his old man could really get his teeth into — that he could really *squeeze*. He was a master of it — a true charmer. But extorting them of their antique furniture was one thing, trying to sell them beauty products was another thing altogether.

'I hope the new girl who comes to clean has left the place looking nice. I never really know. They come and go, these young things. They cost the earth and none of them really wants to be looking after a dotty old bat like me.'

'Hired hindrance, Mrs Brooks,' says Bunny, and Mrs Brooks chuckles as she taps her way through the kitchen with her white, cleated stick.

'Exactly, Mr Munro,' she says, as Bunny remembers, with a sudden plasmatic surge in his leopard-skin briefs, Mylene Huq from Rottingdean, bucking and screaming and begging Bunny to come on her face.

Bunny follows Mrs Brooks into the living room and it is heavy with dead air as if time itself had ossified into something immobile and unyielding. The shelves are crammed with ancient books covered in a patina of dust and there is the terrible spectral absence of a television set. The open-lidded, upright Bösendorfer along the far wall, with its rictus of flavescent teeth, would be a nice little earner for some enterprising antique dealer in a couple of years – thinks Bunny – and he gestures pointlessly at the piano and enquires of the old blind lady, 'Do you play?'

Mrs Brooks makes monster claws of her arthritic hands and giggles like a little girl. 'Only on Hallowe'en,' she says.

'You are a very trusting lady. Do you always invite strangers into your home?' asks Bunny.

'Trusting? Nonsense! I have one foot firmly planted in the grave, Mr Munro. What would anyone want from me?' and with her antenna-like stick clicking against the furniture, the old lady makes her way to the chintz-covered armchair and lowers herself into it.

'You'd be surprised,' says Bunny, looking at his watch and suddenly remembering an alcoholic dream he had had the night before that involved finding a matchbox full of celebrity clitorises – Kate Moss's, Naomi Campbell's, Pamela Anderson's and of course Avril Lavigne's (among others) – and trying unsuccessfully to stab holes in the lid with a blunt knitting needle while the little pink peas screamed for air.

'I may be blind, Mr Munro, but my other senses have yet to desert me. You seem like a nice man.'

Mrs Brooks offers Bunny the chair opposite her and Bunny has the sudden urge to turn around and make a run for it – he feels a kind of foreboding in the room – but instead he sits and places his sample case on the little Queen Anne table in front of him. Bunny realises to his surprise that there is an oversized transistor radio on the table that has been playing classical music the whole time he has been there.

Mrs Brooks swoons dramatically, and then rocks back and forth and says, with great reverence, 'Beethoven. Next to Bach, no one does it better. Streets ahead of Mozart. Beethoven understood suffering in the most profound way. You can feel his deep belief in God and his raging love for the world.'

'It's all a bit over my head,' says Bunny. 'I'm just a working stiff.'

'Auden said it all. "We must love one another or die."'

Mrs Brooks' misshapen hands twitch on the armrests of her chair like alien spiders and her rings make an unsettling clicking sound. Outside Bunny can hear the bitching squawk of seagulls and the low drone of the seafront traffic.

'Have you read Auden, Mr Munro?'

Bunny sighs and rolls his eyes and snaps open his sample case.

'Bunny,' he says. 'Call me Bunny.'

'Have you read Auden, Bunny?'

Bunny feels a needle of irritation tweak the nerve over his left eye.

'Only on Hallowe'en, Mrs Brooks,' says Bunny, and the old lady laughs like a little girl.

The Punto is parked on the Marine Parade and Bunny Junior rests his head on the window and watches the steady stream of people walking past and wonders exactly what it is he is doing. He feels like he has learned the Patience Law and wonders when his dad is going to teach him how to actually sell something. The boy thinks there may be a chance that not only is he going blind with advanced blepharitis, but he is going insane as well, and has looked up the word 'Mirage' in his encyclopaedia and it says 'An optical illusion resulting from the refraction of light causing objects near the horizon to become distorted.' He has also found 'Apparition' and it says 'The visual experience of seeing a person (living or dead) not actually present,' but none of this makes much sense to him. He has come to believe that his mother is looking for him and that she has something important to tell him, and he thinks that if he remains where he is she will, in time, find him. He is glad he has learned the Patience Law. It has been helpful. He also thinks that there is something that he has to tell his mother but he can't think of what it is because he is too hungry. He wishes he had eaten his Cornish pasty in the café at lunchtime. He sees a group of youths mooch by, stuffing handfuls of chips into the holes in their hoods, and a hungering noise issues from the pit of his stomach.

He looks behind him and can see, across the road on the promenade, a booth with 'FISH AND CHIPS' written in large letters on its candy-striped awning. The sea breeze brings down a delirious waft of fried potatoes and vinegar and Bunny Junior closes his eyes and inhales and, once again, whatever the animal is that's trapped in his guts lets out a demonstrative moan.

The boy knows he is not allowed to get out of the car but he is becoming increasingly worried that if he doesn't eat something soon, he is going to die of hunger. He knows that he has three one-pound coins in the pocket of his trousers. He imagines, with a certain amount of pleasure, his father returning and finding him dead in the Punto. What would that say about his Patience Law? The boy sits there and counts to one hundred. He looks over one shoulder then the other. He opens the door of the Punto and climbs out, jiggling the coins in his pocket.

Down to the pedestrian crossing – he thinks – then over the road, two minutes tops. He feels a sudden surge of panic move up the nerves in his legs and explode in his stomach and he puts his hand on his chest and feels his heart pounding through his shirt. Then he puts his head down and sets off.

He arrives at the pedestrian crossing just as the red man blinks on and he waits a full three minutes for the green one. In that time, a man dressed in white tracksuit bottoms and a white polo shirt sidles up to him. He has plucked eyebrows and thinning black hair,

'No school today?' says the man, smiling and playing with the little embroidered polo player on the breast of his shirt. The man's eyes are so blue and clear, and his teeth so straight and white, that Bunny Junior has to squint when he looks at him.

'Taking a sickie?' enquires the man – but it is not a question, rather the naming of some perverse and diabolical act.

The light changes and Bunny Junior charges across the street and doesn't look back, saying the word 'fuck' under his breath over and over again because now he doesn't feel hungry in his stomach any more, now he wants to shit his pants. He feels to his core the terrible knowledge that he should never have left the refuge of the Punto.

At the fish and chip booth there is a small queue and he joins it and stands there, hopping from foot to foot. He turns his head tentatively in the way you do if you think there may be a monster or ogre or something behind you, and sees the guy in the tracksuit on the other side of the road fiddling with the polo player on his shirt. He seems to have forgotten about Bunny Junior until he raises his head and smiles and lifts up his index finger and moves it back and forth.

Bunny Junior turns away and watches the man in the fish and chip booth with the wire mesh basket and Popeye arms until it is his turn to order. He notices that the man's arms are covered in thick, black fur.

'Chips, please,' says the boy.

The man behind the counter fills a small waxed-paper cone with chips and says, 'One pound.'

The boy says, 'Salt, please.'

The man sprinkles salt on the chips from a large, stainless steel saltshaker.

The boy says, 'Vinegar, please.'

The man puffs on his cigarette and pours vinegar from a bottle onto the chips. He hands the paper cone to the boy and the boy gives him the money and turns around and sees his mother walking away from him down the promenade. She wears an orange dress and her blonde hair is tied back in a ponytail.

'Maybe I should report you to the authorities,' says the

man in the white tracksuit bottoms, who is suddenly standing next to the boy, talking out the side of his mouth and twisting the little polo player on his shirt. Bunny Junior swings away from the man because he thinks the man wants to eat him. He sees his mother get swallowed up by the crowd and, with a roaring in his ears, takes off after her, wishing his mother would stop disappearing all the time.

The boy notices that the people look like the undead or aliens or something as he weaves his way through the crowd. Everybody seems a foot taller and their arms have grown longer and their faces are mask-like and their jaws are slack. He looks this way and that and cannot see his mother and under his breath says that word again. He stops, looks up and down the promenade and stuffs a handful of chips in his mouth. He looks over the wrought-iron railing, down to the lower promenade, and sees, with a burst of love, his mother talking to a group of people who are sitting in an outdoor café. She is smoking a cigarette and Bunny Junior wonders when she started doing that. He thinks the first thing he'll do when he is reunited with his mother is tell her to just put that cigarette out. He stuffs another handful of chips into his mouth and descends the stairs, two at a time, the paper cone held above his head like he was the Statue of Liberty or an Olympic torch-bearer.

It is hotter down on the lower promenade and hellishly bright. The boy wishes he had brought his shades because his eyes are itching like nobody's business and everyone has got hardly any clothes on. The boy recoils at the mass of hairy arms and dead flaky skin and congealed make-up and stinky rings of sweat and cadaverous age spots and rolls of white fat as he winds his way through the crowd towards his pretty mother.

He walks up to the café, gasping for air and wondering what to do with his chips. Sensing the boy's presence, his mother turns around.

'Hello,' she says, in a warm, familiar voice.

Bunny Junior can see that her features have been slightly modified.

'Are you all right, sweetheart?' she says and puffs on her cigarette.

There is something in the way she says this that makes the boy step forward and wrap his arms around his mother's waist and rest his head against her stomach. He feels, at this moment, a vast sense of sad love for his mother, and at the same time wonders why she is not nearly as soft as he remembered her to be. Her stomach seems full of rocks and when he touches her breasts they feel small and hard.

'Excuse me?'

The boy can hear something extrinsic in her voice – an unrecognisable and alien quiver of agitation maybe, or embar-rassment, he isn't sure, and it makes him want to let go of her, but he doesn't know how to, so he clings on harder. The woman – whoever she is – squirms and pulls at him and little stabs of pain shoot up his arms as she manages to prise herself free.

'Stop that,' she says. 'Where is your mother?'

The boy looks up at her and sees that she has a nose like a little brown hook and that her hair is not really blonde at all, but mouse-coloured, and her dress, which is actually pink, smells of cigarettes and old coconuts.

The woman reaches out to touch the boy on the head but

he rears back and she accidentally knocks the cone of chips flying. The chips scatter across the floor of the restaurant.

'Oh, dear, I am sorry,' she says.

But the boy is spinning now, spinning and turning and running for his *fucking* life.

21

'This Replenishing Hand Cream has almost magical restorative powers. The effects are instantaneous,' says Bunny. 'Allow me to show you.'

'On these fossilised old things, I doubt it,' says Mrs Brooks. She removes her rings and holds out her monstrous claws. Bunny squeezes some cream into his hands and reaches across the table and takes hold of the old lady's fingers and gently massages the cream into her knotted knuckles. Her arthritic hands actually creak under Bunny's touch. Mrs Brooks rocks back and forth, marking the space around her with her metronomic sway.

'It's been many years since someone has done this to me, Mr Munro. You have certainly charged an old girl's batteries!'

Bunny says, in mock surprise, 'My God, Mrs Brooks! Your hands look like a young girl's!'

Mrs Brooks laughs a tinkling, happy laugh.

'Oh, you silly man,' she says.

Bunny Junior charges up the steps and along the promenade, doing his best not to touch the killer zombies, past the fish and chip man with his fuzzy blow-up arms and over the zebra crossing where the child-eaters operate, and when Bunny Junior sees the yellow, shit-splattered Punto he feels a palpable sense of relief, like he is back where he belongs. He pulls open the door and flops into the passenger seat, his feet doing their lunatic dance, his heart as heavy as an anvil or an anchor or a death. He presses down the lock on the door and rests his head on the window and screws up his eyes and remembers how his mum used to get pretty nutty some days – like the time he found her sniffing his dad's shirts and throwing them around the bedroom or sitting on the kitchen floor crying with crazy lipstick smeared all over her face. But even though she had what his dad told him was a 'medical condition', she always smelled nice and she always felt soft.

There is a sudden rapping on the window as loud as gunshots. The boy's blood turns to ice. His blood turns to ice and he covers his eyes with his hands and says, 'Please don't eat me.'

He hears the sound again and looks up to see a female police officer tapping on the glass.

The police officer is young, with cropped hair and a pretty face, and as she mimics winding down the window, she smiles at Bunny Junior and the boy notices, to his relief, attractive indentations appear at the corners of her mouth. He winds down the window. He sees she has an almost invisible frosting of soft blonde hair on her top lip, and when she leans in the window he hears the new leather of her utility belt creak. Bunny Junior smells something shockingly sweet as she says, 'Are you all right, young man?'

The boy presses his lips together in the imitation of a smile and nods his head.

'Shouldn't you be in school?' she says, and Bunny Junior guesses the ogre in the white tracksuit has turned him in and he has no idea how to answer this question. He fiddles with his Darth Vader and shakes his head.

'Why not?' says the police officer, and Bunny Junior hears a little blurt of static come from her radio transmitter that sounds so much like a fart that he giggles for a second.

'My dad says I don't have to go to school today,' he says, and suddenly he is sick to death of adults – police officers with truncheons and creeps in white tracksuits, zodiac-symbol-wearing wackos and women who crow like roosters, fat men in dresses and mothers who go and kill themselves, and he wonders, with fury, where his fucking father is. Almost immediately Bunny Junior feels bad for thinking that and erases it from his mind.

'Why is that?' says the police officer.

'I'm sick,' says Bunny Junior and sinks back in his seat and, with a dramatic flourish, approximates what he considers to be a reasonable imitation of a boy dying a million deaths.

'I see. Well, shouldn't you be in bed then?'

Bunny Junior shrugs and says, 'I guess.'

The police officer points into the car and says, 'Who's that?'

The boy waggles his Darth Vader and says, 'Darth Vader.'

The police officer stands up straight and claps her hand to her chest and says, in a mock-serious voice, 'May the Force be with you.'

Bunny Junior notices the little indentations appear in the corners of her mouth. Then they disappear and she puts her head back in the window and says, 'Where's your dad, then?'

* * *

The silver bracelet that Bunny wears on his left wrist clinks, then echoes quietly around the room. Mrs Brook's hands twitch in her lap and they do indeed look younger. She wears a blissed-out smile on her tiny, wrinkled face, and as Bunny licks the stub of his pencil and finishes filling in the order form, he feels, in a remote way, vindicated. He thinks he has outdone himself. He has sold this elderly lady a vast amount of beauty products that she will never use, but in doing so, he has made the old trout happy. But Bunny also feels a jittery discomfort in his body, a caffeinated restlessness to the order of his blood. He has felt this way all afternoon, and has assumed it was a basic quotidian hangover (he had overdone it a bit this morning), but through the window he can see a dark menace of starlings falling and ascending above the gusting sea and he understands, suddenly, that the discomfort he is feeling is actually a rising terror of sorts – but a terror of what?

'You will receive the products within ten working days, Mrs Brooks,' says Bunny.

'It's been an absolute pleasure, Mr Munro.'

It hits Bunny then and he realises he has known it was coming all along. He feels it moving up through his bones and he feels his heart adjust itself in preparation. He notices that the radio has inexplicably stopped transmitting and the room has darkened a fraction and the temperature has dropped. He experiences a lack of feeling in his fingertips and a lifting of the hair on the back of his neck. There is a brief crackling of the electrics in the overhead light. He knows more than he knows anything that if he raises his head and looks over at the living room wall, he will see his dead wife, Libby, sitting on the brocaded piano stool by the Bösendorfer. She will be wearing the nightdress that she wore on her wedding night

183

and the night she hanged herself. He can see a smudge of orange in the far corner of his vision and an accusatory upward motion of an arm or something. He hears the starlings begin to twitter manically and peck and scratch at the window. The air begins to throb and warp, and when he hears great, heavy, doom-laden chords being hammered out on the piano, he throws his hands over his ears and makes an unsuccessful attempt to scream.

Mrs Brooks begins raking the air with her claws.

'Beethoven!' she shouts, deliriously, a curlicue of fog at her lips.

'She had a medical condition,' pleads Bunny.

'What?' says Mrs Brooks.

'Eh?' he says, keeping his head lowered.

Bunny feels an unsolicited and volcanic rage rip through his insides – a rage towards everything – this wife of his, who even beyond the grave hunts him down in order to wag a defama-tory finger; this arthritic old bitch with her lacks and loopy needs; his spaced-out kid waiting in the car; his father dying of cancer; all the rapacious, blood-sucking women; the fucking bees and the starlings – *What does everybody want from me?!* He curses his own insatiable appetites, but even as he does so he tries, with a Herculean act of will, to divert his thoughts onto the shiny genitalia of a starlet or celebrity or *anything*, but can't think of one because the starlings are dive-bombing against the window and the piano chords are so loud now he thinks his head is going to split in half. Mrs Brooks grabs his hand with her mangled claw and says, 'We must love one another or die!'

'Eh?' says Bunny, keeping his eyes averted, keeping them down, keeping them closed.

He hears Mrs Brooks say, 'It is just that you seem so sad.'

184

'Eh? What? Sad?' says Bunny and wrenches his arm away and slams shut his sample case. The old lady looks about blindly, her outstretched hand uselessly scraping the air.

'Forgive me,' she says, full of self-reproach. 'I'm terribly sorry to have upset you.' Her hands pound at the aggrieved space in front of her. 'I'll see you out,' she says.

Bunny stands, head still inclined, his hands over his ears.

'Don't bother, Mrs Brooks,' he snarls and reaches down and deftly and noiselessly scoops up the old lady's wedding rings from the table and slips them into the pocket of his jacket. 'I'll make my own way,' he says.

Bunny turns defiantly towards the Bösendorfer just in time to see the empty brocaded piano stool and the air wobble with his ghost-wife's departure. He turns away, pats his pocket, flicks his pomaded forelock from his eyes and thinks – Fuck you all.

22

Outside Bunny stands on the footpath and allows the pale remnants of the afternoon sun and the gentle sea breeze to pass across his face and take with it the cloying atmospherics of the old lady's dust-covered home – a place where ghosts appear. His shirt is soaked in sweat and he shivers as he looks around and notices that the starlings have gone. He still thinks he can hear the pounding, funereal piano chords coming from Mrs Brooks' flat, but he can't be sure.

He walks down to Marine Parade and as he turns the corner he becomes aware of several things at the same time. First, a female police officer is standing by the Punto talking into a radio transmitter or walkie-talkie or something. Second, she is wearing a blue gaberdine uniform that makes her tits hum with a custodial authority that hits Bunny right in the dick, and finally that she is definitely not a dyke because her arse is high-up and unbelievably fit. It is only as he strides towards her, the piano booming in his head, that he wonders what the fuck she is doing there.

'Can I help you, officer?' says Bunny.

The police officer stops talking into her radio transmitter and there is a squelch of static. Bunny clocks the weighty, hardcore accoutrements – handcuffs, truncheon, mace –

hanging from her belt, and also her torpedo-like breasts and, despite his grim disposition, he experiences a kind of alchemical transmutation in his leopard-skin briefs where a mild-mannered mouse morphs into a super-powered hard-on from Krypton and he wonders, obscurely, if society would not be better served if they kept this particular officer away from the general public – like a desk job in a place where it was freezing cold all the time or something.

'Is that your son?' says the police officer.

'Yes, it is,' says Bunny, draping a practised hand over the front of his steepled trousers and clocking the number on her epaulette – PV388.

'He tells me . . .'

'You *spoke* to him?' interrupts Bunny and looks in the window of the Punto and sees Bunny Junior slumped in the passenger seat looking decidedly out of sorts, his head lolled back, the tip of his tongue hanging out the side of his mouth.

'He tells me he is feeling ill,' says the police officer.

'And?' says Bunny. But he's had enough of this.

The police officer says, all business, 'What is your name, sir?'

'My name is Bunny Munro,' he says, leaning in and snuffling like a rabbit. 'Is that Chanel?'

'Excuse me?' says the police officer.

Bunny leans in closer and sniffs again.

'Your scent,' he says. 'Very nice.'

'I will ask you to stand back, sir,' says the police officer and her hands drop to her belt and hover around the can of mace snug in its little holster.

'That must have knocked you back a few bob.'

The police officer repositions herself, planting her feet firmly on the ground. Bunny senses that she is new on the job and notices an activated, keyed-up gleam in her eye and a fleck of foam on her lower lip, as if this was the moment she had been waiting for all her professional life, and indeed, beyond.

'Take a step back,' she says.

'I mean, how do you afford that on a policeman's wage?' says Bunny, thinking he may have got that thing about her not being a dyke wrong, and thinking he would probably be best served if he kept his mouth shut.

'Would you like to continue this conversation down the station, sir?' says the police officer, her hands dancing around her belt as if she can't decide whether to mace him or club him.

Bunny steps forward, blood flushing at his throat.

'The thing is, officer, that boy you just questioned in the car is frightened. He is scared out of his fucking wits. His mother just died in the most terrifying of circumstances. I can't begin to describe the effect that this has had on him. It's a fucking tragedy, if you must know. Right now, my son needs his father. So, if you don't mind . . .'

Bunny notices the muscles relax in the police officer's thighs as she softens her stance. He notices a slight incline of the chin and a twinge of humanity around the edges of her eyes. Bunny thinks – No, he was right the first time, she is definitely not a dyke, and under another set of circumstances things might have panned out differently. He actually feels a throb of sadness as the police officer steps aside and permits Bunny to pass, open the door of the Punto, get in and drive away.

As he negotiates the late-afternoon traffic, Bunny pats Mrs Brooks' wedding rings in his pocket, registers the after-scent of the police officer's perfume and is almost blown out of the driver's seat by a blizzard of imagined pussy, glittering and

sleek and expensive and coming at him from every direction
– Jordan's, Kate Moss's, Naomi Cambell's, Kylie Minogue's,
Beyoncé's and, of course, Avril Lavigne's – but spinning up
through all of that, in an annulus of tiny handcuffs and resting
on a cartoon cloud of Chanel, comes the humble vagina of
the police constable, number PV388.

Back on top – thinks Bunny, obscurely, as he turns into a
Pizza Hut and hits the men's room with a vengeance.

Bunny folds a slice of pizza in half and stuffs it into his mouth.
Bunny Junior, shades on, does the same. There are so many
jalapeños on the pizza that tears run down the side of Bunny
Junior's face and his nose streams.

'She wanted to know why I wasn't in school. I think it's,
like, *illegal*, or something,' says the boy with a barb of irony
his father does not detect.

'And?' he says.

'I told her I was sick, Dad.'

'And?' says Bunny.

'And she wanted to know where my mother was!' shouts
the boy and drops his piece of pizza, gulps down his Coke and
rubs at his forehead. 'And she wanted to know where my *father*
was!' Tears well in the boy's eyes.

'Bitch,' says Bunny and stuffs another piece of pizza in his
mouth.

'Why *aren't* I in school, Dad?!' shouts Bunny Junior and
wipes a great streak of snot from his nose with the back of
his hand. Bunny looks at his son, flat-eyed, and rotates the
bracelet on his wrist. He sucks his Coke and says nothing for
a while.

'Take those glasses off,' says Bunny.

The boy does so, and in the hard-boiled light his swollen eyes itch and dazzle. Bunny pushes the pizza tray to one side and speaks in a voice so quiet the boy has to crane forward to hear him.

'I'll ask you straight up, Bunny Boy. What would you rather do? Be with your dad or hang out with a bunch of snotty-nosed little fuckers at school? You want to amount to something? You want to learn the business or walk through life with your arse hanging out of your trousers?'

'Can I put these glasses back on? It hurts in here. I think I might be going blind,' says the boy, squinting up at his father. 'I think I need some eye drops or something.'

'Answer the question,' says Bunny, 'because if you want to go back to school, just say the fucking word.'

'I want to be with you, Dad.'

'Of course you do! Because I'm your dad! And I'm showing you the ropes! I'm teaching you the trade. Something some mummified old bitch with a bloody blackboard and a piece of chalk wouldn't have the faintest idea about.'

The boy's eyes stream in the people-hating glare and he dabs at them with a napkin and slides his shades back on and says, 'I think I might need a white stick and a dog soon, Dad.'

Bunny doesn't hear this, as his attention has been drawn to an adjacent table where a mother sits eating pizza with what must be her daughter. The young girl is wearing gold hipster hotpants and a lemon yellow T-shirt that says 'YUMMY' and shows her belly. She wears fluorescent pink nail polish on her fingers and toes. Bunny is thinking that in a few years' time the girl would be seriously hot, and the thought of this has Bunny considering revisiting the bathroom, but then the girl's mother says to Bunny, 'I don't like the way you are looking at my daughter,' and Bunny says, aghast, 'What do you think I am?!' and then says, 'Jesus! How old is she?' and the woman says, 'Three.' Bunny says, 'That's not to say that in a few years . . . well, you know . . .' and the woman picks up a piece of cutlery and says, 'If you say one more word, I'll stick this fork in your face,' and Bunny replies, 'Wo! You suddenly got very sexy,' and the woman scoops up her daughter and moves away, saying, 'Arsehole,' and Bunny waggles his rabbit ears at her and says to Bunny Junior, 'I learned the trade with my old man, out on the *streets,* you know, the front line. We'd drive around in his van, find some rundown old place, a real drum – flaky paint, overgrown garden – owned by some rich biddy with fifty fucking cats, and in he'd go, and before I had time to eat my sandwich, out he'd come with a nice little Queen Anne dressing table. He had a gift, my old man, the *talent,* and he taught me the art – how to be a people person. That's what we are doing, Bunny Boy. You may not be able to see it right now, but I am handing down the talent to you. Do you understand?'

Bunny Junior says, 'Yes, Dad.'

His father stands and says, 'OK, then.'

'I might have to learn Braille,' says the boy.

'Bitch,' Bunny says under his breath.

There is a crack of thunder, a flash of lightning and it begins to rain.

23

In the corner of the room, on a small black television, a bull elephant fornicates epically with its mate. Bunny, who lies on the bed fully clothed and wholly drunk, can't quite believe what he sees. A storm wails against the windows – thunder, lightning, cats, dogs – and in the bed next to Bunny the boy lies curled in a deep, embryonic sleep. Neither the trumpeting mastodon nor the hammering rain can wake him.

In one practised motion Bunny decants a miniature bottle of Smirnoff down his throat, shudders and gags, then repeats the action with a little green bottle of Gordon's gin.

He closes his eyes and the black wave of oblivion gathers strength and moves towards him. But Bunny finds his thoughts straying towards the three young mothers he visited yesterday morning – was it only yesterday? – Amanda, Zoë and especially Georgia. Georgia with the big bones and the violet eyes. Georgia with the gone, gone husband.

Somewhere in the back stalls of his consciousness Bunny hears the triumphant bull elephant blow a super-sized bucket of custard into his happy consort. The windows buckle as the storm pounds and down in the bassbins he hears the infra-sonic reverberations of thunder. Bunny imagines, dreams even, Georgia naked and angled across his knee, her great, white globoids trembling beneath his touch, and it feels as if these apocalyptic rumblings of weather and his goatish visions were in some weird way connected and prophetic because, deep down, Bunny knows, more than he knows anything in the world, his mobile phone is about to ring and that Georgia will be on the line.

Bunny opens his eyes and gropes about for his mobile phone just as it begins to vibrate, juddering about on the bed to the super-sexy ringtone of Kylie Minogue's 'Spinning Around', and he visualises Kylie's gold lamé hotpants and his dick magically reanimates, hard and erect, as he flips open the phone and says, 'What's the story, morning glory?'

He puts a Lambert & Butler between his lips and torches it with his Zippo and smiles to himself because he knows – he knows the story.

'Is that Bunny Munro?' comes a voice, soft and timid and from another world.

The room swims as Bunny throws his legs over the edge of the bed and sits up and says, 'And who might that be?' – but he *knows*.

'It's Georgia,' says Georgia. 'You were at my house yesterday.'

Bunny draws on his cigarette and blows a syzygy of smoke rings – one, two, three – then reams the last one with his index finger and says, out of a dream, 'Georgia with the violet eyes.'

'Is it . . . did I . . . have I called too late?'

Bunny slips his socked feet into his loafers and says, with genuine emotion, 'You won't believe what I'm watching on the Discovery Channel.'

'It's too late . . . I can call back,' says Georgia, and Bunny thinks he can hear the low breathing of a sleeping child and a terrible, protracted loneliness coming down the line.

'Have you any idea just how big an elephant's dick is?!' says Bunny.

'Um . . . maybe I should . . .'

'It's . . . aah . . . it's fucking *elephantine!*'

Bunny leaps to his feet and the room turbinates and unravels and Bunny claws at the air futilely and shouts, 'Timber!' and lands like a felled tree between the two beds.

'I've made a mistake,' says Georgia, and Bunny raises himself on his hands and knees.

'Georgia . . . Georgia, the only mistake you made was not to ring me sooner. I've been lying here, going off the hinges thinking about you.'

'You have?' she says.

Bunny stands, the phone clamped to his ear and looks down at his sleeping son. He experiences a wave of sentiment so strong that he can barely find the presence of mind to pick his car keys up off the bedside table.

'Didn't you feel it yesterday?' said Bunny, his voice low. 'The chemistry . . . sparks were going zip, zip and zap, zap!'

'They were?' says Georgia.

Bunny conducts a villainous panto-creep from the hotel room, leaving the TV running and closing the door behind him. The hallway is the colour and texture of whale blubber and Bunny moves down it with footsteps both comic and monstrous, the cloacal stream of mustard-coloured carpet roiling beneath his feet.

'You know they were! E-leck-tricity, baby! Zap, zap! Zip, zip!' he says into the phone.

'Well, you seemed like a nice kind of guy,' she said.

'Thunderbolts and lightning! Very, very frightening!'

'Um, Bunny?' says Georgia.

'Mamma mia! Mamma mia! Mamma mia, let me go!'

'Are you all right, Bunny?'

Bunny negotiates the stairs, one at a time, at a perilous backward angle, hanging sloth-like from the banister, whereupon he flings out an arm and sings in an insane operatic voice, 'Beelzebub had a devil put aside for me! For me! For me!'

He makes his way through the unpeopled lobby of the Empress Hotel and all the while Bunny thinks – This is strange. Where is everybody? He passes the vacated reception desk and his voice grows serious.

'I'm going to tell you something, Georgia, because I don't think there should be any bullshit between us. You know, lies and stuff . . .'

Georgia's response seems otherworldly, distant, dreamed. 'Um . . . OK,' she says.

'Because I've had it up to here with that shit, all right?' says Bunny.

'OK,' says Georgia. 'What is it?'

'I'm drunk.'

Bunny jams another Lambert & Butler in his mouth, torches it, then steps out the front door of the hotel onto the seafront and is hit by a gale force of such brutality he is pummelled to his knees. His jacket flaps over his head and he shouts into his phone, 'Fuck me, Georgia! Hang on a minute!'

Bunny sees, in slow motion, a vast wave of seawater explode against the promenade wall, then be picked up by the wind and carried, surrealistically and in sheet-form, across the road and dumped on top of him. Bunny scopes the Punto, then crawls towards it, the salted rain tearing at his face. He notices that the coastal road is deserted and that most of the streetlights are down. He hears, above the clamour of the storm, a grinding and twisting of metal, and a crack of lightning reveals the skeleton of the West Pier. The wind hammers at the Punto and Bunny, with considerable effort, prises open the door and, in time, clambers in. He sits, drenched, and watches an over-cranked POV shot of green seawater pool at his feet and he says, stunned and not of this earth, 'Georgia?'

'What's going on, Bunny? Are you OK?'

Georgia's voice sounds unlike anything he has ever heard before, and he wonders whether he hears anything at all.

'Just a second,' says Bunny.

He looks at himself in the rear-view mirror and sees a man who could well be himself but somehow is not. He is not as he remembers himself to be. His features seem unrelated to each other and a general subsidence has occurred. His eyes have sunk into their orbits and there is a debauched slackness to his cheeks and when he attempts to smile he reminds himself of Mrs Brooks' leering, yellow-toothed Bösendorfer. His face is scoured raw by the salted rain and his helixed forelock hangs across his face like a used condom – but it's not that – he just looks like a different person and he wonders where he went.

'Georgia, listen to me. This one's coming at you, baby, straight from the heart. OK?'

'OK.'

'How would you feel about a lonely, lovesick, slightly drunk, middle-aged man coming to visit you in the middle of the night?'

'What, now?' but the voice seems electronic, like a recorded message.

'I'm taking that as an affirmative,' says Bunny.

'Bunny, where are you?'

He turns the key in the ignition and, with an uncharacteristic confidence that makes Bunny think – What's up with the Punto? – the car roars into life.

'Where am I?' Bunny says, 'Oh, Georgia, I'm all over the fucking place!'

Bunny forceps the phone and tosses it on the seat next to him. He notices that the two pools of water at his feet have drawn together to become one larger pool and he feels a palpable but unidentifiable sense of emotion at that. He closes his eyes and he hears a great, black wave crash against the seawall and spew its jet of foam over the Punto and the car judders at the impact and he hopes he has not fallen asleep. He opens the glove compartment, takes out the sales list, finds Georgia's address and moves out onto the depopulated street. Bunny notices that a power-line has blown down and he can see it writhing like a black snake, fizzing and showering sparks and moving towards him down the rain-drenched street. He feels as though the black snake is seeking him out, and that if it reaches him he will die. He also thinks he could be seeing things and that this is all a mirage or an illusion or a monstrous vision or something, and he says through his teeth, 'Thunderbolts and lightning, very, very frightening.' Then he jams his foot on the accelerator and moves – in slow motion – down the street.

As Bunny navigates the streets, and Georgia's voice recedes, he thinks, with a cybernetic certainty – I am the great seducer. I work the night. Sheets of darkness that his headlights can barely penetrate wall him in but Bunny feels like he could lie back and close his eyes and the trusty Punto would know exactly where to go. Once he has left the coastal road, the wind abates and the night stops throwing down any more rain and Georgia's large white backside fits snugly into the pornographic think-bubble that hangs over his head. A spectral silence envelops the car and Bunny hears nothing but his own steady, inevitable breaths.

Out of the night the great hulk of the Wellborne estate looms up, like a leviathan, black and biblical, and Bunny parks the Punto by the now empty wooden bench – gone is the fat man in the floral dress, gone are the hooded youths. Bunny steps out, his suit drenched, his hair plastered to his head, but he does not care – he is the great seducer. He works the night.

He enters the dark maw of the stairwell and his eyes burn from the acid stench of urine and bleach and he does not care. He feels his genitals leap in his fist as he squeezes them through his sodden trousers and mounts the stairs three at a time even though he cannot really recall speaking to Georgia at all. He shivers in his freezing, waterlogged suit and works the night. He does not care.

Bunny winds his way down the gangway but must retrace his steps because he has missed Flat 95 due to there not being any lights on. He presses his face up to the window and thinks he can see the lambent flicker of a candle or nightlight or something in a back room and he smiles because he knows – he feels it humming all along his spine – more than he knows anything in his entire life, that Georgia is waiting in that dimly lit back room, naked and on all fours, knees spread wide apart, breasts swinging, backside raised to the heavens and her fucking pussy hovering in the air like the most wonderful thing imaginable in this rotten, stinking, infested *fucking* world, and all he has to do is reposition his erection in his trousers (which he does), then push on the door (that has been left on the latch) and it will swing open (which he does and which it doesn't), so he taps on the door and whispers 'Georgia', through the keyhole. This has no immediate effect, so he bangs on the door with his fist and then gets down on his hands and knees and calls her name in the loudest whisper he can muster through the cat-flap. Then he calls her name again.

Suddenly, very suddenly, all the lights go on. The door opens and a man appears in his underwear with a large, empty, Teflon-coated saucepan in his hand. Bunny has a very good view of an extremely crude representation of a depraved-looking Woody Woodpecker, leering and smoking a cigar, tattooed on the inside of the man's ankle. Bunny sees, also, that the man has an infected toenail.

'Who are *you?*' says Bunny, looking up from the floor.

He sees Georgia in an ugly bombazine dressing gown standing behind the man with the saucepan, and Bunny shouts, pointing at the man, 'Who is *he?*'

Georgia, her hand resting protectively on the man's broad and illustrated shoulder, peers down with a look of genuine confusion on her face and says, 'Mr Munro, is that you?'

Bunny shouts, 'I thought he was fucking gone, gone!'

The man with the tattoo on his ankle – where did he get that? Prison? Primary school? – hands the saucepan to Georgia and leans down and says in an end-of-things whisper, 'Who the fuck are you?'

Bunny, who is attempting unsuccessfully to stand and who is not in any way concentrating on details, thinks the man simply said, 'Fuck you,' and instantly regrets replying, in kind, 'Well, fuck you too.'

The man actually yawns, scratches his stomach, then backs up four paces, runs down the hall and boots Bunny so hard in the ribs that he spins in mid-air and lands, with an expulsion of air, on his back. Bunny places an arm over his head to shield himself from the next blow.

'Please, don't,' he says quietly.

But the blow does not come and he takes his arm away in time to see the door kick shut by a purulent yellow toe.

Back in the Punto, Bunny opens his trousers and undertakes a wank of truly epic proportions – it just goes on and on – and when at last he goes over the edge, Bunny lets his head fall back and opens his mouth as wide as he can and exhales the last remnants of reason, in an elephantine bellow, that echoes through the weather-beaten night, across the Wellborne estate. He realises, in a shadowy way, for a brief moment, that the weird imaginings and visitations and apparitions that he has encountered were the ghosts of his own grief and that he was being driven insane by them. He knows more than he knows anything that very soon they will kill him. But more than any of that, he wonders what was wrong with that bitch Georgia anyway. Jesus.

24

When Bunny enters the lobby of the Empress Hotel he is pleased to see things have returned to normal – the world seems to have reassembled itself. For some reason the Empress Hotel reminds Bunny of a sad and unsuccessful comb-over but he is too fucked-up to work out why. It is six o'clock and the early risers move through the lobby like the living dead. These scrubbed and scoured lobby-lurkers exude from the pores of their skin an eye-watering miasma of raw alcohol but Bunny doesn't recognise this as his own private funk is such that people naturally keep their distance. His sour and sodden clothes, the metallic stench of abject terror and the bouquet of his own substantial hangover, form a force field around him. He also looks like a maniac. He feels a real sense of achievement that he has managed to cross the lobby in the manner of a biped and not on all-fours. He wonders whether this may work to his advantage as he leans across the reception desk and says, 'I need the key to room seventeen. I've locked myself out.'

The man sitting behind the counter has a smudge of dead hair plastered across his skull and a nose that reminds Bunny, with a redux of dread, of a cat-flap. On a TV mounted on the wall above his head the news plays out. He is reading the local newspaper through a 'Mystic Eye' magnifying card and he looks up at Bunny and lays the newspaper and the 'Eye' on the counter.

'The crap they print in these things. It's enough to make you want to slit your wrists. Day after fucking day . . .' he says.

He performs a dentured smile and, without concern, enquires, 'What happened to you?'

'The key to room seventeen, please,' says Bunny.

The receptionist picks up his 'Mystic Eye' and peers at Bunny.

'Fucking hurricanes, avian flu, global warming, suicide bombers, war, torture, mass murderers . . .'

For a moment Bunny thinks that the receptionist is giving a terminal prognosis based on Bunny's appearance, but realises that the receptionist is tapping at the newspaper with his finger.

'Plagues, famine, floods, fucking frogs . . .'

'The key . . .'

'Little children murdering other little children, bodies piling up in mounds . . .'

'The key . . .'

The receptionist swings his arm around in a dramatic arc and jabs his finger at the TV.

'Look at that fucking guy,' he says.

But Bunny does not need to look, because he knows. He recognises the familiar shrieking, stampeding crowd, and even though he knows what the receptionist is about to say, it doesn't stop a chill wind clawing its way up his spine and circling around his tortured skull.

'He's here!' says the receptionist, and then points his finger at Bunny and says, 'It's biblical! It's Reve-fucking-lations! If we could all just be a bit nicer to one another!'

Bunny lifts his head back and notices an antique chandelier hanging greasy and fly-spotted from the ceiling. The crystal teardrops make patterns of ghastly light across the walls. Bunny leans across the counter and looks at the receptionist.

'Listen, you loopy old cunt. My wife just hung herself from the security grille in my own bloody bedroom. My son is upstairs and I haven't the faintest fucking idea what to do with him. My old man is about to kick the bucket. I live in a house I'm too spooked to go back to. I'm seeing fucking ghosts everywhere I look. Some mad fucking carpet-muncher broke my nose yesterday and I have a hangover you would not fucking believe. Now, are you gonna give me the key to room seventeen or do I have to climb over this counter and knock your fucking dentures down your throat?'

The receptionist reaches up and turns down the television, then directs his attention to Bunny.

'The thing is, sir, it is against hotel policy to give out two keys.'

Bunny gently lays his head on the counter and closes his eyes and points of refracted fairy light orbit around his skull.

'Please don't,' says Bunny, quietly.

He stays like that for a time until he feels the key to Room 17 slipped into his hand.

'Thank you,' he says, and picks up the newspaper. 'May I have this?'

Bunny moves across the lobby and cleaves apart a team of tracksuited table-tennis players who look to Bunny like they come from Mongolia or somewhere.

'Ulaanbaadar!' shouts Bunny, despite himself.

The guy who is possibly the coach breaks into a smile and the whole team cheer and give Bunny the thumbs-up sign and pat him on the back and say, 'Ulaanbaadar!' and Bunny sadly mounts the hotel stairs.

Bunny walks down the hall and looks at his watch and sees the time is 6.30. He puts the key in the lock and, as he does so, he becomes aware of a strange sound coming from Room 17. It is non-human, conversational and very scary. He thinks, as he opens the door, that it is also oddly familiar.

Bunny enters the room and sees two things at approximately the same time. First, the eccentric and unsettling sound that has frightened him is coming from the Teletubbies, who are on the TV. Po is engaged in a freakish, mutant conversation with Dipsy. Then Bunny notices that Bunny Junior is standing motionless in the centre of the room, between the two beds. He is staring at the television set and his face has drained of blood and his eyes are wide in his head and he is standing in a pool of his own water, the front of his pyjamas soaked in urine. The boy turns to his father and makes a fluttering gesture with his left hand and says, in a faraway voice, 'I couldn't find the remote.'

'Shit,' says Bunny, beneath his breath.

He walks past his son and sits on the edge of his bed. The bed is hard and unforgiving and covered in tiny, empty bottles. On the floor lies the butt of a dead cigarette.

Bunny moves his hand across his face and says, 'You better change.'

The boy passes his father, holding the tops of his pyjamas with one hand and covering his mouth with the other, and says, 'I'm sorry, Dad.'

Bunny says, 'It's OK,' and the boy disappears into the bathroom.

Bunny tosses the newspaper onto the puddle of urine. He looks at the television and sees Po and Dipsy holding hands in a violently green field full of oversized rabbits. Bunny looks down at the newspaper and sees a black-and-white CCTV grab of the Horned Killer and a headline that reads, 'HERE AT LAST'. He trances out, in slow motion, on the water absorbing into the newspaper and tries not to take it personally when he sees that the soakage is taking on the shape of a rabbit.

He looks up and finds his son standing in front of him dressed in a pair of shorts and a T-shirt. The boy climbs up onto Bunny's lap and puts his arms around his neck and rests his head on his chest. Bunny places a cautious hand on the boy's back and stares out.

'It's OK,' he says.

The boy squeezes his dad close and starts to cry.

'I'm ready,' says Bunny, obscurely, to nobody in particular.

PART THREE

DEADMAN

25

The boy thinks his father looks weird, sitting there eating his breakfast in the dining room of the Empress Hotel, but it's hard to really know for sure as it seems a long time since he has looked anything else. His eyes keep darting all over the place – no sooner have they looked over there, than they look over here, and as soon as they look over here, they are looking somewhere else. Sometimes he is rubbernecking over his shoulder, or searching under the table, or checking who is coming through the door, or squinting at the waitress like he thinks she is wearing a disguise, like a mask or veil or something. He keeps holding his ribs and sucking air through his teeth and wincing and generally making strange faces. Sometimes he does these things sped-up and sometimes he does them slowed-down. Bunny Junior feels time is playing tricks on him. For example, it feels like he could grow from a little boy into a wrinkly old man in the time it takes his father to lift his cup, bring it to his lips and take a slurp of tea, and other times it seems like his father is doing everything revved-up and super-fast, like racing around the breakfast room or running off to the bathroom. Bunny Junior feels like he's been 'hitting the road' for a million years but realises with a chilly, drizzly feeling that this is only the third day.

His dad keeps saying something about the client list but as far as Bunny Junior can see the list is pretty much finished. He wonders what will happen when there are no more names left on the list. Will they go home? Will they just get another list? Does this just go on and on for ever? What did life have in store for him? What will he amount to? Is there some alternative life waiting to be lived? Then his dad forks an entire sausage into his mouth and the boy can't help but smile at this truly impressive display. That's the thing with his dad – thinks the boy – just when you're about to get really angry with him, he goes and does something that leaves you completely awestruck. Well – he thinks – I love my dad and that's a good thing. I mean – he thinks – you've got to hand it to him.

Bunny Junior watches a glob of ketchup run down his father's chin and land on his father's tie. This particular tie is sky-blue and there are cartoon rabbits printed on it, with little stitched crosses for eyes, lounging around on white cotton clouds. Bunny is too busy scanning the breakfast room to notice the mess he is making, so the boy reaches across the table and dabs at the spot with a damp napkin.

'That's better,' says the boy.

'I don't know what I'd do without you,' says Bunny, looking around the place like his head was on some kind of crazy, floppy spring.

'You'd be a bit of an old pig,' says the boy.

Bunny stands up and looks under his chair.

'I said, "You'd be a bit of an old, fucking pig",' says Bunny Junior, a bit louder.

The boy has been reading his encyclopaedia at the breakfast table and, as well as 'Apparition' and 'Visitation', he has looked up 'Near-Death Experience'.

The boy looks at his father and, for no particular reason, says, 'Hey, Dad, it says in my encyclopaedia that a Near-Death Experience is a striking occurrence sometimes reported by those who have recovered from being close to death.'

His father stands abruptly and bumps the table and there is a rattle of crockery and the little white porcelain vase falls over with its sad and solitary flower and they both watch, in slow motion, the water soak into the tablecloth. Bunny Junior picks up the flower (a simulated pink English daisy) and puts it in the buttonhole of his father's jacket.

'There you go,' says the boy.

'We've got work to do,' says Bunny. He scrapes back his chair and says, 'We've got important business to attend to.'

Bunny pulls up the collar of his jacket and wraps his arms around himself.

'Is the air conditioning up too high in here?' he says, with a shudder.

'I guess,' says the boy, and he picks up his encyclopaedia and follows his father out of the breakfast room of the Empress Hotel.

At the reception desk, Bunny hears a pretty Australian back-packer chick with pink highlights in her hair and a dusting of translucent powder on her freckles say to her friend, 'Hey, Kelly, did you see this?'

She points to a tabloid newspaper on the counter.

Kelly has blue hair and wears a loose cheesecloth dress and Tibetan beads around her neck. She looks at the tabloid and sees a photograph of the Horned Killer, flanked by two over-weight policemen. The killer is shirtless and six-packed and smeared in red paint, his hands are cuffed, his fake joke-shop horns still perch on his head. He stares resolutely into the camera. The headline reads, 'GOTCHA!'

'Wow, Zandra, they got the guy,' she says.

Zandra traces the contours of the killer's body with one plum-coloured fingernail and says, 'Looks kind of cute, though.'

Kelly looks over her shoulder at Bunny, who has moved in close and is craning his neck and trying to see the front page of the newspaper.

'Who?' she says, distracted.

'The devil guy,' says Zandra.

Kelly elbows Zandra and says, under her breath, 'My God, girl, you are incorrigible!' then looks over her shoulder at Bunny again.

'Wash off the body paint. Lose the plastic horns . . .' says Zandra.

'Girl, you are *rampant!*' says Kelly, from the side of her mouth.

'Yeah,' says Zandra, 'I know,' and with a little grunt adjusts her backpack, adding, 'I wouldn't mind his shoes under my bed *at all!*'

'Sssh,' says Kelly, under her breath.

'Sorry,' says Zandra, 'I mean, *hooves!*'

Kelly turns around and faces Bunny.

'Could we have a little room here, please?'

Bunny raises his hands in the air and takes a step backwards.

'Sorry, Kelly,' says Bunny, 'It's just that I think we are having our childhoods stolen from us.'

Bunny moves across to the receptionist, with his wisps of white hair and his catastrophic hinged nose, and pays his bill, and as he turns away the receptionist shoots out his hand and grabs Bunny by the wrist. He looks at Bunny through his 'Mystic Eye' and points at the newspaper.

'Did you see this? They are saying here that this devil guy's horns aren't fake. They're real.'

As the automatic door hisses open Bunny Junior feels a sense of relief to be leaving the Empress Hotel and he says to his father, 'A Near-Death Experience generally includes an out-of-body event in which people travel through a dark void or tunnel towards the light.'

The sun beats down and steam rises from the wet and dazzling streets. The glare hurts the boy's eyes and he slips on his shades and wonders if he is actually dead. He thinks – Is this why I keep seeing my mother? He pinches the flesh on his thigh until his eyes water, and out on the sea a bank of condensed mist moves across the water towards them, like an unsolicited memory.

'In a Near-Death Experience people have reported encountering religious figures!' shouts Bunny Junior, jumping up and down, and rubbing the bruise on his thigh and thinking – ouch, ouch and *ouch!* 'One may even encounter deceased loved ones!'

His father keeps walking in a peculiar way and beating at his clothes with his hand and looking over his shoulder, and the sea mist continues to roll towards them, like a great white wall, blurring the line between the real world and its fogbound dream or something.

'There you go,' says the boy, helping his father, who has fallen over on the sidewalk, to his feet. 'Look what you've gone and done,' he says, pointing to a little triangular rip in the knee of his trousers.

'I don't know what I'd do without you,' says his father as he takes a long drink of something from a bottle, opens the door of the Punto and, face first, falls in.

When the Punto doesn't start, his father pounds the steering wheel, then actually clasps his hands together in supplication and petitions God and all His saints for assistance, and the insubordinate Punto, as if taking pity on him, coughs and splutters into life with a promise of taking him where he wants to go.

'A Near-Death Experience is often accompanied by strong feelings of peacefulness, Dad,' says the boy.

'Grab the client list,' says Bunny, resting his head on the wheel and playing with the hole in his trousers.

The boy says, 'It . . . is . . . often . . . accompanied . . . by . . . strong . . . feelings . . . of . . . peacefulness,' and he leans over and takes a tissue from the glove compartment and together they dab at the messy little scrape on his dad's knee.

'There you go,' says the boy.

Bunny parks the Punto outside a tumbledown bungalow on the hill between Peacehaven and Newhaven – the residence of Miss Mary Armstrong, the last name on the list. The front yard is overgrown and littered with all manner of junk – used appliances and broken machines – a refrigerator, a vacuum cleaner, a washing machine, a bathtub full of yellowed newspapers, a ruptured kayak, a ruined Chesterfield settee and a motorcycle, dismantled and forgotten. Standing in the centre of the yard is a grotesque sculptural abstraction made from welded steel and strips of brightly coloured, spray-painted plastic.

'What a shit-hole' says Bunny. 'They just get worse and worse.'

There had been three names left on the client list, but the other two names had turned out to be non-starters and a complete waste of time.

The first was a Mrs Elaine Bartlett, who lived on the fourth floor of a block of flats in Moulsecombe. Lying on the floor of its only working elevator was a bombed-out kid with a can of air freshner in one hand and a Tesco bag in the other and a Burberry cap on his head. This normally wouldn't have been a problem, except the boy had emptied the contents of his bowels into his shorts and these were pulled down around his skinny, little ankles. The boy had managed, rather heroically, thought Bunny, to graffiti in green spray paint on the elevator wall, 'I AM A SAD CUNT'. Bunny had stepped into the elevator, then stepped out and allowed its doors to judder shut. He contemplated momentarily climbing the four flights of stairs to Mrs Elaine Bartlett's flat and realised, to his credit, that there was no way he was going to make it up them in his present condition, so he staggered back to the Punto.

The next name on the list, a Mrs Bonnie England, living over the hill in Bevendean was not at home in her semi-detached brick-clad box, or so the guy who answered the door and claimed to be her husband maintained. Bunny could see this was clearly untrue, as the woman in the grease-stained pinafore, standing next to the guy who opened the door was obviously Mrs Bonnie England. Bunny didn't press the point, primarily because Mrs Bonnie England was the animate equivalent of the fouled elevator in Moulescombe — a prime stomach-churner with the proportions and sex appeal of a Portakabin. Bunny had simply made a deferential apology for inconveniencing them (the husband was the red-faced, super-pissed-off type, and Bunny was tired of being beaten up) then backed respectfully away and fell over her rubbish bins. Lying on his back on the concrete walkway, Bunny watched Mrs Bonnie England and her husband hold each other's hands and laugh at him.

'Ouch,' said Bunny.

As Bunny limped back to the Punto, he noticed, to his complete surprise, the ripe and rotund figure of River – the waitress from the breakfast room at the Grenville Hotel – walking down the street in her purple gingham uniform with the white collar and cuffs. He rubbed his eyes as if he were seeing things, like she were a mirage or a visual fallacy of some sort or something. She seemed like she had walked out of another lifetime, a less complicated and happier age, and his cock leapt at the memory of her, and his heart pounded like a military drum and he started to cry.

'Hey!' said Bunny, running up to her, dabbing at his cheeks. 'What are you doing, River?'

River took one look at Bunny and screamed. She veered savagely in a wide and reckless arc and sped up, taking wild glances over her shoulder.

'Hey!' said Bunny. 'It's me! Bunny!'

River broke into a run, the various parts of her body pumping and pulsating beneath her uniform.

'Hey, I've been having a really hard time!' said Bunny, his hands thrown out to the sides.

'Stay away from me!' she cried. 'Just stay away from me, you fucking maniac!'

'But, River, didn't we have a good thing going?!' shouted Bunny, but he could hear her sobs as she charged away, her footsteps like gunshots down the street.

'What was wrong with that girl, Dad?' asked Bunny Junior, when his father got back in the Punto.

'I think she has a medical condition,' said Bunny.

26

Outside Mary Armstrong's bungalow, Bunny leans across and says to Bunny Junior, with a belch of inflammable breath, 'All right, wait here, I won't be long.'

'What are we going to do, Dad?' says Bunny Junior.

Bunny takes a slug from his flask and slips it into the inside pocket of his jacket.

'Well, son, we're going to shake the money tree, OK? We're going to shaft some mugs and milk the jolly green cow,' says Bunny, jamming a Lambert & Butler into his mouth. 'We're grubbing the mullah and gleaning the beans. We're divesting the greater public of their spondulics. We are, as they say in the trade, raping and looting.' Bunny torches his cigarette with his Zippo, scorching his quiff and filling the car with the stench of singed hair. 'We're trying to make some fucking boodle! Are you with me? And I've got a very good feeling about this one.'

'Yes, Dad, but what are we going to do with ourselves *after* we make the boodle?'

'We are vampires, my boy! We are vultures! We are a frenzy of piranha flenching a fucking water buffalo or a caribou or something!' says Bunny, with a madman's grin on his face. 'We are fucking *barracuda!*'

The boy looks at his father and a stone-cold realisation hits

him – he sees in the appalling orbits of his father's eyes a resi-
dent terror that makes the child recoil. Bunny Junior sees, at
that moment, that his father has no idea what he is doing or
where he is going. The boy realises, suddenly, that for some
time he has been the passenger on an aeroplane and that he
has walked into the cockpit only to find that the pilot is dead
drunk at the controls and absolutely no one is flying the plane.
Bunny looks into his father's panic-stricken eyes and sees a
thousand incomprehensible dials and switches and meters all
spinning wildly and little red bulbs flashing on and off and
going beep, beep, beep and he feels, with a nauseating swoon,
the aeroplane's nose tip resolutely earthward and the big blue
fiendish world come rushing up to annihilate him – and it
scares him.

'Oh, Daddy,' he says, and straightens the little pink daisy
in his father's lapel.

'We just have to open our great jaws and all the little fish
will swim in,' says Bunny, trying with great difficulty to
extricate himself from the Punto. 'I've got a good feeling about
this one.'

Bunny Junior gets out of the Punto, moves around to the
driver's side, opens the door and helps Bunny out and his
father performs a little shuffling two-step and starts to laugh
out loud for no reason. Everything goes whoosh as the boy
falls out of the sky.

Bunny walks up the oil-splattered concrete drive. He opens
his flask of Scotch and empties it down his throat, then tosses
it over his shoulder and it lands among the strew of garbage
that lies about the overgrown yard. He mounts the steps to
the bungalow, with its grimy pebbledash walls and shattered
windows, and knocks on the front door.

'Miss Mary Armstrong?' says Bunny, and the door creaks open but there is no one there. Bunny strokes the hank of hair that lies, limp and doomed, over one eye and feels compelled to enter.

'Miss Mary Armstrong?' calls Bunny, and takes a furtive step across the threshold. 'Anybody home?' he says.

Inside, the atmosphere of dread and desolation in this dilapidated old house is so powerful Bunny can taste it, like rot, in his mouth, and he whispers to himself, 'I deal in high-quality beauty products,' and closes the door behind him.

The kitchen is dark, the blinds drawn, and Bunny breathes in a sour, animal stench. The door to the refrigerator has been left open, and a pulsing, jaundiced light emanates from it. Bunny notices the refrigerator contains a solitary, diseased lemon, like a premonition, and over by the sink he sees a dog of an indeterminate breed lying motionless on the grimy linoleum floor. He moves through the kitchen and realises, dimly and without concern, that he has left his sample case in the Punto, and finds that at some point in that prat-fall of a morning he has skinned the palms of his hands and that they are slick with watery blood. He wipes them on his trousers and enters the darkened hallway and, as he does so, Bunny becomes aware of a strange, atonal, squealing sound.

'Miss Mary Armstrong? Miss Mary Armstrong?' he calls out and squeezes his penis through his trousers, tugging at it, and letting it grow large and hard in his hand.

'I've got a good feeling about this one,' he says to himself and, in that instant, experiences a kind of weariness of the soul and sits down on the floor and leans back against the wall. He pulls his knees up to his chest and puts his head between them and does a drawing of something with his index finger in the accumulated dust on the floor.

'Miss Mary Armstrong?' he says to himself and closes his eyes.

He remembers a crazy night he'd had at the Palace Hotel in Cross Street, not that long ago, with a cute, little blonde chick he'd picked up at The Babylon. He remembers himself standing by the bed, huffing and puffing, his barked cock feeling like he'd been fucking a cheese-grater or something, and cursing the fact that he hadn't had the foresight to bring any lubricant with him. He remembers giggling to himself and thinking what a crazy party he was having and that he might go one more time, even though it looked like the Roofies were wearing off and the girl was showing signs of waking up. I mean, how much punishment can one swinger take! Then there was a knock on the door – three simple, unassuming raps – and to this day Bunny can't work out what possessed him to open the door. The coke, maybe. The booze, probably. Whatever.

'Room service,' he had said to himself, with a giggle.

He opened the door and standing there was his wife, Libby. She looked at Bunny, naked and glazed in sweat, and then looked at the comatose girl spread-eagled on the bed, and all the years of aggrieved rage seemed to drain from her eyes and her face became as inanimate as a wax mask and she simply turned and walked off down the hall. When Bunny returned home the next morning, Libby had changed; she didn't mention the night before, she stopped giving him a hard time, and she just kind of floated around the house, watching TV and sitting around and sleeping a lot. She even had sex with him. I mean, who would have guessed it, he thought.

'Women,' Bunny says, shaking his head and he starts to cry again.

After a while, Bunny stands up and slaps the dust from his trousers, then moves down the darkened hall as if he is walking into a great wind and, in time, he arrives at a black door. The piercing sonic oscillation is louder here and Bunny puts his hands over his ears and peers closely at a large poster of an extremely sexy girl taped to the door, and even before he realises who it is – the curtain of ironed hair, the zany black-rimmed eyes and the pornographic cupid-bow mouth – he feels new tears scald his cheeks and he reaches out and traces, with his finger, the tender contours of her infinitely beautiful face, as if by doing so he could bring her miraculously to life. He says, in the manner of a mantra or prayer or incantation or something, 'Avril Lavigne. Avril Lavigne. Oh, my darling, Avril Lavigne.'

And without even considering what may exist on the other side of that black-painted door, Bunny pushes it gently open and addresses the room as though it were an alternate and mysterious universe, saying, through his sobs, 'Hello, I am Bunny Munro. I represent Eternity Enterprises.'

Bunny Junior closes the encyclopaedia. He has been reading about the 'Midwife Toad' and is astounded to think that the male carries the eggs on his legs until they hatch! What a world we live in – he thinks. What an amazing world.

He picks up the client list that lies on the seat beside him and, holding it out in front of him, carefully and deliberately, tears it into strips. He puts one strip of paper into his mouth, sucks it to a soft pap and swallows it, then repeats the action until he has ingested the entire list. That — he thinks — puts an end to that.

Wisps of mist curl around the Punto and Bunny Junior watches the monstrous, swallowing fog roll down the street towards him, like an imagined thing, making phantoms of everything in its path. The boy leans back and closes his eyes and allows himself to be devoured by it.

Later, when he opens them again, he sees his mother sitting in her orange nightdress on a low cream brick wall opposite the Punto. She is smiling at him and beckoning him to come join her. Fiddleheads of mist play around her face and when she moves her hands the fog trails from her fingers like purple smoke. Bunny Junior opens the door of the Punto and steps out, like a tiny cosmonaut, into the vaporous air. He floats around the front of the Punto, down along the footpath, and sits on the wall next to his mother. Immediately, he feels a pulsing warmth and he looks up at her.

'I'm so sorry, Mummy,' he says.

His mother puts her arm around him and the boy rests his head against her body and she is soft and smells of another world and she is truly his mother.

She says, 'Oh, my darling child, I am sorry too,' and presses her lips into his hair. 'I wasn't strong enough,' she says, and then, taking the boy's face in her hands, says, 'But you're the strong one. You always were,' and the boy feels the splash of his mother's tears like they were real.

'I just miss you so much, Mummy.'

'I know,' she says,

'Don't cry,' says the boy.

'You see?' says his mother. 'You are the strong one.'

'What will we do about Dad?' says Bunny Junior.

His mother runs her fingers through the boy's hair, then says, not unkindly, 'Your father cannot help you. He is truly lost.'

'That's OK, Mummy,' says the boy. 'I am the navigator.'

His mother plants a kiss in the boy's hair and whispers, 'You have a such a good little heart.'

'Is that what you wanted to tell me?' says the boy.

'No, I am here to tell you something else,' she says.

'Can I ask you something first?'

'OK,' she says.

'Are you alive, Mummy? You feel like you are. I can hear your heart beating,' says the boy, and he holds his mother tight.

'No, Bunny Boy, I am not,' she says. 'I died.'

'Is *that* what you wanted to tell me?'

'Yes, but I want to tell you something else. I want to tell you this. That no matter what happens, I want you to persevere. Do you understand?'

The boy looks up at his mother.

'Yes, I think so,' he says. ' What you are saying is that something really bad is going to happen and you want me to be strong.'

His mother puts his arm around him and smiles and says, 'You see?'

Bunny steps into the room at the end of the hall. A single naked bulb burns dimly overhead and in this airless hideaway the squealing note is violent and invasive, and Bunny squints into the dark to find its source. Over by the far wall an electric guitar leans against an amplifier, feeding back. It takes Bunny some time to notice a young lady sitting on a ruined settee in the middle of the room. She does not seem to be moving. She is very thin and wears a pale yellow vest and a pair of pastel-pink panties and nothing else. Bunny can see the outline of the cobbled bones of her shoulders, the exaggerated angles of her knees, her elbows and her wrists. One spidery hand sits cupped in her lap, a cigarette burning down between her fingers. Her head is slumped forward and her straight, brown hair hangs like a curtain over her face.

'Miss Mary Armstrong?' says Bunny taking a step towards her.

The girl jerks suddenly upright and raises her head, and says, in a slow and hollow croak, 'She don't live here no more. Do you want to see Mushroom Dave?'

The girl's eyelids close and her head falls forward again.

'Mushroom Dave . . . isn't . . . here . . .' she mutters to herself.

Bunny crosses the room and throws the switch on the guitar amp and the room is suddenly silent and magic. He sees suspended around the light bulb glittering motes of dust and he moves across the room and stands before the girl, a ribbon of blue cigarette smoke at her fingertips.

The girl lifts her head and all the muscles of her forehead are employed in an attempt to raise the lids of her eyes. Her hand flutters in mid-air and Bunny can see the fine, bird-like bones of her fingers through her paper-thin skin. The ash from her cigarette falls away and lands intact on the front of her vest. Her eyes are a green of ferocious, chemical intensity and her pupils are non-existent, and Bunny takes a step backward and says tenderly, 'Oh, baby, look at you.'

The girl lowers her head again, in short, sharp increments, until her chin rests on her chest, and her hair falls across her face. Bunny reaches down and puts his fingers under her jaw and raises her head again and sees that the poster on the door was not Avril Lavigne at all but a picture of this sad girl before him — the same pert nose, kohled eyes, straight brown hair, nymphomaniacal upper lip and slender, puppyish body. Bunny feels, in the most obscure of ways, that the resemblance to Avril Lavigne is not just fortuitous, but supernatural. Bunny finds himself sucked, with a great rush of blood, into a vortex of association; where the fairy girl before him — with her blueing lips and trickle of bright blood in the crook of her arm, the mortal weaponry of hypodermic syringe and blackened spoon on the table in front of her — was indeed the accelerated collision of time and desire, the coalescence of all the spinning particles of need, like the motes of dust around the light bulb, brought into being by Bunny's corrupted griefs. In this dim, sequestered room Bunny had walked through the looking glass, into death itself, hers and perhaps his own.

'Let me take that,' says Bunny and removes the cigarette butt from between her fingers and drops it into an overflowing ashtray. 'We don't want to burn the house down,' he says.

He kneels before her and gently brushes the cigarette ash from the looped fabric of her faded yellow vest.

'Oh, dear,' he says, and lights a cigarette of his own, takes a puff or two and then crushes it out in the ashtray.

He slips his hands under her cotton vest and her body spasms and slackens and he cups her small, cold breasts in his hands and feels the hard pearls of her nipples, like tiny secrets, against the barked palms of his hands. He feels the gradual winding down of her dying heart and can see a bluish tinge blossoming on the skin of her skull through her thin, ironed hair.

'Oh, my dear Avril,' he says.

He puts his hands under her knees and manoeuvres her carefully so that her bottom rests on the edge of the settee. He slips his fingers underneath the worn elastic of her panties that are strung across the points of her hips, slips them to her ankles and softly draws apart her knees and feels again a watery ardour in his eyes as he negotiates a button and a zipper. It is exactly as he imagined it – the hair, the lips, the hole – and he slips his hands under her wasted buttocks and enters her like a fucking pile driver.

27

The great bank of mist has rolled by and Bunny Junior sits alone on the low brick wall and plays with his Darth Vader figurine, and although the ghost of his mother has gone, he can still feel the cool imprint of her farewell kisses on his eyelids like tiny twin promises. She is, like the song says, within him and without him and all about him. He is the strongest one and he is protected – that was her promise. Ah, promises, promises – he thinks – and he swings his feet and smiles and hums to himself and jumps his Darth Vader along the wall and watches an old black BMW roll down the street and turn into the driveway of the house with all the rubbish in the yard.

Bunny Junior sees the driver's door open and a tall lean man leporello from the car like a set of dirty postcards. His hair is bleached blonde and he wears tight faded jeans, a black T-shirt and pink loafers. The boy notices a cool tattoo of a scorpion on the man's neck, and thinks he looks like a very tough customer indeed – a real barracuda.

The man scopes the street, to the left and to the right, with a reflexive, practised regard, and Bunny Junior watches as he drops his bunch of keys, curses, bends down and picks them up. Then he mounts the steps, flicks his cigarette into the yard and enters the house, slamming the door behind him.

Bunny Junior swings his legs on the wall and thinks about what his mother told him, and he smiles to think that after all he is just a kid, and that's all he has to be . . . a kid. A kid who likes Darth Vader, a kid with an amazing memory and who could retain all sorts of fascinating facts, a kid who was interested in the world, a kid with 'a good little heart', a kid who could even talk to ghosts. The adult world he was moving about in didn't have to make sense to him – why everyone looks like zombies, why his mother died, why his father acts like a mental case half the time.

He remembers with a quickening of the heart the girl on the bicycle, and he wishes he could tell her that this is what she was – just a little girl – and as she grows up maybe she doesn't have to turn into one of them – cock-a-doodling up the street all the time.

He knows something terrible is going to happen, but for some reason it doesn't worry him all that much. He feels he has become immune to this crazy grown-up world like you do to influenza or leprosy or radiation or something. He feels like he has been given an antidote and he could be bitten by every snake on the planet and he would still be able to walk away. He thinks that ghosts are better protection than real people, and he wishes he could tell the girl on the bicycle that as well.

Bunny Junior hopes nothing really bad happens to his dad, because even though his mother said that he was lost, and even though he probably wasn't very good at being a father in the way he has seen other fathers be on TV and in magazines and in parks and stuff – for example, when they buy the ointment to stop the child from going blind or throw a Frisbee around in the public gardens or something – he loves his dad with all of his heart and he wouldn't in a million years swap him for another one. Who would? Like when he is funny, he is an absolute scream – like look at him now as he jumps down the steps of that run-down old house with all the busted refrigerators and bathtubs and junk, with his trousers around his ankles. Tell me a dad who'd do that!

A few seconds later, the front door of the house flies open and the man called Mushroom Dave rockets out of that forlorn little house with the sole intention of burying a golf club into the back of Bunny's head. Bunny knows this because Mushroom Dave has a nine iron cranked in the air and is screaming, in a voice full of slaughter, 'You're a fucking dead man, you freak!'

Bunny intuits, as he charges across the yard, that to run is most likely a waste of time and that, in all probability, the catastrophe that had been seeking him out his entire life has finally found him and the Day of Judgement is at hand.

But he also thinks, as a matter of good policy, that he should just get the fuck out of there.

But as he crosses the front yard loaded with all that useless impedimenta, Bunny finds that every old washer, bathtub and refrigerator has conspired to punk his progress and, with each tumble and fall, he senses, in a premonitory way, the apocalyptic whisper of the death-dealing nine iron ruckle the air around his cranium. He knows, more than he knows anything in the world, that Mushroom Dave is right, he *is* a fucking dead man.

But, in an act of athletic agility that surprises even him, Bunny leaps over an old cast-iron, clawfoot bathtub (actually worth a few bob), pulling up his trousers at the same time, scrambles across the footpath, yanks open the door of the Punto, piles in and slams the door behind him. He hits the lock buttons, and with his heart thundering in his chest he turns the key in the ignition and the Punto does not cough and does not wheeze – and does not start.

'You fucking piece of shit!' cries Bunny, and then to Bunny Junior, 'Lock your fucking door! We're all gonna die!'

Bunny looks up and sees Mushroom Dave's murderous face, like a terrible melted mask, and he clocks the horizontal sweep of the golf club and hears the gun-crack explosion of his side window and the bright shattering of cubed glass as it implodes inwards and showers Bunny in vicious little zircons.

Bunny tries the key again and the Punto, as if outraged by this attack upon its person, roars perversely into life at exactly the moment that Bunny realises that the boy is actually not in the car at all and that Mushroom Dave is screaming and bringing the club around again.

Bunny hits the accelerator, veers crazily into the street, just as Bunny Junior appears out of nowhere, in his shorts and his T-shirt, and walks almost casually into the path of the Punto.

'Dad,' he says.

Bunny slams on the brake and the Punto screeches to a halt and Bunny Junior stands motionless in front of the car and in that instant there is a moment of true intimacy between the father and his son. Their eyes lock and nobody moves and nobody says anything, yet a current of understanding passes between them, obscure and intangible, but that has something to do with shame and terror and death.

Mushroom Dave moves towards Bunny Junior, with polyps erupting across his brain and scarlet mayhem in his face and a black scorpion writhing on his neck. He raises the club above his head and says, 'You're fucking dead, you little cunt.'

But Bunny Junior stands there and does not move. He feels his mother's kisses on his eyelids and he remembers her promise – that she is within him and without him and all about him – and he feels protected and he realises that his granulated eyelids no longer hurt and that the light of the day feels less painful and he feels that this man before him is just one more ugly customer in one more insane episode in an endless parade of demented incidents that collect around the affairs of adults like limescale or something. He feels it is just another part of the great rain of seagull shit that pours for ever over the doings of grown-ups – with their destructor faces and homicidal golf clubs and their filthy violent mouths and squirming black scorpions – and he simply does not feel impelled to move – and still Mushroom Dave draws closer and time grinds down and everyone floats like motes in space and Bunny starts screaming something inaudible and despairing but the boy cannot hear it because Bunny is hammering the Punto's horn at the same time – and still the boy does not move – and with a great adult grunt, Mushroom Dave brings the nine iron around and the boy reflexively shifts a fraction to the left and feels the sting of the club whiffle against his ear, followed by an immense crack of metal on metal as it slams against the bonnet of the Punto. Bunny Junior places his hand to his ear and when he draws it away and looks at it he sees a smudge of blood on his fingers and the boy makes a kittenish cry and evaporates into the thin and menacing air then reappears in the passenger seat of the Punto.

Bunny roars off down the empty street as the golf club comes down again and blows out the rear window of the heroic little Punto. Bunny Junior rubs his ear, turns around and sees through the hole in the back window Mushroom Dave turn and run towards the house, tossing the nine iron into the yard and disappearing inside.

'He was what you might call one of the crazy guys, wasn't he, Dad?' says Bunny Junior.

The boy reaches into the glove compartment and extracts a Kleenex and touches it against the tip of his ear and looks at the blood and says, 'He got me, Dad.'

Bunny says nothing, the wind blowing through the non-existent side window, his forelock whipping around his eyes, his jacket glittering with sequins of shattered glass. Bunny pulls into the side of the road, turns off the ignition and stares straight ahead, his hands locked around the steering wheel. He takes a series of breaths. He reaches under his seat and pulls out his emergency quarter-bottle of Scotch. He twists off the cap and swallows half of it. He shoves a Lambert & Butler into his mouth, lights it and takes a deep drag, and says to Bunny Junior, 'Don't ever fucking do that again.'

'Do what, Dad?' says Bunny Junior.

'Leave the fucking car.'

'Mum wanted to talk to me,' says the boy.

'Christ! Look what that bastard did to the Punto!' says Bunny, brushing the shattered glass from the dashboard. Bunny eyeballs the boy and says through clenched teeth, 'This is not some fucking game we're playing here.'

'I know it's not, Dad.'

'This is the real fucking deal!' he says.

Bunny realises then that, in all the commotion, the car radio has turned itself on and Kylie Minogue's 'Spinning Around' is playing and he hears that crazy throbbing synthesiser and Kylie singing all achy about how she is up for fucking *anything* and he begins to tremble all over, shake and tremble, shake and tremble and jitter all over and his heart begins to palpitate like a jackhammer and his teeth start chattering like some clockwork skull and he draws back his arm, opens his mouth and with a great existential moan, puts his fist through the car radio.

'That fucking song!' he screams.

And then his mobile phone goes off.

'Christ!' he shrieks and claws his phone from his jacket pocket, flips it opens and screams, 'What!'

'Bunny?'

'*What!*'

'It's Geoffrey, are you all right, my man?'

'No, Geoffrey, I'm not fucking all right! I'm not fucking all right, at all!'

'Listen, Bun, a Miss Lumley called the office. She says she's your dad's carer. She sounds . . . well . . . super-pissed-off. She says you've got to go to your dad's place, pronto. She says it's real urgent. She reckons, and I quote, that it's "a matter of grave importance",' says Geoffrey.

'What? Now?' says Bunny.

'She says your dad's really sick or something.'

There is a silence at Bunny's end of the line.

'Just passing on the message, bwana,' says Geoffrey.

Bunny lobsters the phone, tosses it on the dashboard and pounds at the steering wheel till his hands ache.

'Fuck,' he says. 'Fuck! Fuck! And *fuck!*'

'Where are we going, Dad?'

Bunny starts the Punto.

'We're going to see your granddad,' says Bunny. 'My father.

234

The great Bunny Munro the First,' he says, and Bunny slams his foot on the accelerator and careens off, jemmying the Punto into the early-afternoon traffic that flows along the coastal road. 'That's where we're fucking going,' he says.

Bunny Junior sees a great band of bruised thunderheads garnering together over a grey and swollen sea and flocks of seagulls like scraps of shredded newspaper thrown across a sky so full of insult and injury that it looks like it is about to burst into tears or piss its pants or something. He can smell the fish and the salt on the wind, and hear the breakers erupting over the sea wall, and he turns to his father and touches the tip of his ear and says, 'I think it's gonna rain, Dad.'

And sure enough Bunny Junior sees the first fat drops of rain thud on the dented bonnet of the Punto, and then the sky rips open and it all comes pouring down.

28

In a run-down terrace off the Old Steine, the carpets are threadbare and the light bulbs don't work and on the faded ruined wallpaper there is a willow pattern of frotting Chinamen or Chinamen blowing each other or something – Bunny can't quite work out which – as he mounts the stairs like it's the last place on earth he wants to be. His ribs ache and his knees are skinned and his hands are barked and his nose resembles a poisonous red toadstool and there are holes in the knees of his trousers and his quiff looks intestinal, flopping across his forehead like something from the stomach of something.

Bunny Junior follows close behind, and as he passes each landing he sees the storm lashing at the windows and prays that the bin liners that his father gaffer-taped to the blown-out windscreen of the Punto hold fast because he has left his encyclopaedia on the back seat and if anything happened to that he doesn't know what he'd do.

Coming down the stairs of the building, Bunny runs into Miss Lumley, dressed in a blue nurse's uniform, with a satchel in one hand and a bunch of keys in the other and her little upside-down watch bobbing on her starched bosom.

'Just the man I want to see,' she says.

'What happened to the lift?' says Bunny, gasping for air

and sweating into his shirt so profusely that it clings to his ribs.

'It's broken,' says Miss Lumley, dryly. 'It's been that way for months, Mr Munro.'

Miss Lumley is in her fifties, with a pleasing and compassionate face that has been temporarily disfigured – reddened and soured and frazzled – by being employed in the execution of some unpalatable duty. She peers over the top of a pair of black-framed spectacles and dangles the keys out in front of her.

'I quit,' she says.

'What?' says Bunny.

'Your father is dying, Mr Munro. He needs continuous professional care.'

'I thought that's what you were doing,' says Bunny.

'He needs to be in hospital, Mr Munro.'

Miss Lumley takes a step forward and presses the keys into Bunny's hand and looks him up and down.

'What happened to you?' she asks.

'He won't go into hospital, you know that,' says Bunny, leaning against the wall for support, the weight of the last few days hanging across his shoulders like bags of cement.

'Perhaps you could both go in,' says Miss Lumley, reaching up and gently touching the side of Bunny's nose. 'You look worse than he does.'

'You don't look too hot yourself,' says Bunny, and smiles and reaches into his jacket pocket and pulls out his flask of Scotch.

'Drink?'

Miss Lumley smiles back. 'It's not been easy. I am a patient woman, Mr Munro. I have tried my best. I simply will not subject myself to the level of abuse I have been receiving.

I'm sure you understand. Your father is a very sick man,' she says, placing her hand on her chest. 'Here,' she says, then taps her head, '. . . and here.'

Bunny takes a hit from the flask, sticks a Lambert & Butler in his mouth and Zippos it as Miss Lumley looks down at Bunny Junior.

'Hey, darling,' she says.

Bunny Junior waggles his Darth Vader figurine.

'I got hit in the ear,' he says.

Miss Lumley bends down and, pushing her spectacles up the bridge of her nose, examines the boy's tiny wound.

'I've got something for that,' she says and opens her satchel and produces a small tube of antiseptic cream and a box of plasters. She dabs a small amount of the cream on the tip of his ear and covers it with a tiny circular, flesh-toned plaster.

'You have been in the wars,' says Miss Lumley, closing her satchel.

'You should see the other guy,' says Bunny Junior, and looks up at his dad and smiles.

Miss Lumley turns to Bunny.

'He's a sweetheart,' she says.

Bunny sucks on his Lambert & Butler, his hand trembling, an electrified nerve jumping under his right eye, a rivulet of perspiration trailing down the side of his face.

'Seriously, Mr Munro, are you OK?'

'Hey,' says Bunny, 'it's visiting day.'

'I understand your pain,' says Miss Lumley, placing her hand on his arm. She picks up her satchel. 'Get your father to a hospital, Mr Munro,' and she disappears down the stairs.

Bunny jiggles the bunch of keys in his hand, wraps his fingers around them and looks at Bunny Junior.

'Oh, man,' he says. 'Here we go.'

The boy looks back at him with his dismantled smile, his head angled to the side, and then together – father and son – they mount the final set of stairs.

Bunny tucks in his shirt and rearranges his hair and straightens his tie and drains the remainder of his flask of Scotch and sucks the last gasp out of the Lambert & Butler and turns to Bunny Junior and says, 'How do I look?' and without waiting for an answer knocks three times on the door of Flat 17 and takes a precautionary step backward.

'Piss off, you bitch!' comes a roar, from inside. 'I'm busy!'

Bunny leans close to the door and says, 'Dad! It's me! Bunny!'

Bunny hears a terrible hacking from within. There is a clacking sound and scrape of furniture, a chain of raw expletives and the door opens and Bunny Munro the First stands in the doorway, small and bent, dressed in a brown Argyll jumper with snowflakes and a white polar bear on the front, a nicotine-coloured shirt and a mangled pair of brown corduroy slippers. The zipper gapes open in his trousers and faded blue tattoos peek from the sleeves of his jumper and the open neck of his shirt. The skin on his face is as grey as pulped newspaper and the gums of his dentures are stained a florid purple, the teeth bulky and brown. A sullage of colourless hair spills down the back of his egg-shaped skull, like chicken gravy. He brings with him an overpowering stench of stale urine and medicinal ointment. In one hand he holds a heavy cleated walking stick and in the other, a grimly unpleasant handkerchief. He looks at Bunny and clacks his dentures.

'Like I said, *piss off!*' He slams the door in Bunny's face.

'Oh, man,' says Bunny, putting the key in the door and turning it. 'Just don't say anything,' he says to Bunny Junior out of the side of his mouth, and together they enter the room.

The bedsit is small and unventilated and filled with a layer of stale cigarette smoke. The storm hammers at the windows behind lace curtains yellow with age, and in a tiny kitchen to the side, a kettle shrieks. The old man has sat himself in a sole leather armchair in front of the TV, his walking stick resting across his knees. Behind him a mahogany standard lamp with a tasselled shade casts a fierce light on the back of the old man's elongated skull. On the TV, a pornographic video involving a teenage girl and a black rubber dildo plays out in colour-saturated reds and greens. The old man pushes his gnarled fist into the lap of his rancid grey trousers, claws at his crotch and proclaims, 'The fucking thing don't work!'

The old man looks up from his chair and rubs at his jaw and out of one shrewd eye he scrutinises Bunny's unfortunate demeanour. He sucks air through his psychedelic dentures, points at Bunny's red rosette nose and says, 'How did you get that? Raping an old lady?'

Bunny touches Mrs Brooks' rings in his jacket pocket and with a twinge of shame or something says, 'What you need is a nice cup of tea, Dad,' and walks into the kitchen and turns the screaming kettle off.

'No, I don't,' says the old man. 'What I need is to get my fucking rocks off!' and he scrabbles at the flies of his trousers again.

Bunny crosses the room and hits the switch on the TV.

'Perhaps we can turn this off, Dad,' he says.

'Give us a fag, then,' snorts the old man and wipes at the foam in the corners of his mouth. 'That fucking bitch stole mine.'

Bunny crosses the room and hands his father his pack of Lambert & Butlers and the old man sticks one between his lips and puts the pack in the top pocket of his shirt. Bunny lights his father's cigarette as Bunny Junior walks across the room to a little birdcage sitting on an antique Sutherland end-table by the window. Inside it, on a perch threaded with ivy, sits a tiny mechanical bird with red and blue wings. Bunny Junior runs his fingers along the gilded bars of the cage and the little automata rocks on its perch.

'Come on, Dad, let's make you a nice cup of tea,' says Bunny.

'I don't want a *nice cup of tea*,' sneers the old man and drags on his cigarette, then presses his handkerchief to his mouth and embarks on a seemingly endless bout of coughing that bends his old body double and brings dark, yellow tears to his eyes.

'Are you all right, Dad?' asks Bunny.

'Eighty fucking years old and I go and get lung cancer,' he says and spits something unspeakable into his handkerchief. 'Yeah, I'm just fucking great.'

'Is there anything I can do, Dad?' says Bunny.

'Do? *You?* You must be fucking joking,' says the old man.

Bunny Junior turns the gold key in the front of the bird cage and the automata jumps to life and sings a song in a series of short sweet notes, its beak clacking open and shut, its red and blue wings lifting and falling. A look of immense pleasure passes across the boy's face.

'Don't break that thing. It's worth a bloody fortune,' says

the old man who is attempting to pull the zipper up on his flies, working at it with his twisted fingers.

'Sorry, Granddad,' says the boy.

The old man stops what he is doing and looks up at Bunny, the cigarette clamped between his dentures, threads of skin like worn rubber bands looping at his throat.

'What did he call me?' he says, jabbing a finger at the boy. 'Is he taking the piss?'

'He's your grandson, Dad. You know he is,' says Bunny. The old man turns to Bunny Junior, who watches the little mechanical bird as it sings and dances on its perch.

'Leave that bloody bird alone and come over here to Grandpa.'

With small, cautious steps Bunny Junior moves towards his grandfather, but the old man beckons him closer and leans towards the boy and cocks a thumb at Bunny, who stands clicking his Zippo and pointlessly patting at the pockets of his jacket for a cigarette. The old man says conspiratorially to the boy, 'I hope you break his heart. I hope you break it like he broke mine.'

'Leave him alone, Dad,' mutters Bunny, 'and give us a fag.'

'Fuck off and buy your own,' says Bunny Senior and looks at Bunny from the corner of one yellow, dewy eye, then rolls his tongue around his mouth and hawks into his handkerchief. Bunny Junior turns to the birdcage and twists the key again.

'I just spoke to the woman who looks after you. Miss . . . What's her name?' says Bunny.

'Cunt-face.'

'She says you need to go to the hospital, Dad.'

Bunny Senior raises his walking stick above his head, his face purple with rage.

'You tell that bloody bitch if she ever sets foot in my place again, I'll break this fucking stick over her back! You hear me? I'll poke her . . .' and the old man makes an obscene penetrative gesture with the walking stick and bares his dentures, '. . . in the anus. I'll pull her fucking guts out.'

'Jesus, Dad,' says Bunny.

'I'll fucking *eviscerate* the bitch,' and rolls his huge round tongue around his lips. He hacks into his handkerchief again and holds it up for Bunny Junior to see. He shouts, 'See that? That's my fucking lung!' then points at Bunny with his walking stick. 'Your fucking dad, I tried to teach him the business,' he snarls. 'I showed him the most lovely things a boy could see . . .'

'Come on, Dad,' says Bunny.

'And he ends up peddling toilet brushes!'

'Beauty products.'

'Door to fucking door,' snarls the old man, contemptuously.

'By appointment,' says Bunny.

'Fucking amateur.'

'I work through a reputable company,' says Bunny.

'You're the bloody Bog Roll Man,' says the old man and puts his head between his legs, moans mortally and coughs his guts out. He wipes at his eyes with his handkerchief and sucks on the cigarette.

'Dad, you need proper medical attention,' says Bunny.

'You broke my heart. You dashed the cup from my lips, you little cunt.'

'Dad, you need . . .'

'Don't you come round here telling me what I need.'

The old man addresses Bunny Junior, with one raised finger, taps the pocked bulb of his snout and says, 'I was an *antique dealer*, boy. I had a nose for it.'

'Dad . . .' says Bunny.

'You want to end up a bloody nobody like him?'

'Dad . . .'

The old man looks at Bunny and sneers.

'Shut your fucking hole. You are beyond recall. You are a lost cause. But we might just be able to save the kid,' and the old man slams the arms of his leather chair. 'If he'd just use his ears . . .'

Bunny Senior hacks into his handkerchief. His face grows purple with the effort and he takes some time to compose himself and then his eyes glaze, dimmed in memory and loss, and he speaks in a sly, soft voice.

'Down on Tom Tiddler's ground, we were, picking up gold and silver.'

'We should go, Dad,' says Bunny to the old man. 'Come on, Bunny Boy.'

'I had a nose for it. I could smell a piece of Chippendale, the box of Georgian silver under the stairs . . . a pretty little bit of French, a tasty little bon du jour. Those old girls, give them a few words, and that special look . . . well, can we do business, then, madam? I'd have the Sheraton escritoire off the old bitch for a song . . . yes, a lovely bit of serpentine . . . and there would be not a straight line on it . . .'

Bunny Senior makes gentle curves in the air with his hand and says in a state of awe, 'I was a fucking master of the art.'

Bunny finds himself wavering on his feet, the whisky hitting him from all different directions at the same time, and he looks around for somewhere to sit but he can't find anywhere and anyway he feels if he doesn't have a cigarette soon then he will gnaw his bloody arm off, and he says to the old man, who has now closed his eyes and is reeling in his seat and making motions in the air like he is describing the contours of a well-endowed woman, 'You sure you don't want me to make you a cup of tea before we go, Dad?'

The old man drops his hands, opens one cruel eye and regards Bunny.

'You make me want to vomit,' he snarls.

The mechanical bird winds down and stops singing and grows still on its little perch and Bunny Junior turns and takes a step forward and stands in front of his grandfather.

'My dad could sell a bicycle to a barracuda,' he says.

There is a sudden anti-sound like a retracted implosion of air that presses around Bunny's skull and forces him to throw his hands over his ears, stretch wide his mouth and pop the pockets of air in the joints of his jaw. He feels as though he has been plunged to the bottom of a dark and soundless ocean, the hydrostatic pressure so intense it feels like knitting needles hammered into his eardrums. Not a word is spoken and Bunny floats aghast in this petrified state.

Then, just as suddenly, all the sound comes rushing back and the old man jams his cigarette into a saucer on the butler's tray beside him and shouts, 'What did you say?'

'Dad,' says Bunny. '*Please.*'

The old man raises himself to his feet and stands crooked as a question mark, as if his ancient spine had lost the power to support his furious, bulbous skull. 'Do you mock me? *Do you mock me!?*' he shrieks.

'Dad, don't!' implores Bunny, moving forward, one arm outstretched in front of him, but there is all this whisky in his bloodstream and he stumbles over a walnut footstool – where did that come from? – and falls flat on his face.

With a roar, the old man lunges, like an animal, towards

the boy and jabs him viciously in the ribs with his walking stick and knocks the child to the ground.

'*Do you fucking-well mock me?!*' he screams.

Bunny Junior stares at his father, stunned. Bunny climbs to his feet and sees his father's bloodless knuckles tighten around the handle of the walking stick and witnesses a terrible and familiar bearing of his dentures and a great hurtling-away of the years.

'Don't, Dad,' he says, quietly.

Bunny Senior rears around – this tiny, wicked man – and raises his walking stick above his head and beats at the air and makes ready to bring it down on Bunny.

'What did you say? *What did you say to me?!*'

Bunny cringes, nearly to the floor, screws shut his eyes and throws his hands over his head and whispers, 'Sorry, Dad,' and waits.

In time, Bunny opens his eyes and sees his father sitting back in his cracked leather armchair, his walking stick lying on the floor, rubbing his wrists against his temples, his yellow, deathbed fingers clawing the air like a rack of tiny, mangled antlers. He groans, then examines Bunny through a merciless, solitary eye and says, 'Look at you.'

The boy stands now, silent and frozen and alone. He looks down at his father, who is folded in a heap on the floor. The old man claws the ground for his walking stick, then points it at Bunny and says to the boy, 'Get him out of here.'

Bunny Junior walks over to his father and Bunny raises himself to his feet. The old man explodes into another bout of coughing, hauled from the depths of his lungs. Bunny opens the door and he and the boy step out.

'Son?' says the old man.

Bunny turns around and looks at his father. The old man holds the fouled handkerchief out in front of him, yellow water running from his eyes.

'I'm dying, son,' he says.

Bunny's eyes fill with tears.

'Dad?' he says, and he makes to step back into the room but the old man reaches out with his walking stick and, with a last enfeebled lunge, pushes shut the door.

29

The rain beats down upon the Punto and lashes at the green
bin liners that are taped over the shattered windows, that
have, by some miracle, held fast and not capsized and poured
water all over Bunny Junior's encyclopaedia and made him
have to commit suicide or something. Purple thunder
rumbles overhead and sends veins of lightning crackling
across the sky. Bunny Junior clutches his encyclopaedia to
his chest, like it is his only friend in the world – except at
this moment it is no help and he just doesn't know what to
think. He knows that within the pages of the encyclopaedia
there is all the information anyone could ever need to know
– the answer to all things. But he *still* doesn't know what
to think. He knows that Edgar Rice Burroughs wrote *Tarzan*
of the Apes, and he knows that there are four-eyed fish that
can see above water and below water at the same time, and
he even knows that Joseph Guillotin did *not* invent the guil-
lotine, but what he doesn't know is what to do about his
dad, who has tears running down his face and who is not
saying anything and has no idea where he is going or what
he is looking for and is driving around and around in circles.
He has stopped at a shop and bought a packet of cigarettes
and a bottle of whisky and he is smoking like a chimney

and drinking like a fish and driving like a maniac and crying like he doesn't know what.

For some reason he keeps thinking about the little mechanical bird in the cage, with its colourful wings and pretty little song, and that makes him wish all over again that his dad would stop crying, so he could have a turn.

'Dad?' says the boy as Bunny steers the Punto into an empty parking space outside a small café on Western Road. People huddle together under a striped and dripping canvas awning, smoking and drinking coffee, dressed in T-shirts and miniskirts and flip-flops, unprepared for this heavy summer rain.

'I spoke to Mummy today,' says the boy, over the top of his encyclopaedia that he keeps pressed to his chest.

A spavined old vagrant hobbles past wearing a flesh-coloured eye-patch and sodden rags wrapped around his impossibly swollen feet. He has soiled the front of his trousers and wears an undersized T-shirt that shows the matted fur on his stomach and says, 'SHIT HAPPENS WHEN YOU PARTY NAKED'. He taps a tin cup against the window of the Punto and peers inside, scrutinises the occupants through his single, crazed eye, shakes his head in consternation and shuffles off into the rain.

'What did you say?' says Bunny, turning and looking at Bunny Junior as if he had only just realised that there is a nine-year-old boy sitting beside him.

'I spoke to my mummy today.'

'What?' he says again.

'It was really her, Dad. We talked for ages.'

'You what?' panics Bunny, and starts slapping at his jacket and looking everywhere at once. He slugs at the Scotch and drags on his Lambert & Butler and blows bones of smoke out his nose and shouts, '*You what?!*'

'She says she's coming to see you soon,' says Bunny Junior.

'Eh?' says Bunny, beneath the clamour of the rain, and then does the thing with the whisky and cigarettes all over again.

'Dad, I think I should go back to school,' says the boy.

'Eh?' says Bunny, and he looks across at the café and finds, amid the knot of people sheltering from the rain, three women sitting around a table, deep in conversation, drinking coffee and smoking cigarettes. One is a blonde and one is a brunette and one is a redhead.

'I think we should go home, Dad,' says the boy.

'Where?' says Bunny, and a spasm of panic moves across his face and he begins to claw away the bin liner taped to the window, then peers out at the three women. A great torrent of rain gushes in, drenching him, and he shouts into the deluge, 'What?'

'I think it's time we went home, Dad,' says Bunny Junior, and suddenly he feels a frightful woe in his guts. He reaches over and places his hand on his father's shoulder as if to pull him back from some deplorable turn of events.

'Dad?' he says.

'Wait here,' says Bunny, jerking his shoulder away.

Bunny throws open the door of the Punto and decants himself into the gutter, the booze ramping through his veins. He scampers across the footpath, stands upright and pats in vain at his decommissioned dishrag of a quiff, tugs at his tie with the dead rabbits on it and ploughs blindly through the plastic tables and chairs and says to the three women with their cigarettes and cappuccinos, 'I'm Bunny Munro. I am a salesman. I sell beauty products.'

The women look at each other in bewilderment and the blonde, who has a smudge of chocolate froth on her upper lip, actually starts to laugh, covering her mouth with her long-fingered hand.

Bunny starts to hop up and down, waggling his hands behind his head, and says, manically and with great urgency, 'I sell rich, hydrating, age-targeting lotions that soften the skin and exfoliate surface cells for a younger, smoother look!'

'Excuse me!' says the blonde, who has stopped laughing, but Bunny is screaming now, under the thundering sky and with all the rain coming down.

'The skin is awakened to its fullest potential and infused with a surge of new beauty, stimulating your feelings of pleasure and well-being!'

Bunny falls to his knees and wraps his arms around the long and shapely legs of the woman with blonde hair and burrows his face into her lap and feels all the psychic strings that bind him to the rational earth snapping like rubber bands in his skull, and he bellows into her dress, 'What am I gonna do?!'

'Waiter!' cries the woman. '*Waiter!*'

Bunny looks up at the woman and sees the stripe of chocolate froth on her lip through a film of tears.

'Will you fuck me?' he says.

The woman rears back, her long fingers at her mouth. The brunette and the redhead scrape back their chairs.

'Waiter!' they scream.

Bunny stands and from the corner of his eye sees Bunny Junior's face like a little scared balloon framed in the window of the Punto and he throws out his arms and addresses the shrinking customers with the whole of his voice.

'*Will somebody please fuck me?!*'

Thunder rumbles across the sky and Bunny hears the women scream — many of them, all of them — horrified and familiar as he grabs at them, his teeth bared, his mouth gaping wide, jumps at them, leaps at them – and an Italian waiter with a blue jaw and black apron grabs Bunny around the chest, wrestles him from the café and drags him down the street.

With a shove, the waiter deposits Bunny on the wet footpath outside the Punto and stalks away.

Bunny wrenches open the car door and piles in and looks at the boy. He turns the key in the ignition, guns the engine and looks at the boy. He zooms into the rainy street just as a maroon 'DUDMAN' concrete mixer truck veers into the oncoming traffic, its barrel rolling, its windscreen wipers frantically lashing at the storm. Bunny clocks the tanned, tattooed arm hanging limp from the window and looks at the boy. The mixer truck blows its horn – once, then once again – then speeds up and ploughs head-on into the Punto. There is a brutal compaction of metal and an explosion of glass, and as Bunny goes flying past, he looks at the screaming boy.

30

Bunny opens his eyes and the world is filmed in red. He realises, in a distant way, that he is on his hands and knees in the middle of a street. He can hear far-off wailing and feels an immense rain beating down upon him. He sees that the ground beneath him is pink with his own blood. He crawls a couple of paces and wonders what he is doing. He looks behind him and sees a little yellow car twisted around a maroon concrete mixer and he slowly stands up. He looks at his hands and wonders why he is holding a child's encyclopaedia. He looks back at the crumpled yellow car and in his mind's eye he sees the face of a boy.

Then there is a boom of thunder and Bunny looks up at the black clouds that move overhead and he sees a silver pitchfork of lightning leap from the sky and with an intake of breath he throws out his chest and sucks the lightning into his heart and the encyclopaedia flies from his hand with a loud *bang* and a webbed scar blossoms across his body and he crashes, stiff as a plank, onto the rain-filled street.

31

First there is the darkness. But Bunny feels he has always been aware of the darkness. Then there is the smell – a rancid stench of body odour with a tang of terror-crazed, female blood trapped within it – and Bunny realises as he inhales this stink that he is, indeed, alive. He finds he is swimming up from the most silent and suffocating depths of the deepest and blackest of seas. He realises that this thing that smells so badly and is squatting beside him has reached way down into the watery darkness and dragged him gasping for air to the surface. He can feel its heat against his lower body but there is something debauched and obscene about its proximity. The thing that is sitting beside him leans across and locks him in an embrace. He can feel, in its form, a plasticity – an absence of bones – and that the creature is quite possibly reptilian by nature. When it speaks, its breath smells of shit and the stench adheres to the contours of his face like a dishcloth or winding-cloth or something.

'They got me, those motherfuckers,' it says.

The words crawl across Bunny's face and seep into his nostrils, his mouth, his ears.

'They have done me down, my brother,' it says.

Bunny can sense that whatever this thing is, it is naked.

He can feel its erect phallus pressed against his stomach, pulsing with sexual heat, as it leans across him.

'Twenty-five to life, they gave me!' it wails, suddenly, clinging to Bunny. 'Twenty-five to life – with no fucking pussy!'

Bunny feels the creature crawl up on top of him and the scorch of its penis – long and thin – shift against his stomach and an insistent knee separates his thighs.

'*Help me!*' it moans.

Bunny tries to move but cannot. He attempts to open his eyes but they feel as though they have been stitched shut with a needle and thread. Then he realises he can see tiny pinpoints of light appearing from the world beyond.

'But I've been watching you,' says the voice, with a sudden, cloying intimacy. 'You're a fucking trip, man!'

Bunny feels a greased arm taking leverage around his neck.

'You're out of this world, baby. You're in a league of your own!' he says.

Bunny feels the pulsing phallus, move down his stomach, slide across his groin and slip between his legs.

'You are a fucking *inspiration!*'

Bunny struggles, in vain, but is impotent to move his arms or legs.

'You have the *talent, boyfriend!* You are a *master of the art!*'

Bunny sees the points of light connecting, expanding, and the black slats of his eyelashes drawing apart. He opens his eyes and his pupils contract painfully against the incursive light.

'Here's something to remember me by,' says the voice, in a whisper, 'until we meet again.'

Then he sees the smeared, scarlet face with its black hole of a mouth, its raw, red tongue, its yellow eyes, its goatish horns, all come down upon him like a lover, and he experi-ences a searing penetration between his splayed buttocks.

Then, at the point of climax, hot and liquid against his ear, he hears the demon's grievous moan, rising from his memory.

'My true intent is all for your delight,' he thinks it says, but he can't be exactly sure.

32

The night is a deep velvet blue and the moon an alabaster balloon and the planets and the stars are spilled across the heavens, in handfuls and heaps, like gold coins. The smell of brine lives deep within the breeze that blows up from across the ocean and speaks, in a secret way, to the crowd of women who walk down the main sodium-lit thoroughfare – it speaks of deep, feminine mysteries and unawakened and illimitable desires, of silver-haired mermaids and bearded, trident-waving mermen and the looped humps of sea monsters and bejew-elled cities drowned beneath masses of unreadable water. No one can remember a night quite so magical in Bognor Regis for years.

Bunny stands at the window of his chalet and watches the crowd as it moves down the lamp-lined path and passes the swimming pool, pink and magical, where a reinforced concrete elephant in a yellow tutu spurts strawberry-coloured water from its upraised trunk. Bunny smiles to himself as the crowd of women, unsuspecting, pass the giant fibreglass rabbit, goggle-eyed and buck-toothed, that stands like a bizarre avatar or tribal fetish beside the water-slide. On a little track circling the main swimming pool sits a brightly coloured electric train for children, its engine adorned with the same rapturous face of a circus clown that Bunny remembers from when his father brought him here as a child. He remembers, too, the fun fair, with its world-class monorail and Apache Fort and Dutch windmill that the crowd drifts past, as it winds its way around the empty swings and deserted slides and abandoned seesaws of the children's playground.

A black rag of cloud slides across the surface of the moon and Bunny sucks on a Lambert & Butler and watches someone point at the Gaiety Building and someone point at the putting green (with its huge golf ball balanced on a thirty-foot golf tee) and someone point at the amusement arcade and everyone ascend the stairs and enter the Main Hall of Butlins Holiday Camp in Bognor Regis.

Standing at the window, there is a certain determination in Bunny's posture, his feet firmly upon the earth, his chin raised, his shoulders serious and square and a look of concentration, but also mourning, around his eyes.

Over the entrance to the Main Hall the Butlins mission statement blinks in a candy-pink neon, 'OUR TRUE INTENT IS ALL FOR YOUR DELIGHT', and Bunny can see through the arched windows of the hall the crowd of women milling around, their invitations in their hands, staring at each other and wondering what they are doing there.

'Our true intent is all for your delight,' says Bunny to himself and he throws back his head and drains the contents of a can of Coca-Cola.

Bunny has put on a fresh shirt — thick red stripes with a contrasting white collar and cuffs — and the bizarre webbed scar curls from the open neck of his shirt like crystals of frost. He has loaded extra pomade into his hair and arranged his lovelock so it sits on his forehead with a new, almost yogic serenity. His cheeks are freshly shaved and he smells heavily of cologne and there is a thin, embossed cicatrix above his right eye, an inch long, that looks like it has been sculpted from pink plasticine.

'What did you say, Dad?' says Bunny Junior.

'I said, our true intent is all for your delight,' says Bunny.

'What does that mean?' says the boy.

'I don't know.'

Bunny Junior sits sunk in a beige corduroy beanbag, his own scar across his left eye, faint and pale, like a distant, ghosted echo of his father's. He is dressed in a white T-shirt and a pair of blue gaberdine shorts and flip-flops.

Bunny turns to the boy, sucks on his cigarette, expels a funnel of smoke into the room and asks, 'Will you be all right, Bunny Boy?'

'*I'll* be all right. But will you?' says Bunny Junior.

Bunny crumples the can of Coke and lobs it into the sink in the tiny kitchenette and says, 'Yes, I'm ready,' then slips on his jacket, throws his arms out to the side and says, 'How do I look?'

'You look good, Dad,' says Bunny Junior. 'You look ready.'

'Well, yeah, because there is something I've got to do,' says Bunny.

'I know, Dad,' says the boy, and he picks the scorched remnants of his encyclopaedia, with its rain-swollen pages, off a low laminated coffee table.

'You go wait for me down at the swimming pool, and I'll come by and pick you up later,' says Bunny.

'Yeah, Dad, I know.'

Bunny sucks the last gasp out of his Lambert & Butler, crushes it in an ashtray, checks himself in the mirror (for the hundredth time) and says, 'Sure you do, Bunny Boy.'

Bunny Junior lies back in the beanbag and opens his ency-clopaedia and peels apart the ruined pages until he finds a definition of the word 'Fantasy'.

'A fantasy is a situation imagined by an individual which does not correspond with reality but expresses certain desires or aims of its creator. Fantasies typically involve situations that are impossible or highly unlikely,' reads the boy and closes the encyclopaedia. 'Who would have guessed that, Dad?' he says, secretly pinching his leg.

'See you, Bunny Boy,' says Bunny, and he opens the door of the chalet and steps outside into the cool evening air.

Outside the night air carries within it only the faintest idea of a chill but it is enough for Bunny to register a shiver run through his body. At least he hopes it is the breeze and not some eleventh-hour lack of resolve, because, as he walks down the path towards the Main Hall, he feels a rising but not alto-gether unexpected suspicion that the course of action he is about to embark upon may not be as straightforward as he has planned.

He stops walking for a moment, puts a Lambert & Butler in his mouth and looks up at the night sky for guidance or strength or courage or something, but the moon appears coun-terfeit and merely cosmetic, the stars cheap and gimmicky.

'Oh, man,' he says to himself. 'What happened to the night?'

Bunny Zippos his cigarette, takes a deep drag, holds it in his lungs and comes to understand that there is simply no point in turning back, he must do what he came here to do, and he expels a resolute stream of blue smoke into the air and moves on. He leaves the path, makes his way around the side of the Main Hall and enters the stage door of the Empress Ballroom.

The carpeted stairs are rank with cigarette smoke and stale beer, and as he climbs them, Bunny sees within the bizarre amorphous pattern of the flock wallpaper a gallery of sinister faces with elongated and spiteful eyes. He sees these as a congregation of accusatory faces – a grotesque collection of the aggrieved – and he hopes that they are not some kind of premonition of things to come.

He traces his finger along the raised scar over his right eye and walks down a short hall, and as he draws closer he hears the dull murmur of the crowd gathering and he thinks he can hear, on the soft-pedal, a note of anxious expectation growing within it. He also senses, deeper down, a reverberation of malice and mistrust that he knows is imagined, or at least anticipated, but nevertheless implodes within him like a sadness.

'Oh, man,' he says again and he enters the cramped back-stage area of the Empress Ballroom.

Bunny sequesters himself into the wings and, hidden there, takes a deep breath and pulls back one of the red velvet, star-spangled curtains and sees that the interior of the Empress Ballroom, with its purple-and-gold satin ceiling and its ornamental balconies, is filled to capacity with the crowd of women that he had observed walking up the main path. He feels his heart constrict and a bubble of dread rise in his chest.

On the tiny glittering stage, a three-piece band dressed in pale green velour jackets begins to play an instrumental version of a soft rock classic that Bunny feels is both familiar and foreign at the same time.

261

Bunny puts a Lambert & Butler in his mouth and pats his pocket for his Zippo.

'Need a light, friend?' says a voice.

Bunny turns and sees a tall, lean-looking figure standing, like a tower of obtuse angles, in the shadows. He has a cigarette dangling from his mouth and what appears to be a saxophone hanging around his neck. The man strikes a match and the flare of the flame reveals him to be a blue-eyed, handsome man in his early fifties. He sports a black moustache, wears a hairnet and is dressed in the same pale green velour jacket that the other band members are wearing. He reaches over and lights Bunny's cigarette.

'Shouldn't you be on?' says Bunny, keeping his voice low.

The musician takes a drag of his cigarette and blows a considered plume of smoke into the air and says, 'No, man, they haul me in on the third number.' Then he takes a step back, sucks on his cigarette again and gives Bunny the once-over. 'Hey, man, I love the quiff. What are you?' he asks, 'A joke-man? A magician? A singer?'

'Yeah, something like that,' says Bunny, and then adds, 'I dig your moustache.'

'Thanks, man. The missus don't go for it much.'

'No, it looks good,' says Bunny.

'Well, it's a commitment,' says the musician and takes a final drag on his cigarette and with a swivel of his black leather boot grinds it into the floor.

'I can see that,' says Bunny.

'But I do love my wife,' says the musician, tracing his fingers along his moustache, a distant look in his eyes.

Bunny feels a wave of emotion erupt in his throat and he

presses his lips together and turns his face away, so that it is momentarily lost in shadow.

Suddenly, out of nowhere, a tiny man in a red tuxedo with white piping and gold buttons the size of milk bottle tops and an immaculate strawberry-blonde toupee pushes past Bunny and bounds onto the stage. He executes, with a shimmy and a shake, a series of rolling gestures with his hands that brings the band's song to a close.

The musician with the moustache leans in close to Bunny and behind his hand speaks to him out of the side of his mouth.

'Hey, did you hear the one about the junkie who shot up a whole packet of curry powder?'

'No,' says Bunny, who has pulled back the curtain again and is anxiously scanning the crowd on the dance floor of the Empress Ballroom.

'Yeah, well, now he's in a korma.'

On the stage the diminutive Master of Ceremonies skips up to the microphone, pops his cuffs and throws his arms out wide and says in a voice that surprises Bunny in its depth and insistence, 'Hi-di-hi!'

The audience responds with a smattering of non-committal applause.

'I can't hear you!' says the MC, in a singsong voice, 'I said "Hi-di-hi!"' and then walks to the lip of the stage and points the microphone at the audience.

'Hi-di-hi!' says the audience, in unison.

'That's better! Are we gonna have fun tonight?'

The crowd, swept up, clamours its assent, with foot stomps and hand claps.

'We are gonna dance!' says the MC, and the little man does a nifty twisting movement with his tiny feet, his pink toupee shimmering in the stage lights, the buttons on his jacket twinkling. 'We are gonna sing!' he cries, and yodels horribly, then cocks his thumb over his shoulder at the band and says in a panto-whisper, waggling his thick black eyebrows, 'I better leave that to the professionals!' The crowd laugh and whistle and applaud. 'And when the lights go down,' says the MC, winking suggestively, 'maybe make a little love!'

The crowd hoot and stomp their feet as the little man shuffles around the stage making suggestive movements with his tiny, gloved hands and grinding his child-like hips.

Bunny feels a thread of perspiration wind its way down the side of his face and he pulls a handkerchief from the pocket of his jacket and presses it against his forehead. The musician looks at Bunny with an expression of concern or sympathy or something.

'What are you doing here, man?' he asks.

'I'm just trying to put things right, you know,' says Bunny.

'Uh-huh, I hear you,' says the musician. 'We've got to love one another or die, brother.'

'Yeah, I heard that,' says Bunny, and again a swell of regret blooms within him and he puts his hand up to his heart.

'It's super-glue, baby,' says the musician, and blows softly into his saxophone. 'It keeps the heart of the world pumping.'

Bunny peers around the curtain again, and the mirrorball that hangs from the ceiling of the ballroom has begun to revolve and splinters of silver light dance across the faces of the crowd and Bunny sees Georgia, standing in the front row, a thing of certain beauty, proud-looking, almost regal, in a cream chiffon evening dress with scarlet sequins sewn across its bodice like a spray of arterial blood. Her yellow hair hangs in loose ringlets around her lavender eyes and she sways, back and forth, to some inner song, a content smile upon her face. Zoë and Amanda stand each side of Georgia dressed in identical indigo trouser suits. Bunny notices that Zoë now has the same candy-coloured hair extensions as Amanda, and they look happy.

Standing nearby, Bunny sees the Tae Kwon Do black belt, Charlotte Parnovar, dressed in a Mexican peasant skirt and a white embroidered blouse, and as Bunny unconsciously traces his fingers along the lumped bridge of his nose he sees that her face looks softer, less severe, all evidence of the unsightly cyst on her forehead gone.

Bunny sees Pamela Stokes (Poodle's 'gift') with her arm around the waist of the cuckolded Mylene Huq from Rottingdean, both smiling and stealing shy and coquettish glances at one another.

Bunny recognises Emily, the cashier from McDonald's, dressed in a snug yellow top and tight red trousers, her skin glowing, gazing about the Empress Ballroom as though she has never seen anything so beautiful in her life and applauding enthusiastically as the strange little MC, with the pink toupee, raises his hand to quieten the crowd.

'But seriously, folks, before the fun begins, we've got a gentleman who has come along tonight and wants to say a few words to you.'

Bunny wipes his face with his handkerchief and says to the musician with the saxophone and the moustache, 'I guess this is me.'

'Knock 'em dead, brother,' says the musician, and he pats Bunny on the back. 'Knock 'em dead.'

Bunny takes a final, firing-squad suck of his Lambert & Butler and grinds it out on the floor. Then he pulls the curtain aside, pats at his lovelock and walks onto the stage as the MC executes a dainty little two-step, throws out his arms and says, 'So without further ado-da-do, could we have a big round of applause for Mr Bunny Munro!'

33

Bunny walks onstage to blind and uproarious applause. He enters an apron of red light that spills across the stage like splashed ink. He registers the foot stomps and cheers and whistles, and for a brief moment Bunny feels the air of compacted dread loosen around his heart and thinks that, all things considered, his plan may not be so foolhardy as he had previously thought and sending out the invitations to these women was perhaps not such a dumb idea after all. But as he stretches out his hand and sees the blood-coloured light pool in his palm like a cup of gore, he understands that nothing in this world is ever that easy. Why would it be? He walks closer to the lip of the stage, plants his feet firmly on the floorboards and peers into the audience.

He sees, with a shamed stricture of the heart, the old blind lady, Mrs Brooks, in dark glasses and pink lipstick, seated in a wheelchair. Her skin looks considerably younger, Bunny notices, and as she performs her metronomic rocking and claps her ringed hands together, she appears sprightly and newly energised. Behind her, a pretty young carer stands, one hand resting affectionately on the old lady's shoulder.

To one side of her, Bunny sees, dressed in a dazzling mulberry taffeta cocktail dress, the young girl from The Babylon Lounge in Hove that Bunny date-raped. She is sharing a joke and laughing together with a dark-eyed beauty in sateen drainpipes and gold pumps that he had a similar thing with after a night at The Funky Buddha. Bunny feels a shamed flush of blood to the throat.

He sees a girl with long, ironed hair and crazy kohled eyes and cupid-bow lips, and he recognises her as the Avril Lavigne look-alike from the bungalow in Newhaven. Beside her stands Mushroom Dave, tapping his foot and dressed in a black suit and tie, his arm thrown protectively around her shoulders, a lit cigarette dangling from his mouth. He whispers something to the girl and they look at each other and smile.

And so it goes, Bunny looks over there and looks over here and looks somewhere in the middle and sees someone from this place and then someone from that place and someone from some other place altogether. On and on it goes, faces rising from the mossy depths of his memory, each with their burning attendant shame – Sabrina Cantrell, and Rebecca Beresford, and Rebecca Beresford's beautiful young daughter – and over there, caught in the roaming spotlight, he sees Libby's mother, Mrs Pennington, who is smiling now, smiling and rubbing the shoulders of her stricken, chair-bound husband.

More and more he sees them, standing at the front of the stage, swaying on the dance floor, standing on tiptoes at the back of the hall, waving from the little ornamental balconies – all of them and all the others, in every shape and form and incarnation, some half-recalled and some half-forgotten and some barely a smudged fingerprint on his memory – but all looking glorious and radiant and altogether perfect.

From this council estate and this broken-down apartment

and this one-bedroom flat and this down-at-heel hotel, from this dying seaside town and from that dying seaside town, Bunny sees them all coming towards him, from down the days and months and dreadful years of his life, the great teeming parade of the sorrowful, the grieving, the wounded and the shamed – but look! Look at their faces! – all happy now and happy and altogether happy in the eternally beautiful Empress Ballroom at Butlins Holiday Camp in Bognor Regis.

Then, as Bunny steps, squinting, into the spotlight and taps the microphone twice with his index finger, he sees, at the very front of the stage, River the waitress from the breakfast room of the Grenville Hotel – looking more lovely than he can imagine anyone could ever look – stepping angrily from the crowd and thrusting forth her arm and extending one purple finger and screaming through her teeth, '*My God, it's him!*'

Suddenly the atmosphere undergoes a momentous change. The applause, like an inverted roar, is sucked from the room and there is a whirl of confusion and all the furious light bulbs of recognition ignite at the same time. Then follows a howl of outrage that breaks across Bunny with such force that he is propelled backward and almost knocked off his feet.

Bunny steps back to the microphone, leans in and says, into the purgatorial storm, 'My name is Bunny Munro. I sell beauty products. I ask you for one minute of your time.'

Bunny stares down at the audience and begins his testimony.

Bunny tells the crowd how he was involved in a head-on collision with a concrete mixer truck. He tells them how he was struck by lightning. He explains how his nine-year-old

269

son was almost killed. He talks, to the audience, in terms of a miracle or a wonderment, and he puts forward the question as to why he was spared.

'Why was I spared?' he asks, in slow motion, crackling yellow lightning fracturing the purple-and-gold ceiling. The stage lights shift and move across Bunny's face in reds and purples and deep greens, and the mirrorball slowly revolves and sprinkles him with particles of jewelled light, and everything feels like it has come climbing up from a dream.

He tells the crowd of the shameful nature of his life. He talks explicitly and in detail about the people he has taken advantage of – how he has treated the world and everything in it with utter contempt.

'I was a salesman, all right,' says Bunny, 'peddling misery, door to door,' and he closes his eyes and surrenders to his own swooning testimony and his body is picked up and sent floating about on little prayers of refracted light. He places his hands inside his shirt and traces his fingers along the embossed scar that the electric charge has written into his body and talks about the nature of love and how frightened it made him feel, how the very existence of it terrified him and had him running scared and, with beads of red perspiration blossoming in the palms of his hands, he talks about the suicide of his wife and his own accountability in that dreadful act. He talks about the terrible absence of her in his life and in the life of his boy.

He tells the crowd of his crisis of conscience and how he had seen all the things he had done and all the misery he caused pass by him in an unbroken chain and he tells them how he was literally possessed by the Devil as coloured water pools around his feet and flows like a river across the apron of the stage.

Once again he asks of the audience, why he had been spared.

'Why was I spared?' he asks, again, in slow colour motion.

He says that after a while he had given up thinking about why he had not died and started to think about how he could live his life differently in the future. He tells the audience that his father is dying of lung cancer and that his intention is to go and look after him. He tells the audience that he is going to try to move through life with a bit more dignity from now on. But most of all, he tells the audience that he is going to go and look after his little boy, Bunny Junior.

At first the crowd berate him. They boo him, hiss him and shake their fists at him. Then Mushroom Dave moves forward and expertly flicks a cigarette and it explodes in a shower of sparks against Bunny's chest, which serves to further increase the force of the crowd's disdain. Charlotte Parnovar starts springing up and down on her toes, throwing threatening shapes and looking like she is about to jump up on stage and impart a little more peace, integrity and respect by busting Bunny's nose again. River keeps thrusting her finger at Bunny and shrieking incomprehensibly. A wine glass spins through the air and shatters on the stage behind him. Libby's mother, Mrs Pennington, screams in rage from the centre of the room, her face a horrible mask, the bone of her finger jabbing at him from inside her long black glove.

But Bunny soldiers on.

He says that the well-being of his son is the most important thing to him in the world and that he knows he can't wind back the clock and undo all the things he has done, but, with the crowd's help, he could at least turn the tide on his wretched life and move on with a little self-respect. He implores the crowd to listen to him.

Perhaps it was the blind lady, Mrs Brooks – who knows? – but someone, somewhere, says, 'Quiet! Let him speak,' and the ramping crowd, in time, gains some composure, and when Bunny talks about the depth of love he has for his nine-year-old son, a sudden unexpected groundswell of sentiment moves through the people and someone, somewhere, shakes their head and calls out, 'You poor man,' and slowly the crowd's rage falls away and they begin to listen.

Then Bunny moves forward and he holds his hands out to the sides, the red sweat leaking from his wrists like blood and fire blossoming across his chest, and he says, 'But first I need your help,' and he bows his dripping head, and then he raises it again.

'I am truly sorry,' he says.

Bunny takes a step forward and experiences a contra-zooming of the crowd that causes him to clutch at the memory of them.

'Can you please find it in your hearts to forgive me?'

Tears pour down his cheeks – red tears, purple tears, green tears – and Georgia sobs quietly and Zoë and Amanda give her consolatory hugs and the girls from The Funky Buddha and The Babylon Lounge wipe tears from each other's eyes with balled-up Kleenexes and there is a great surge of collective emotion as you might see on TV or somewhere, and the audience begin to applaud – because they are human and so much want to forgive – and Bunny moves forward and descends the three short steps into the crowd.

River the waitress approaches Bunny and throws her arms around his neck and cries strawberry tears upon his chest and forgives, and Mushroom Dave embraces Bunny and forgives, and the little junkie chick smiles up at him through her ironed hair and kohled eyes and forgives and all the girls from McDonald's and Pizza Hut and KFC hold onto Bunny and kiss him and forgive and Mrs Pennington moves forward with her wheelchaired husband and lifts her arms up and Bunny embraces her and together they weep and together they forgive and Bunny moves through the crowd and feels a chill in the air and notices a ghost of frost curl from his lips as Charlotte Parnovar dressed as Frida Kahlo hugs him with her muscular arms and forgives and the blind Mrs Brooks reaches out to him with her ancient hands and forgives and people kiss him and hug him and pat him on the back and forgive – because we so much want to forgive and to be forgiven ourselves – and Bunny sees Libby, his wife, through the crowd, dressed in her orange nightdress and as he moves towards her the crowd parts and he smiles into a prism of light and green oily oversized tears fall down his face and he says, 'Forgive me, Libby. Oh, Libby, forgive me.'

'Hey, don't worry about that,' she says, with a dismissive wave of her hand. 'There is plenty of time for that.'

'I went a bit crazy. I just missed you so much,' says Bunny, and purple blood drips from his brow and pours from his hands and runs relentlessly across the dance floor.

'Hey, I've got to go,' says Libby. 'Bunny Junior will be all right now.'

'Does that mean you're going to stop haunting me?'

Bunny hears the siren of a police car or an ambulance or something, from a million miles away, wailing mournfully through the psychedelic night. He thinks he hears a great rain, crashing all around him, like applause.

'Haunting you?' she says, with a furrowed brow. 'What do you mean?'

'I just miss you so much.'

'I never *haunted* you,' she says, flickering and strobing all about the place.

'Well, what are you doing now then?' says Bunny, mopping at his face with his handkerchief, his blood adding a scarlet patina to the rain-pocked water running freely along the gutters.

Libby laughs. 'Hey, Bunny, I'll see you in a minute,' and moves off and disappears like a ghost or spectre or something, under the streaming umbrellas of the weeping crowd.

As Bunny walks down the main thoroughfare, the sky is wide and mostly clear and full of ordinary lights. The Butlins mission statement blinks above his head and he hears the band start up in the Empress Ballroom and a cheer from the crowd and the sound of a saxophone carried on the cool, salted air. Scraps of blue cloud drift across the moon like spilled ink and he wipes his hand across his brow and loosens his tie.

'Oh, man,' he says, with the kind of narcotic euphoria a dying creature may experience before its lights blow out.

Bunny can see his son waiting for him at the edge of the pool, in a hoop of light thrown down by the streetlamp. His flip-flops are placed carefully beside him and he trails his feet, thoughtfully, in the water.

'Hi, Dad,' says the boy.

'Hi, Bunny Boy,' says his father.

Bunny puts his hand lightly upon his son's head and runs his fingers through his hair.

'Check this out,' says Bunny. 'Come on.'

The boy climbs to his feet, looks up at the heavens and makes an unsolicited observation about the sky looking like a giant swimming pool full of black ink and stars, then follows Bunny over to the brightly coloured electric children's train sitting on its silver tracks. He trails puddled footprints of pink water behind him, the moon duplicated in each of them – the police sirens, the ambulance sirens, getting louder.

'I remember this from when I was a kid,' says Bunny, and he climbs into the front carriage. 'Hop in,' he says.

Bunny Junior climbs up next to his father and makes himself comfortable and Bunny points to the train's control panel and its big yellow plastic key.

'See that key?' says Bunny. 'Turn it.'

Bunny Junior looks up at his father, his lips pressed together, and feels a fluttering around the region of the heart.

'Don't be afraid,' says Bunny, 'this time you're driving,' and places his hand on the boy's head.

Bunny Junior reaches down and turns the big yellow key and the little train springs to life and it begins to shunt along its tracks. Bunny throws his arm around the boy and the child smiles wide and begins to laugh. The train circles the swimming pool and Bunny Junior sees reflected in its waters all the treasures of heaven and he looks at the rain dripping off his father's head and he feels the rain running down his own face and the boy starts to laugh out loud. Bunny rings the train's silver bell and Bunny Junior rings the silver bell and scarlet blood flows down the gutters and from one end of the Holiday Camp to the next can be heard the laughter of a father and son and the ringing of silver bells.

As the train completes its circuit and slows to a halt, Bunny asks the boy, 'Do you want to go again?'

Bunny Junior looks at his father and reads his face and shakes his head, and says, 'No, it's OK, Dad.'

He watches his father climb out of the train.

'Come on, I want to sit by the pool,' shouts Bunny. 'It's much too loud here.'

Together they walk back to the pool. Bunny takes his shoes and socks off and dangles his feet in the rain-pocked water as Bunny Junior sits down beside him. Bunny puts his arm around his son, squinting into the sudden white headlights.

'Ah, Bunny Boy,' he says, and draws him close and presses his lips into his hair and breathes in his pungent, little-boy odour.

'Fuck,' says Bunny, quietly, and shakes his head.

Bunny Junior reads his father's face some more and sees the raised white scarring like a lace handkerchief at his throat and thinks he smells the tang of scorched flesh and sees the water pooling all around him.

'I've got to lie down a minute,' says Bunny, but the boy can't hear him for the screaming umbrellas.

By the edge of the pool – and in slow motion – Bunny falls away and lies upon his back, his feet dangling in the riffled water. The boy reaches over and strokes his father's brow.

'I'm going to close my eyes for a bit,' says Bunny, clutching for a moment at Bunny Junior's T-shirt.

Bunny Junior leans down and kisses his father.

'No, don't close your eyes, Dad,' he says softly and kisses him again.

Bunny shuts his eyes, his arms relaxing at his sides.

'Just for a bit,' he says. 'It's better.'

'No, don't close your eyes, Dad,' says the boy.

Bunny tilts his head away and he opens his eyes again for a fraction of a second and sees Penny Charade, the twelve-year-old girl he met at Butlins when he was a boy, dressed in her yellow polka-dot bikini, her long wet hair hanging down, sitting on the other side of the swimming pool, her caramel-coloured legs moving the surface of the water. She smiles at Bunny with her violet eyes.

'I just found this world a hard place to be good in,' says Bunny, then closes his eyes and, with an expiration of breath, goes still.

'Oh, Daddy,' whispers Bunny Junior.

The rain hammers down and black thunderheads boom and send lightning crackling across the sky. The crowds weep and scream from under their dripping umbrellas and beneath the canvas awning of the café on Western Road. Bunny Junior lays his head down on his father's chest and puts his arms around his neck and kisses him a final time.

He looks behind him and sees the maroon concrete mixer truck on its side. He sees the sheared tattooed arm dangling by a cord of skin tissue from its window. He sees the mangled Punto, wrapped in folds of smoke and steam, its passenger door hanging open. He feels the sting of his grazed hands and knees. He sees his blackened encyclopaedia lying on the road, curling grey smoke. He hears the last soft beat of his father's heart.

'Oh, Daddy,' he says.

The boy wipes the blood and the storm from his father's face and sees rushing towards him through the curtain of rain, in slow motion – just like life – the emergency services, with sirens whooping and lights screaming, and ambulance drivers in their streaming rubberised jackets and firemen with water running from their golden helmets and police officers with their heavy utility belts, in slow motion, rushing headlong towards him – just like in life – and the paramedics with their clattering gurneys rushing and rushing towards him and the leaden rain coming down, and the awed and weeping crowd, like statues, but, in their way, full of noise and rushing too – just like life – all suddenly clamouring, like a vast agency of protection, for the boy's attention.

Bunny Junior watches a policewoman with long blonde hair trailing behind her like moulded plastic and her radio transmitter squelching its own private language and her warm, merciful, adult face smiling down at him as she kneels on the street and says, 'Come on, little man, let me help you,' and Bunny Junior gently pushes her outstretched hand to one side and, standing, stands up above.

Acknowledgements

I would like to thank John Hillcoat for providing the original spark for this novel and Doug Leitch for his generosity and local knowledge. Also Simon Pettifar, Warren Ellis, Tony Clark, Rachel Willis, Brock Norman Brock, Sebastian Horsley, Ray Winstone, the Bad Seeds, Jamie Byng and my editor Francis Bickmore for their advice, support or unwitting influence.

I would also like to thank Kylie Minogue and Avril Lavigne with love, respect and apologies.